Known for her wide-ranging articles, opinions and commentaries on everything from current affairs to health, fashion and motoring, *Daily Telegraph* columnist Celia Walden has written for *Glamour, GQ, Elle, Porter Magazine, Harper's Bazaar,* Net-a-Porter's *The Edit, Grazia, Stylist, Standpoint, The Spectator* and Russian *Vogue.* Born and raised in Paris, Celia studied at the University of Cambridge. She and her husband now divide their time between London and LA. Her first novel for Sphere, *Payday,* was a Richard & Judy Book Club pick.

Also by Celia Walden

Payday

THE SQUARE

Celia Walden

SPHERE

SPHERE

First published in Great Britain in 2023 by Sphere
This paperback edition published in 2024 by Sphere

1 3 5 7 9 10 8 6 4 2

A CIP catalogue record for this book
is available from the British Library.

ISBN 978-0-7515-8321-2

Typeset in Minion by M Rules
Printed and bound in Great Britain by
Clays Ltd, Elcograf S.p.A.

Papers used by Sphere are from well-managed forests
and other responsible sources.

Sphere
An imprint of
Little, Brown Book Group
Carmelite House
50 Victoria Embankment
London EC4Y 0DZ

An Hachette UK Company
www.hachette.co.uk

www.littlebrown.co.uk

For Elise

PROLOGUE

Weird what you remember – after. How some tiny subset of neurons could have registered that 'Boogie Wonderland' was playing as I left the party and came to find you. That one of the security guys at the garden gate was grinding his fag butt into the pavement as I crossed the lane.

There are bits missing. I don't know whether the door to Addison Mansions was wide open or ajar, or what I was thinking, Leila, as I watched you take your last gurgling breath.

But then everything was clear again. The blood that had stippled the blinds, marbled the wall and run in ragged rivulets to the skirting board. The thoughts running through my head. *You had it coming. From the day you arrived in Addison Square, you had this coming.*

CHAPTER 1

COLETTE

'I'm going to need a few more minutes.'

From her crouched and cramped position beneath the desk, Colette angled her face up at her client and forced a smile.

She needn't have bothered. He was back to pacing up and down his study, and as she returned to the tangle of cables wedged between desk and wall, Colette did her best to ignore the rhythmic stick and wheeze of his soles against the hardwood floor.

Those slippers summed up everything she disliked about Adrian Carter. There was the pomposity of the oxblood velvet and the pretension of their pointed tips. Paired with the middle-class, middle-aged West London summer uniform of linen shirt and chinos, they were obvious in their intent, banal in their cultivated eccentricity: *I'm not just an off-duty suit. I've got kooks and kinks. Layers.*

She'd seen similar slippers in Shepherd's Bush market, laid out in rainbow stripes. But these were more likely to have come from a real Moroccan medina; one of the exotic conferences the TV agent was forever jetting off to, and Colette pictured Adrian, the statesman-like patron, slowing to survey the footwear in a souk: 'Aren't these jolly!'

'You OK with me switching off the router?'

'You what?'

'Then I'm just going to check the software's done its thing, but you should now be bug free.' Hitting the right tone – one that was clear but never patronising – was the hardest part of being an IT consultant.

'It means switching off this lot,' Colette stressed, holding up the overloaded extension lead.

'Do it.' He didn't look up from his phone.

'At some point we should really transfer some of these to another power outlet . . . '

'At some point,' Adrian's tone was so tetchy it bordered on disbelief, 'we will. But not at this precise point, when I've got seven, no, six minutes until an urgent Zoom call it's not currently looking like I stand a hope in hell of making. I'd assumed this would get sorted hours ago.'

Adrian liked his passive tense. How or by whom didn't matter, just that it 'got sorted'. And 'hours ago'? Given he'd only called Colette two hours ago, when after a quick attempt to fix the problem from her flat – using

TeamViewer – she had been forced to drive over to Addison Square, this seemed unrealistic. But now wasn't the moment to point that out.

'Bloody thing's had a mind of its own this past week,' he muttered. 'How the hell did I get this bug anyway?'

Without waiting for an answer, he made a call.

'Dom? It's me. Listen I've been floored by some bug.' A laugh. 'No. Worse. The tech kind. And I've got our person on it but I'm going to need you to host the meeting until I can join ...'

'Our person?' How about Colette? The same 'person' who retrieved seven years' worth of your family memories – two sets of ultrasounds included – when you thought you'd deleted them all. The 'person' who dug out that work file you thought you'd overwritten, has painstakingly talked you through every TV glitch you've ever had and just sped over here, at 8 p.m. on a Friday night, to deal with your 'emergency'.

Beneath the desk Colette exhaled slowly. The smack, stick and wheezing had resumed, closer now, louder, and she swivelled on her haunches to find herself blocked in by two chino-clad calves, the points of Adrian's preposterous babouches inches from her own feet.

It wasn't personal. Reaching for something on his desk, Adrian had forgotten the woman wedged beneath it in the way one might forget a sleeping collie.

'Adrian?'

'Mmm ...'

'I'm going to need to get out.'

With an exaggerated sidestep her client let her through and hoisting herself upright Colette slipped back into his chair and pressed 'refresh' on one of the open tabs at the bottom of the screen.

It took her a moment to make sense of the image that sprang up: a fleshy blur of pinks and browns, with what she first mistook for a wound, glistening crimson at its centre. Doubtless some Netflix gore-fest Adrian had been watching. Then the freeze frame released itself.

There was male grunting, panting, thrusting and a high-pitched female whine that was more animal than human. Two, no, three men. A young woman spreadeagled on a leather sofa. Her hands were tied above her head; her lower limbs being manipulated like a doll's. Male laughter, raucous, from behind the camera; jokey comments exchanged in a Slav language she couldn't identify.

Colette froze, waiting for her client to lunge forward and stab at the keyboard in the way people did when some shameful little proclivity was exposed on a job. The feral wails speeded up, perforated by the smack of a palm against bare flesh, but still he didn't move and when his eyes met hers they weren't embarrassed or aroused but amused: 'Not your thing?'

His gaze moved dispassionately down her body, from her cropped hair and glasses to the Velcro straps of her sandals. There it lingered, as though tickled by these final details. Adrian Carter wasn't 'perving'; he was jeering. Any woman over fifty would be jeer-worthy to a man like him. From the speakers a single shrill cry broke into a sob, and he added: 'Hard to tell what you're into.'

What felt like minutes must only have been seconds. Then, with one last glance at Colette's face, Adrian tapped a button on his keypad. The grunting and bleating stopped.

The image vanished. And as though the whole thing had been a mirage, as though she'd imagined it all, her client deadpanned, 'We sorted?'

'I just need ...' To her irritation Colette found that her voice came out hoarse with embarrassment. Gluey with shame. All the shame Adrian hadn't felt she had somehow taken on. '... to do one last reboot.' He was openly smiling now; he was enjoying her discomfort. 'Then we're done.'

'How's it going?'

Colette turned to see a pretty, full-faced woman peering through the crack in the door: Adrian's long-suffering wife.

'Slowly,' he groaned, leaning in to follow the white oblong's sluggish progress across the screen, and she got a waft of cedar aftershave.

'Hi, Emilia.' She managed to raise a stiff hand in greeting.

'A cuppa, Colette, or some iced water?'

'Not now, Em,' her husband snapped. 'For fuck's sake not now.'

The spasm of hurt on Emilia's face was swallowed up immediately by her smile: too broad, too bright. A smile adept at papering over cracks.

'Sorry,' she whispered, pulling the door shut. 'Let me know if you need anything.'

As they both stared at the screen, Colette could feel the heat exuding from Adrian's damp torso, hear the impatience pushing through every nasal whistle, and in silence they both followed the line: *6 minutes remaining; 5 minutes remaining; 4 minutes ...*

'Come on. Come on ...'

Abruptly, as though tired of its own teasing, the screen brightened into a familiar seascape, and although the last thing Colette wanted was to extend her time at number 46 Addison Square by another second, part of her felt dismayed that the device hadn't seen fit to torment him a little longer.

'We're in.'

She was packing up her things when the *Mad Men* theme tune rang out: Adrian's cretinous ring tone for as long as she'd known him.

'Yup?'

Maybe it was the length of the pause that followed, or her client's sudden stillness, registered out of the corner of her eye – but his reaction was curious enough to make Colette glance up.

Whoever was calling wasn't just unwelcome but unnerving. The levity in his face had drained away along with the colour, and his voice dipped to a murmur as he spat out: 'How did you get this number?' Then: 'No. Sorry. Not happening, love. Hanging up now.'

Adrian didn't move, staring at the phone in his hand, as though it were an unknown quantity – or a threat.

Colette cleared her throat.

'I'll let you get on.'

Zipping up her rolling Tumi briefcase she pulled it out into the hallway. 'And you'll remember to log out of TeamViewer, bec—'

But already he was kicking his study door shut: 'Will do. You're a star, Lynette.'

For a moment she just stood there. Then, to no one, 'It's Colette.'

CHAPTER 2

SYLVIA

Loss. They tell you it happens to you all over again, every morning. That for a few minutes when you first wake up your pain's been wiped clean – then *boom*: you're bent over double. You can't move. You can't breathe. You can't see anything but the black hole left in your life.

They also tell you there are three stages of grief. Or is it five? Either way 'denial' is the first, and there's 'anger' somewhere along the road towards 'acceptance'. But most of all they tell you that it's 'normal'. That you're normal for feeling whatever you're feeling.

What the fuck do *they* know?

Securing the hook on Reggie's leash, Sylvia slammed the front door, stepped out onto the pavement and breathed in deeply.

'What the fuck do they know?' she repeated out loud, and the shock of the profanity in that somnolent square made her smile.

That was another thing she'd been relishing since Archie's death (or 'her release' as she secretly thought of it – and what would you have to do to get a fifty-two-year sentence?). Not only would she never again be kept awake by her husband's restless left leg, and never again be forced to sit through David Attenborough's awe-struck murmurings, but if she wanted to be a foul-mouthed pensioner, she could bloody well scatter her F-bombs around the streets of West London.

Archie had felt the same way about women swearing as women in dungarees: not so much critical as saddened on an almost existential level. He'd never known about her silent asides. ''Course I don't mind you popping to the club, *you old twat.*' 'Enjoy your pub night with *those pompous arses.*'

In the moments she hadn't felt able to face another day married to a man she had never really loved, unleashing that internal vitriol had been therapeutic.

She'd stopped doing it when Archie was diagnosed. Because she wasn't a monster, and having her sentence cut short had made her generous. She would do whatever she could to make her husband's last months as pleasant as possible, but after that – now – the world was hers for the taking. Not that she intended to jet off to far-flung places. After all, the only person she was interested in was right here in Addison Square.

Up ahead, on the corner, a figure was slouched against the railings. In football shorts and an oversized T-shirt, young Felix was all pale, right-angled limbs, his head hanging heavy on his neck in that uniquely teenage way, as though the sheer prospect of life was too exhausting to bear. Only as she approached could Sylvia see that beneath the curtain of ginger hair, Felix's eyes were alert, darting up and down the lanes to either side of him.

Sylvia was opening her mouth to shout out 'good morning' when, after a last quick scan, Felix took off.

'Someone's up to something.' She smiled down at Reg. 'Am I right?'

Behind the symmetrical façades of those Georgian terraced houses, the rest of her neighbours would only just be waking up, sticking kettles on and rousing heavy-limbed children. Aside from the newspaper delivery guy, the odd jogger and the Filipina nannies hurrying to work, the square was usually empty at this hour, and as she walked purposefully down a lane strewn with fox debris, Sylvia inhaled the clean, acetous notes of high summer morning.

She checked her watch. In five minutes the delivery vans would start their rounds. Then, at some point within the next fifteen, the real reason for these early morning walks would open the green door up ahead. Sometimes she would be spotted; other times not. Either way she would be there, watching.

Somewhere behind her a wolf whistle rang out and glancing back she caught a flash of brown limbs and neon pink as a figure jogged past on the other side of the square: Leila. Seconds later the white van man responsible appeared, neck craned to gorge on the young French woman's backside before it disappeared from view.

Sylvia snorted.

'Men,' she replied to Reggie's questioning ear cock. 'They go a bit funny over pretty girls.'

In fairness, Sylvia mused, with a practised upward eye-flick at the drawn bedroom curtains above that green door (she was a bit too early today), everyone had gone a bit funny over the square's glamorous newcomer. Funny in subtle and very different ways.

'One more lap, Reg?'

The terrier looked dolefully up at her, as if to say, 'Archie never made me do so many circuits.'

'Come on. It's going to be another scorcher. You'll be all floppy later.'

Sylvia had thought it would pass, the defensiveness and slight suspicion that could still be felt towards their new neighbour, and perhaps it would, in time. After all Leila had only moved in six weeks or so ago, and it wasn't unusual for a small community to react that way to a newcomer. Especially when the newcomer looked like her, had a job like hers (Sylvia had never heard of the pop stars she danced for, but everyone else seemed awestruck), was twenty-eight – and foreign.

Were you still allowed to say 'foreign'? Or would her nephews cite that as an example of 'unconscious racism'? Sylvia was not a racist. Unlike the other seventy-somethings forever asking anyone dark-skinned where they were from, she understood that although Leila's parents were Moroccan, she was still French, born and raised. But last she checked French was still foreign.

She thought of the time Archie had taken her to the Wolseley and Nicole Kidman had walked in halfway through their dressed crabs. Some diners had openly gawped at the film star, others had forced themselves not to. Either way the atmospheric shift had been palpable. Maybe there were people who because of their looks, talent or charisma were like celebrities among us; people who upset the delicate balance around them simply by existing. Either way Sylvia couldn't help but feel a little smug that out of all the square residents Leila had only really chosen to befriend her.

Reggie had slowed to a halt. 'It's a lamppost,' she muttered, anxious not to miss her window on the other side of the square. 'There'll be another one on the next corner, I promise.' But now he was doing the backward circling that pre-empted a bowel movement, and as she waited impatiently for him to finish, Sylvia forced herself to remember that the terrier had his uses.

No one would ever question why an old lady should choose to walk her dog past the same front door once, sometimes twice a day. Or indeed why she should slow at that precise point.

Squinting over at the green door Sylvia's heart stilled. Was that a chink of light? Was it opening? With a tug of the leash, she picked up her pace, waiting for the distracted double take, the recognition and the grin. She was ready – pretending to fuss over Reggie on the opposite pavement – when they came.

'Morning, Sylvia!'

'Oh!' A chuckle of surprise. 'Morning.'

'Like clockwork, aren't we?'

Sylvia smiled, nodded, and repeated under her breath: 'Like clockwork.'

CHAPTER 3

COLETTE

Colette stopped singing along to Michael Bolton's 'Go the Distance' when the phone rang, glanced up at the clock above the oven, and went back to making her omelette.

The chimes told her it wasn't her mother (for some reason she'd assigned the 'By the Seaside' tone to the nursing home) and it was still only three minutes to eight. She had to be strict with her morning work hours. God knows the days could be long.

The call would be a client 'emergency', she thought tetchily. Not a 'slight tech issue' or a 'little problem', but an 'emergency', so poorly explained through the initial breathless babblings that Colette would be forced to make the client backtrack, as always, to the precise moment they had overwritten their best man's speech, deleted a year's worth of coursework, or generally had their lives hijacked by a technology they didn't understand.

It was because there were enough 'emergencies' in Colette's world to have her talking clients down off tech ledges from daybreak until the early hours that she had abandoned the in-house big city jobs a decade earlier. Lucrative as those contracts had been, they'd also meant recovering one trader's presentation at 2 a.m., assuring a sobbing PA that there was no way of recalling the email about her 'boss's lame ass '90s boots' from said boss's inbox at the crack of dawn, and talking a technologically dyslexic CEO on Tokyo time through a complex debugging procedure.

Did she miss the money? At first. But as her private client base grew, meeting the mortgage payments on the Mortlake flat she'd bought for the tiny balcony and Thames view alone had become less onerous, and after a few years of matching those city retainers Colette had even been able to move her mother to a plusher care home in nearby Sheen.

What she hadn't missed at any point, however, was the pretence of being 'part of a team'. Because despite the pub nights, birthdays and deal celebrations she'd only ever been invited along to as coats were grabbed and monitors switched off – 'Shit,' she'd once overheard a young trader ask, 'has anyone asked the IT lady?' – Colette had bought into that pretence for years.

Then came the fire drill incident. She'd been in the tech storage cupboard fixing a mouse as all but one of Ellis, Wyatt & Watkins' 474 employees had been disgorged, grumbling, onto Queen Victoria Street. The cupboard door had jammed.

And only when she'd finally freed herself, over half an hour later, nearly dislocating a shoulder in the process, had Colette realised that not one of her 'team' had missed her. Not even the floor's designated 'fire warden'. She'd resigned that afternoon.

Now, although the calls continued to come in at all hours, she had no obligation to answer them.

Breakfast should be sacred. Too many people saw eating as needing to be combined with another activity: reading, binge-watching, talking. She could still picture her mother leaning against the sink in her Peter Robinson uniform at the end of a long day, spooning baked beans into her mouth straight from the can as Colette ate her own frozen dinner alone at the table. The viscous tangerine film that covered her teeth and lips as she bitched about the 'little madams' on the shop floor that day, and how tired she was. How bone tired. But whenever Colette had asked her mum to sit with her at the kitchen table, she would always refuse.

From the way people looked at Colette in restaurants now when she dined out alone, there was something brave about sitting there eating without a prop of any kind, about listening to yourself chew and swallow and enjoying not just the taste but the ceremony of food, without wincing at every clank of cutlery against china. Those were the only moments she ever felt conspicuous.

Pouring the yellow gloop into the pan, she turned on the hob. Then the chimes sounded again.

Above the oven, the digital clock flicked from 7.59 a.m. to 8, and with a small sigh, Colette picked up.

'Colette Burton?'

'Hi.'

A woman's voice, low and soft as a caress.

'Hi.'

'I hope you don't, um, mind me calling so early. My name's . . . ' But Colette already knew. That accent was a bit of a giveaway. 'Leila. We haven't met.' *We have, but it was brief, and I wouldn't expect you to remember.* 'Sylvia Ryan kindly gave me your number. I've just moved to Addison Square, and I need your help with something. A couple of things, actually.'

Tapping 'speaker', Colette put the phone down on the counter and began to tilt the pan this way and that. 'One of them is . . . ' Something about the quality of the pause made her turn and stare down at the screen.

' . . . delicate.'

'Delicate how?' She couldn't help herself.

Another silence. Then: 'I don't really feel comfortable talking about it over the phone.'

Colette allowed herself an eyeroll.

'No problem. Shall we find a moment this week? I'm actually going to be in the square on Thursday.'

'I was kind of hoping for sooner.'

'OK.'

With a few taps, Colette pulled up her calendar.

'I can definitely take a look and see if . . . '

'As in today. As in now?'

Less than an hour later she found herself halfway across Putney Bridge, stranded behind a bus. Strumming on the steering wheel, Colette watched the air around its exhaust pipe quiver in the heat.

There was something sickening about London heatwaves. Toxic. All those scorched-limbed joggers staggering along the pavement beside her, sucking in the fumes. Even the Thames, beyond, looked bilious.

There was only one explanation for her moving her first appointment of the day back two hours and hotfooting it over to Addison Square: she was curious. About the issue so 'delicate' it couldn't be discussed over the phone; about this newcomer who had got all the residents talking.

Their one and only meeting, last month, had been brief. Colette had been at Sylvia's, discussing the digital 'handover' that would need to take place now that Archie was gone, and when they'd gone up to the bedroom to take a quick look at her late husband's Mac and check how much would need to be done, there had been this extraordinarily beautiful French girl perched on the side of the bed trying on a pair of shoes.

The old lady had embarked on a 'therapeutic clear-out' of the house a few weeks earlier, and apparently Leila had been helping her go through her wardrobe. The shoes had been fished out of the 'to be donated' pile. Purring murmurs of admiration as she angled her slender ankle this way and that, Leila had initially refused to take them. 'They're vintage YSL!'

But Sylvia had insisted, and Colette had been touched by the bond being forged between these two very different women with fifty odd years between them.

On the other side of the bridge the roads were clear, and twenty minutes later Colette was inching her way back into a tight space outside Addison Mansions when the chimes started up again.

'Lady, I'm right outside,' she murmured to the rear windscreen. 'Could not have got here any quicker.'

Only when she checked her phone, she saw that it hadn't been Leila at all.

Adrian Carter
Missed call.
1 new voicemail.

How many times had Colette seen her client's name flash up on her screen over the years? It never filled her with joy, but today the pattern of letters felt like an attack on her consciousness, the accompanying visuals causing her stomach to clench and her throat to close up.

Adrian's slippers, Adrian's 'work laugh', Adrian's screen – Adrian's sneer. She was back in his study, to that woman laid out like a sacrificial offering, the damp sheen of those smooth-shaven bodies, the serrated cries. But it was the look on Adrian's face that Colette could still see most clearly. Casual amusement: that was all she was worthy of.

Since her visit to number 46 Addison Square two days ago, the events of that evening had acquired the hyper-reality of a nightmare. As in a nightmare she'd been turned to stone. She hadn't reached forward and turned that filth off; she hadn't even said anything. Yet it had all happened, and somehow that reality had become even more chilling in the hours and days that followed than it had been in the moment.

As her finger hovered over the voicemail message, she pictured Adrian recounting the episode to his friends down the pub. Guffaws of laughter. Heads being thrown back; gold fillings bared. She pulled back her hand, not yet ready to hear his voice.

Over the years Colette had been confronted by enough embarrassment as she sat in front of her clients' screens to wipe out most of her own. Or so she'd thought.

Like every IT consultant she'd chanced upon a lot of porn, the only surprise being how traditional men and women were in their sexual tastes. 'Hot MILFs', 'lesbian roomies', with the odd 'kinky stepmum' or 'diaper dude' thrown in – it tended to be as mainstream as Ocado orders in digital footprint terms. Then there were the naked snaps – of the wife, husband, girlfriend or gay teen boyfriend. And the awkward moments hadn't stopped there.

As she'd delved in and out of her clients' devices there had been accidental sightings of love notes, hate notes and medical notes detailing everything from gynaecological conditions she never knew existed to aborted pregnancies her clients' husbands would never know existed. All of those things she had overlooked using the same vacant expression her job so often necessitated.

'Think of me like a doctor or therapist,' she'd murmur, when something needed to be said to stem the slew of mortified apologies and tortuous explanations. 'I'm a judgement free zone.' As with doctors and therapists, this was a lie. You didn't have to care to judge, and the arrogance implicit in secrets had always bothered Colette, reminding her as it did of school swats, hands curved protectively around their work. As though people were so desperate to know; as though secrets made you special. When as she knew better than most, everyone had something to hide.

So Adrian liked to watch a gangbang as his wife read the kids *The Tiger Who Came to Tea* upstairs. Which made him a sleazy prick as well as rude, vain and misogynistic – all judgements she'd amassed over the years she'd worked with him. But what he'd done the other night? Not so much the absence of shame as the determination to revel in her discomfort? To humiliate her? Three decades in the job and Colette had never come across anything like it.

Shaking her head clear of these thoughts, she took a breath and tapped on his voicemail. 'Speaker' was an afterthought; she couldn't have Adrian's voice in her ear.

'Ah, um . . . '

'Colette,' she mouthed, releasing her seatbelt.

'You're not there.'

'Quick, aren't you, Adrian?'

She felt better for the repartee, even if there was no one here to hear it. But wait: was he calling to apologise?

'So I've been getting these notifications from that malware protection software you installed,' her client went on, and again she felt stupid. Of course Adrian Carter wasn't calling to apologise. 'They're popping up constantly.' A pause. 'They're bloody annoying.'

As her client's semi-sarcastic, nasal drone filled the car she felt a weight gather in the middle of her sternum.

On her way home that night, she had worked through every possible course of action, from confronting her client and the sending of a brief note saying that regrettably she was no longer going to be able to tend to the Carters' tech needs (but could recommend another consultant who would be more than happy to take over) to the imaginary call she would never, in a million years, put into Emilia: 'There's no

21

easy way of saying this, but your husband's a pig of cartoon proportions.'

Only none of these were viable options – not given how many clients Colette had in Addison Square. She would have to explain why she was withholding her services, for a start – and with Adrian as twisted as he was, he might actually enjoy the awkwardness of that conversation, relish the chance to humiliate her a second time.

Then there was the fact that the Carters were amongst her biggest earners. All of which left her with only one option: continuing to work for Adrian with icy professionalism and hoping that life found its own way to even the score.

'Anyway, if you could let me know when you could drop by and work your magic . . . '

'Go away.' Colette stabbed at the phone, missed, and tried again. 'Go. Away!'

A rap on the window made her jump. Her first thought was that the spandex-clad woman smiling through the glass at her was even more otherworldly than she'd seemed that day at Sylvia's. A halo of tight black curls highlighted Leila's sculpted features. Her mouth was small but full, her cheekbones sharp and high, her eyes feline.

Then the embarrassment kicked in. Colette saw herself from Leila's point of view: a middle-aged woman sitting in her car shouting at her phone – and felt her cheeks flood with colour.

She buzzed the window open. 'Hello.'

'Not late, am I?' Wrapped around her tricep was one of those phone-holder armbands that made people look like members of the fitness Stasi. 'Thought I'd squeeze in a quick run before you got here.' A bright white smile. 'I'm Leila.'

Was she really going to pretend this was their first meeting? 'I'm Colette.' Yes, she was.

'Thanks for coming. Lucky you had a window.' Pulling up a foot behind her, Leila curved herself in against the car, pumping her toe against the back of her mesh-panelled thigh in a series of limber gestures that drew a low whistle from two passing builders. 'Shall we go up?'

Leila insisted they take the stairs. 'It's like I always tell my clients: we've all got free gyms everywhere we look. It's just about using them.' She glanced back at Colette, behind her. 'I'm not sure how much Sylvia told you. I'm actually a dancer, but I teach a few cardio classes at that place, Karve, on the high street.'

Leila hadn't said 'I'm not sure whether Sylvia told you', but 'how much', and Colette logged the significance of this: the assumption being that all the residents of Addison Square were talking about her. Which, to be fair, was true.

When Colette followed the young woman inside her flat, she saw that the layout was exactly the same as Zoe and Guy's, beneath.

'Those are the last of them,' Leila gestured with her chin at the cardboard boxes lining the hall. 'Can't believe I'm still unpacking, but I'm almost done. Come through.'

The sitting room was uncluttered, decorated in the sparse, neutral tones every gen-Instagram woman favoured. Hadn't one of her clients – Zoe? Emilia? – said she was some kind of 'influencer'?

'So as I said on the phone,' Leila started, waving Colette towards the sofa, 'I've got a few things I need help with.'

Rather than sit, the young woman walked to the window

looking out over the garden and stood there, fiddling with the matte black band around her wrist.

'That the new PB Wearables smartwatch?' Colette asked. 'I thought it wasn't out until September.'

'It's not, but I'm under contract to them, so I'm supposed to be wearing it in every 'gram for the next two months. At the moment it's basically just an ugly bracelet, though.' She gave a nervous laugh. 'Haven't been able to set it up yet.'

'Ah. Well, I can help you with that.'

'Great.'

Colette waited.

'I've also been having trouble with my WiFi.' Whatever the real reason for Colette's visit, Leila wasn't ready to dive straight in. 'Keeps wanting to connect me to the Mulligans' downstairs.'

Colette nodded.

'That's easily sorted. It'll be the walls and ceilings. They're very thin in these mansion blocks. Your router is . . . ?'

'OMG so thin!' Leila pointed out a little grey box behind the TV. 'A detail the lettings agency hadn't thought to share, you know? I mean, it's fine. I got the place cheap. Landlord knocked a load off the market price because it's a short-term let and I need to vacate a couple of times a week for sale viewings, which actually works out fine. Just would've been nice to know that I was going to get to enjoy my downstairs neighbours' *contretemps* in stereo. Sorry: arguments.'

From her kneeling position by the router, Colette blinked up at her.

In all the years she'd worked for Guy and Zoe, Colette had never so much as heard either one of them raise their voice.

'I mean, couples argue,' Leila went on. 'I'm French; I get that. But wow.'

Back on the sofa, turning her attention to the laptop set down on the coffee table in front of her, Colette made a non-committal noise.

'OK.' With a few last taps she was done and onto setting up Leila's watch.

Both issues were laughably easy to fix. To the point that Colette suspected Leila could have done so herself. Now, as she strapped her smartwatch back on, the young woman chewed at the inside of her mouth. Their eyes met.

'You know that anything you tell me is totally confidential, right?'

Leila paused, then nodded.

'Just that you mentioned something "delicate", and I can promise you that in my line of work, I deal with a lot of sensitive issues.'

Again, Leila nodded.

''Course you do. It's just, well, this ... Put it this way: it was either you or the police.'

Pulling her phone from its Velcro arm-pocket, Leila found what she was looking for and handed it to her.

'Sorry.' Colette looked from the young woman's Instagram page – a little grid of scantily-clad selfies – back up at her client. 'What am I looking at?'

'That's not my page. RealLeila? It's not me.'

Colette frowned.

'Someone's set up a fake account, pretending to be me.'

'Well, I'm afraid that does happen if you're, um, an influencer or, you know, in the public eye. It's not really something that I can do ...'

'You don't understand.' Leila snatched the phone back, tapped on the screen, and held it out to Colette. 'See that?'

It was a close-up of Leila's thighs and buttocks, barely contained by a pair of tiny denim shorts as she lay sunbathing on a lawn.

'Ye-es . . .'

The shot had been taken from behind, and, from the pixilation of the image, quite far away.

'I don't know who took it.'

'May I?' Tapping on the image, Colette zoomed into the strip of flowerbed and corner of lacquered black railings behind. 'This was taken inside the garden.' She'd never set foot in there. Addison Square gardens were for keyholders only. But like every passer-by Colette had peered through those railings and wondered at that secret enclave.

Leila nodded. 'A few of them have been. Others in the lanes of nearby streets. Scroll down.'

There were dozens of shots, many taken from behind: Leila as she walked along the square lanes, a rolled yoga mat under one arm, Leila's neat, denim-clad backside as she pushed through the doors of Boots on the high street. Another of her in a short skirt at the M&S self-checkout, bending over to pick up a bag of shopping.

Feeling a bit sick, Colette scrolled on. There were a couple of Leila's sitting room window, as seen from the east: one, zooming in on what appeared to be a swimsuit, hanging out to dry; another of a blurry grey shape through the window – presumably Leila.

'These started . . . ?'

'When I moved here.'

'That's cyberstalking.' Colette shook her head. 'It's straightforward stalking. And it's illegal. You mentioned the police. Why haven't you spoken to them?'

Wagging her head from side to side, Leila looked away.

'Who wants to get involved with the police unless they have to? And it's pretty clear, isn't it, that this is . . .'

'. . . one of your neighbours.' Although she couldn't quite believe it herself, Colette finished the sentence for her.

'No one else would have been able to get those garden shots. Which is why I called you.'

Only then did Leila sit, leaning towards Colette with her elbows on her knees. 'Sylvia said that you know this square "like the back of your hand". That you know these people inside out.'

'Well, I . . .' Colette stared at her. Things seemed to be taking a funny turn.

'You don't have any idea who might be doing this?' Leila asked.

'Me?' Why on earth would she know? 'I was going to ask you the same. You haven't noticed anyone hanging around?'

'No.'

'But you – you're in a position to find out.'

'Sorry, I don't . . . ?'

It occurred to her that Leila might somehow have misunderstood the nature of her job. Or maybe she was just a bit doolally? Colette had had a couple of odd requests over the years – the guy who wanted her to set up spyware to monitor his wife stood out – but she was struggling to understand what this woman was getting at.

'Aren't they pretty much all your clients? Sylvia said they

were.' Leila paused. 'You're inside their homes, their devices, their heads. If one of them was stalking me, you would know, wouldn't you?' She tilted her head to one side: 'Or *could* know.'

As Colette finally understood what was being asked of her, she felt a jolt of offence. Then she worried she might laugh. That's how inappropriate this was. Sitting up straight, she pushed the bridge of her glasses into her nose.

'I appreciate that this must be very upsetting for you ... '

'Upsetting? It's totally freaking me out. It feels like harassment.' Leila's voice dropped to a whisper: 'Worse. Like I'm being assaulted again and again. Which sounds ridiculous, I know, when there's been no actual contact. No real threat ... ' She shook her head. 'It's hard to explain.'

'No. I can imagine.' She didn't have to. A thought: was the vile Mr Carter behind this? A man like him couldn't have failed to notice his beautiful new neighbour. But abusing her position to spy on her clients? Leila must be truly desperate to be asking this.

'As I said earlier,' Colette went on, trying to keep the extent of her outrage from her voice, 'my job's all about confidentiality, discretion.'

Because that was another thing Leila clearly hadn't understood, and to be fair she was new to the square: an outsider. How could she know that Colette was a part of these people's lives? That – Adrian Carter aside – she was viewed in the same way as a long-time local GP: trusted, valued, indispensable. 'Listen, I've worked here for years and I'm as loyal to my clients as they are to me.'

Leila's mouth twisted into a smirk at this, as though she'd bought what Colette had said ... until that point. And although she felt sorry for this young woman, that signalled the end of the conversation for her.

Standing, Colette heard herself say stiffly, 'No, I'm afraid I can't help. Now, unless there's anything else?'

CHAPTER 4

HAMMERSMITH POLICE STATION
EXTRACT OF RECORDED INTERVIEW
WITH MR ADRIAN CARTER

Date: 16 July
Duration: 66 minutes
No. of pages: 32
Conducted by Officers of the
Metropolitan Police

DC HARRIS: The victim was a beautiful woman. Attracted a lot of attention in the square.

AC: You're going to have to ask me a question if you expect me to answer it.

DC BAXTER: I think what DC Harris is saying is that a woman like Ms Mercheri, well, people take an interest?

DC HARRIS: For the benefit of the tape, Mr Carter is not replying.

DC BAXTER: That was a question, to be clear. Here's another: someone paid particular interest, didn't they?

DC HARRIS: For the benefit of the tape, Mr Carter is shrugging.

DC BAXTER: But that interest was unwelcome, to say the least. Is that where all this started, Mr Carter?

CHAPTER 5

ZOE

'You're sure Ollie's dad knows that I'll be at a meeting with Emilia over the road? That it'll only be you two in the garden?'

'Mum. You've asked me that, like, five times.'

'We're just doing a bit of square party prep. I shouldn't be more than an hour.'

Felix's hair was far too long. She reached out to move his fringe out of his eyes.

'I'm thirteen.' He dodged her hand, rolling his eyes at the smaller boy kicking a football from side to side a few feet away.

'I'm aware. But Ollie's only seven, so I'm just making sure.'

'We're fine.' Felix dug his toe in a divot in the lawn. 'You can go.'

'Can I?' Zoe doffed an imaginary cap. 'Why thank you.'

She looked around. The communal gardens were empty, the once lush, green half-acre broken up by sun-scorched patches. The gates were locked. It was perfectly safe to let Felix and Ollie have an after-school game of football there for an hour.

'Right. Well, we're at that café by the bus stop: Alloro. Done by 5.30 p.m., latest. Any problems, just call. And it goes without saying that you don't leave the garden.'

'Mum!'

'I'm going.'

As she crossed the lawn to the gate nearest the high street Zoe glanced back at the two boys, not for the first time wondering at this curious friendship.

It was a recent development, one she wanted to discuss with Guy, yet something was holding her back. How could she voice the true breadth of her concerns, even to her husband? Ask him why Felix never brought home any of his classmates? Why none of them ever invited her son back to theirs? And what could he possibly have in common with a boy six years younger?

Along the border of the flower bed Zoe spied the glint of a chocolate wrapper and, tutting, stooped to pick it up. As she straightened, a flash of white caught her eye. The garden wasn't empty. There, in the shade of the magnolia tree at the far left corner of the lawn, was their new upstairs neighbour.

Wearing some kind of tight white leotard and short combo, Leila was sitting cross-legged on a rubber mat. She didn't, from this distance, appear to be either reading or on the phone, and Zoe had a few minutes to spare before meeting Emilia. Maybe now would be a good moment both to break the ice – and have that 'chat' she'd been putting off.

'Shall I just do it?' Guy had asked yesterday, when the music had started up again overhead and Zoe had been forced to admit that no, she hadn't yet found the right moment to speak to Leila about it. 'You seem to be making this into . . .' A sigh of impatience. 'It's perfectly normal to tell a new neighbour to keep it down, you know. She probably doesn't realise how much we can hear. But we are going to need to make it clear. Preferably before I lose my mind.'

Zoe had assured her husband she would deal with it. Guy was good at a lot of things, managing whole areas of their life seamlessly, but he could be cack-handed with people and she wanted to get things off on the right foot. That was why Zoe had invited the young French dancer over for a drink the week she'd moved in. Only Leila had never got back to her with a date, which made things a little awkward now.

May the eighth. Seven weeks ago. That was when the removal van had pulled up outside. Zoe remembered because that was also the week the heat had started building and building, every day breaking a new record, the Met office predicting 'red' warnings by the end of this month. Well, maybe now that Leila had settled in, she would remind her about that drink, mention the square party, get her involved, and when she saw the right chink, raise the music issue.

Stretching her mouth out into a welcoming smile, Zoe took a few brisk strides in Leila's direction, noticing as she did so that the young woman was plugged into something.

'Afternoon!'

Her neighbour didn't react.

'Another sweltering day!'

Nothing.

It was hard to tell from this distance, with the sun in

Zoe's eyes, but she could have sworn Leila was looking straight at her.

'Thought I'd come and ...'

She was now directly in her neighbour's line of vision, yet still Leila didn't move from her Buddha-like position. Uncomfortably aware of her limbs and their stiff, puppet-like movements, Zoe attempted an exaggerated wave.

'Hell-o!'

Only then, when she was no more than five yards away, did Leila make the smallest movement, slowly raising a finger and wagging it from side to side in a gesture that was zen, schoolmistress-like and unmistakable: no. *Not now.*

No? Incredulity bubbled up in Zoe's throat, manifesting itself in a small, strangled laugh. That's how you greet your new neighbour? The woman who put together a list of 'useful numbers' and slipped it under your door the day after you moved in? The person who has been trying to do the civilised thing and *get to know you*?

As she turned on her heel and began to retrace her steps towards the gate, however, Zoe lurched from annoyance to embarrassment. Whatever Leila had been doing it was clearly a solitary activity and her face flared as she replayed her repeated, persistent attempts to interrupt her 'moment'. It was still hot when she pushed through the door of Alloro and sat down before her neighbour Emilia.

'You OK? You look ... ?'

Zoe shook her head, not so much in a negative way as an attempt to break her stupor. Bring herself back to the present: to the noisy conviviality of the café, the spluttering of the milk frother and the sweet, floral scent of brewing coffee.

'Yeah. I ... ' She put both hands to her hair, smoothing her bob in the single, symmetrical movement that always helped renew her sense of control. 'Sorry. Bit of a weird one.'

Emilia leaned forward. 'Go on.'

Zoe paused. Leila's hand movement had been so slight. Perhaps she'd misinterpreted it?

'I'm being petty, but you know our new girl?'

'Our . . . ?'

'Ms Mercheri.'

'Ah. Leila.'

They exchanged a look that often accompanies any mention of a superlatively beautiful woman in female conversation: beneath the jokey eyeroll, an acknowledgement of genuine pique.

'She just cut me dead in the garden.'

Emilia frowned. 'How d'you mean?'

'I mean, the woman's been living above us for almost two months and we've still not said more than a few words to each other, so I thought I'd say a proper hello just now, on my way to you.' Zoe was aware that she sounded slightly breathless. 'And she's doing something cross-legged on a mat, all . . . ' Putting the palms of her hands together Zoe mimicked Leila's absurd prayer-like posture. 'And when I approach her, she wags her finger at me. Actually *wags it*. As in: "don't even think about it". Can you believe that?'

A smile crossed Emilia's face. So fleeting Zoe might have imagined it.

'Was she meditating?' she asked.

Zoe paused. 'Maybe. So yeah, I could probably have picked a better moment.'

'Still. Bit rude.'

The waitress appeared, and after the usual anguished 'I

really shouldn'ts' from Emilia they settled on a shared slice of carrot cake with their coffees.

'This is on the committee,' Zoe added.

The words gave her a little swell of pleasure. She needed it. Emilia Carter wasn't just a long-time neighbour but a friend. Yet in between their occasional coffees and walks, Zoe would forget what hard work she had become; how an hour with her could feel like an uphill climb.

She hadn't always been that way. Not so long ago Emilia had been pretty in a milk maid kind of way, vital, but over the years a kind of listlessness seemed to have enveloped her. It sometimes made Zoe want to shake her. But today she was struck by how completely Emilia seemed to have given up.

The floral silk blouse she was wearing looked expensive, but stretched over full, poorly rigged breasts, the fine fabric was coming apart at the seams – and those draw-string trousers were doing nothing to hide her weight gain. The thick blonde hair with a good two inches of roots was twisted up into a makeshift topknot and although Emilia had that eerily good skin – 'fat girl skin', Zoe always thought of it as – a slick of lipstick and a touch of mascara would have made such a difference. 'We're all on a hamster wheel,' she felt like saying. 'Accept that, hop back on and get on with it.'

But Zoe didn't have time to explore the inner workings of Emilia's mind. She had asked her here with one thing in mind: getting her name down on that party spreadsheet.

With less than three weeks left it was time to engage in a little low-level bullying with the Addison Square residents. Especially the ones who believed their artful attempts at deflection had worked. Because, you know what? If you're so disinclined to pitch in with these things, maybe don't move into a square.

Squares are different. Special. Little self-contained communities, close-knit islands bound by old-world pleasures like bonfire nights, cake sales and neighbourly tennis tournaments; they're the promise of a life coveted by everyone. Because in the end, isn't that sense of 'belonging' what we're all yearning for?

'I was going to ask how you felt Sylvia was doing?' Emilia said now.

'She's been amazing. Pretty much got the whole catering side of the party sorted.' Zoe would toss that out, let it sink in. This woman lost her husband of fifty-odd years three months ago. She's still grief-stricken – and *she's* helping out. 'Hopefully it's helping take her mind off things. I did offer to make someone else my deputy when Archie ... Anyway, I'm sure she would have said if she hadn't felt ready.'

'Exactly. Poor thing, though. She must be feeling pretty lost.'

'We've been doing what we can ... '

Well, Zoe had. In Guy's mind, the flowers and condolences they'd given Sylvia the day after Archie had passed were job done.

Later, when their elderly neighbour had started on a big clear out, her husband had agreed that sending over Felix to help her box up some donations for Oxfam was a good idea. But that thing he'd said at the weekend? 'Remember, Sylvia's not a friend; she's a neighbour'? That had put her out. As though one couldn't, shouldn't, be both.

'Anyway, about the party ... '

But Emilia had stopped listening. Zoe followed her gaze

through the window at the jumble of fast-moving pedestrians on the pavement outside; at a sleek figure in white, the back of a head and an explosion of tightly coiled curls from beneath a red baseball cap: at Leila.

'Ha,' she murmured. 'Speak of the devil.'

CHAPTER 6

EMILIA

'You know she's worked as a backup dancer for Keisha?' The vision in the red cap had disappeared. Yet there they both were, still staring through the window at the space Leila had passed through. 'In her last video too,' Zoe added.

Emilia smiled. 'I didn't have you down as a Keisha fan.'

'The kids tell me this stuff.' There was something defensive about her shrug. 'Apparently Leila's also a "fitfluencer".'

'Couldn't quite manage that with a straight face, could you?'

Then, because there was something so predictable and forty-something about their sneering (and that little voice inside Emilia's head was snickering, 'What have *you* ever done for a living?'), 'Although obviously we all follow a bunch of them, so . . .'

Zoe was waiting, unsmiling, one clean-angled brow raised, and Emilia moved quickly on. 'Doesn't Leila give classes at that new place on the high street too? She was banging on about something called "Body Karve" on Instagram the other day.'

'I saw that.'

Zoe Mulligan really had done her homework. Along with everyone else in the square, Emilia was willing to bet. Because Ms Mercheri was new and shiny, with the kind of looks that actively made you uncomfortable. So much so that she'd found herself cutting short any chance interactions with Leila in the garden, conscious of the kicking every second in this young woman's company gave her self-esteem.

What she didn't need at this precise low point in her life was a gorgeous Parisian influencer being thin all over the square. Then again, at least she wasn't in the unenviable position of living in the flat beneath hers.

Emilia leaned forward. 'Someone said she's got over half a million followers.' 'Someone' being Leila's home page. But she didn't volunteer that information, or the fact that in a moment of ego self-harming she'd also signed up to notifications from @Leilaloveslife.

'Just looking at some reel she did the other day made me want to lie down.'

Zoe groaned. 'We're lucky if we manage a Sunday afternoon stroll!'

Emilia was surprised it had taken this long for the marital 'we' to make an appearance. 'We feel so strongly that Freya should learn a third language before she starts secondary school.' 'We love Cornwall in early September.'

Maybe it was sweet that couples like Zoe and Guy merged into one another, became a single entity, but to Emilia it was always a painful reminder of how disconnected she and Adrian had become. She'd felt this acutely in recent weeks. Her husband had been jumpy and bad-tempered, closing his study door in a way he'd never done before, as though wanting to put a physical barrier between them. The Mulligans had celebrated their tenth wedding anniversary last year. Would she and Adrian reach that milestone?

'I'll tell you something else,' Zoe was still on Leila. 'She likes her music loud when she works out up there. It's been driving Guy bonkers. He says he'll have a word, but you know what men are like. Better if I do it, don't you think?'

Emilia took a sip of her coffee. 'I know men are suddenly very happy to get involved when supermodels move in next door.'

A beat.

'Oh, I'm lucky with Guy.' Zoe's smile was tight, as though pulled outwards by invisible threads on either side. 'He's not *that* man.'

The implication being that Adrian was?

Emilia had tried to laugh off her husband's reaction to Leila in the usual jovial wifely ways – 'Daddy's very excited by our new French girl, isn't he?' – but there was something so humiliating about the look on Adrian's face whenever they passed their neighbour in the lane or she was mentioned in conversation. A brightness, an alertness, that Emilia was acutely aware she would never again have the power to provoke in her husband. But now she was 'projecting' – as that therapist had said last year – her own 'feelings of inadequacy' onto Adrian.

'Anyway, enough about Miss "I want to be alone",' Zoe said brightly. 'How are you doing? Hattie not too knackering? I remember how hard it was doing the whole thing again with Freya, four years after Felix – and that's a smaller age gap than you've got. But the idea of dealing with a ten-month-old again now ... I do admire you.'

Beneath the excessive concern on Zoe's face (why did this woman always make Emilia feel like there was something wrong with her?) there was an undercurrent of impatience. They were not friends. Living across the square from one another, even for years, didn't automatically give two people that status, and the truth was that Zoe was far more exhausting to be around than any ten-month-old.

Those energy-levels and rottweiler tactics must have been put to good use at Goldman Sachs, before she'd given it all up to become an uber-mum and uber-neighbour. Then there was the close-talking that Adrian always joked forced him to take a step back whenever they bumped into one another in the square. Did this woman ever just slump on the sofa like everyone else?

Although they were not here, in the nearest café with decent coffee, to discuss the kids, Emilia dutifully batted away a few last questions.

'Honestly, she's been such an easy baby,' she said with a buoyancy she desperately wanted to feel. The café windows were floor to ceiling and choosing a table in the full glare of the afternoon sun had been a mistake. Already, Emilia was suffocating, counting the seconds until she would be released. 'And sometimes I'll get that nice sitter Marta to come in and help out.'

'Good for you. All these women who feel guilty about

having nannies just because they don't work. Never understood it.'

'Well, I wouldn't really call her a nanny,' Emilia protested weakly, conscious that Zoe neither had a job nor a nanny.

'But why not get help if you need it? God, what I'd give to have just a couple of hours to myself.'

You had to admire the work. Although the obvious question would of course be: 'if you're so desperate for me time, why cast yourself as the square's head prefect?' Long before she'd been formally elected Chair of the Garden Committee Zoe had taken on that role.

Emilia could remember variants of her neighbour at school: the industrious ones who set up societies and did the Duke of Edinburgh Award scheme. The ones who went on to alliterate their children's names just so that they could have the satisfaction of saying 'Felix and Freya' ten times a day, showcasing their families as neat, cohesive 'units'.

She also knew that there were civic-minded people in the world who genuinely cared about their communities and saving the town hall. Even if they didn't care and were doing it all for status reasons, Emilia had always been grateful they existed. Because if her neighbour was going to the trouble of setting up the square's Little Free Library, if she was organising every last detail of its two hundredth celebration party, surely that meant Emilia didn't have to?

Zoe hadn't touched the carrot cake she'd insisted on them sharing until now, when she curved her fork around a corner of frosting, inserted the mound of sugar into her mouth, sank back in her chair and closed her eyes.

Those few seconds of feigned ecstasy gave Emilia the chance to marvel both at Zoe's blunt-cut bob – styled to

soften a jaw that was almost masculine in its squareness –
and compact little figure, as immaculate as always in its
long-sleeved pink Breton top and denim skirt.

'On the subject of time for yourself,' Zoe pushed the cake
towards her, 'I'm afraid I'm going to need to steal some of it.'

'For the party.'

Emilia gave a series of small nods, hoping this would help
conceal her horror.

'We've had a bit of a set-back with our MC, Ems.'

There was a type of woman who abbreviated your name
even if the relationship wasn't really 'there' yet (in this case
Emilia was confident it never would be), either out of a
desire to speed up the process – or get what they want. Zoe
Mulligan was that woman.

'MC?'

'Sorry: host. MC's one of Felix's words,' she went on, with
a fleeting smile at the mention of her teenage son, the son
it was impossible to forget was from Zoe's first marriage, so
different was he in colouring to the rest of the family. And
that one imperfect part of her neighbour's life had always
intrigued Emilia. It was hard to picture Zoe failing at anything – let alone something as public as marriage.

A memory came to her: an impromptu gathering in
the garden last summer. Emilia, Zoe and a couple of her
school mum friends sharing a bottle of rosé in the shade
of the gazebo as they watched their children play frisbee
on the lawn. Peering over her sunglasses at Zoe's daughter,
one of the mums had asked where Freya had bought her
pink sundress.

'That FARA place on the high street,' she'd replied, keen
to stress her ethical credentials. The woman had clapped her

hands at that: 'Hilarious. It's my daughter's – we dropped off a bag of stuff last month.' Everyone had laughed. Everyone except Zoe, whose jaw had clenched as she forced a smile.

'You know how we'd got Hugh Campion to be our celeb compère?' Zoe went on. 'Because of some age-old connection to the square?'

Emilia nodded, vaguely remembering a mention of the *Gardening Hour* presenter months ago.

'He's had to pull out. Filming clash. So now I need to find someone else, and it needs to be a proper person.'

Again, Emilia nodded, aware that by 'proper' Zoe meant famous; good enough for Addison Square.

'I know I've said this before, but it's going to be huge, Ems,' Zoe went on. 'Two hundred people for two hundred years! And listen, I'm light on volunteers for both prep and the night itself, and I realise you've got your hands full . . .' A tiny, inorganic V-shaped indentation appeared between Zoe's brows, as though having been Botoxed into submission everywhere else, the muscles of her forehead had chosen to assert themselves with force in that single spot ' . . . but I'd so appreciate Adrian's help getting someone good.'

Was Zoe actually about to suggest that her husband should enlist one of the TV personalities he represented to . . . what? Come and compère a garden party? 'Our budget isn't huge. In fact, we've pretty much drained it already. Who knew marquees could be that expensive? It's a big ask, I know, but with Adrian's connections . . .'

She was. And for free, no less.

From the way Zoe was pressing her lips together as she slid a document across the table, anyone would think she was revealing a government scandal. But no. It was just an

Excel spreadsheet broken down into colour-coded columns marked 'refreshments', 'catering', 'fun & games' and 'short film.' If her neighbour loved spreadsheets and budgets this much, she really should have stayed in investment banking.

Some of the boxes marked 'volunteers' had simply been filled with question marks. *She* was supposed to be the answer to one of those question marks.

'Wow,' Emilia managed. 'You've been so ... organised.'

'Tell me about it. Thought I'd deleted the whole bloody spreadsheet last week. Had to call whatsherface. With the sandals.'

Emilia had what felt like her first easy laugh of the day.

'You're as bad as Ade. He can never remember Colette's name. Calls her "the geek". Every time we hear that little wheelie-briefcase being pulled along the pavement outside ... '

'Oh God,' Zoe shrilled, 'the briefcase!'

' ... it's "Geek to the rescue!"'

Zoe was so amused by this that, swallowing a mouthful of scalding coffee, she began to flap a hand in front of her mouth. But this time, Emilia's laugh wasn't so easy. This had been happening a lot lately. One minute she'd be quoting her hilarious husband, and the next it would hit her that whatever he'd said wasn't that funny – just unkind.

Gazing back down at the spreadsheet Emilia searched for something more to say. Something that would make her sound involved even if that was the last thing she wanted to be. Finding nothing, she reached forward and shovelled the two last mouthfuls of carrot cake into her mouth.

Zoe waited until Emilia swallowed, then clapped her hands together.

'I'm so grateful for your help.'

This was how the Zoes of the world did what they did. At no point had she agreed to help out with this giant fag of a party – yet within an hour she'd been bound and cuffed.

'Right.'

Zoe stood, and as she tucked a curtain of hair behind one ear, Emilia noticed a thick stripe of freshly dried blood along the lobe. Less of a nick than a hefty bash – and a recent one.

'Ouch. You've hurt yourself.'

That little V was back between Zoe's brows. Touching her ear with the tip of a finger, she remembered, smiled. 'I was trying to shift the hall table yesterday. Lost my balance and boom: smack, bang into the wall. That'll teach me. Anyway, this was fun!'

'It was.'

'We'll do it again?'

'Please.'

Outside on the pavement, released from the tyranny of Zoe's demands and the relentless perkiness that always managed to make her feel 'less than', Emilia watched her neighbour stride off down the high street.

Hit by a rare wave of well-being, she stood there for a moment, watching the procession of shoppers with exposed, reddened flesh seek out strips of shade. Then she remembered Hattie, Theo and Marta – who would be waiting to go home – and saw the rest of the day stretching ahead in a series of menial tasks.

She had begun to weave her way through the stationary traffic when the lights changed and a white van man, crawling close enough for her to feel the hot huff of his engine against her flank, suggested she 'watch where the fuck you're going!'

The curse landed like a slap, but as she turned to see the face of such casual vitriol, Emilia heard a male voice behind her retort: 'How about you watch your language, mate?' She smiled in recognition: 'Hugo.'

She waited until they had both safely stepped up onto the kerb to kiss her neighbour lightly on the cheek. The kissing was a recent development. In all the years Hugo Cooper had lived across the square, they had only ever greeted one another with nods and smiles. But they'd been spending so much time together lately. With her neighbour no longer working, his wife away so much and their boys now closer than ever, it felt as though life were pushing them together – and Emilia had found herself looking forward to their playdates more than she should.

'No need to be un-fucking-civil, is there?'

Hugo's hand was still hovering around her elbow and she took in his long lean figure – in a mottled grey T-shirt today, sunglasses obscuring his suede brown eyes – and smiled.

'Seriously, are you OK?'

Amused by the question – as though she were some fragile eighteenth-century lady – Emilia broke into a laugh. 'Yeah. All good.'

Suddenly she was. How many people had that effect on her? Now that her parents were gone there was only really her best friend Caroline, who had kept her promise when she first moved to LA, FaceTiming every Wednesday evening without fail. But then she'd missed a week and Emilia had missed the next, and now they were lucky if they managed to snatch ten minutes once a fortnight.

None of the school mums did, as much as she'd tried to become a part of their clique. And as for Adrian, who was always either out or locked away in his study, her husband had adopted such an infuriating habit of scrolling through his Twitter feed when she tried to speak to him at the end of the day that Emilia had found herself swallowing idle anecdotes and jokes lately, knowing they would only fall on deaf ears. That she would, at most, get a distracted smile and a misplaced 'Yeah?'.

She'd forgotten how good it felt to ramble inconsequentially with another human being – until that still, low-skied Saturday in February. Theo's sixth birthday party, with all the joy and exhaustion that came with it. She'd been so furious at Adrian for leaving early, but Hugo had stayed, helped her clean up afterwards, and the easy banter they'd immediately fallen into hadn't just been a pleasant surprise, but a release. Like coming up for air after holding your breath too long.

'This heat ...' she started.

At that precise moment Hugo said, 'I'm glad I caught you,' and this time they both laughed.

They had turned into the square now, and already, as she had started to at the end of the boys' play dates, Emilia was trying to find a way of extending their time together. 'I was going to ask whether Ollie might be free for a run around in the garden?'

'He is.' It was too quick. 'I mean, we're around.' They were nearing his house, and she slowed her stride.

'Great.' Beneath his shades, Hugo looked tired.

'Yasmeen away again?'

'Lisbon. All week. And there are only so many rounds of

50

Monster Bowling I can play without losing my mind. But obviously it's their playdate, not ours.'

'Obviously.'

'So half an hour? Usual place?' Hugo threw her a parting wave.

Still smiling, Emilia rounded the corner into her side of the square. Maybe today wasn't going to be a write-off. Maybe she'd even have time for a quick shower and a change of clothes before the playdate. Pulling out her phone she checked the time, using the other hand to push open the front gate.

As always the latch was stuck. She pushed again. Harder this time. And when it released itself with a jolt, Emilia went with it, flying forward and landing hard on her knees on the York paving.

As she waited for the pain to hit Emilia registered the torn hem of her skirt, the dots of blood seeping through the fabric over her knee, and the humiliation. Did anyone see her go down? Then her eyes fell on the phone that had landed with an anti-climactic smack, face down, a little way off.

'Shit.'

Flipping it over she saw that the screen was black, a web of silver cracks radiating from a single central bullet hole: the point of impact. It was just a tumble; just a phone. Why this sense of foreboding?

CHAPTER 7

COLETTE

'We definitely can't just fix the screen?'

'I wouldn't recommend it.'

Perched on the edge of the sofa, Colette pulled on the polyurethane gloves she carried with her for precisely these moments. Hospital blue, with ruched elasticated cuffs, they looked like an absurd hybrid of gardening and surgical gloves, but she'd learned not to take any chances.

These devices splintered like ice, into a thousand shards that could slip beneath fingernails and slice into little bare feet like the ones crossed on the sitting room floor in front of her now, where Emilia's son sat staring up at her.

'He should probably put those back on.' Colette nodded at the slippers that had been kicked off beside the sofa.

For a second Emilia didn't react.

Then, leaning forward, she handed them to her son.

'She's right, T. Put them on.'

Beneath a swell of lower back fat the greying elastic of Emilia's underwear was on display, but she was too intent on catering to her son's needs to care, and Colette wondered what it must feel like to be that child – a child so central to someone's existence that dignity was sacrificed without a second thought.

'I think Theo would like a pair of those gloves.' Back on the sofa beside her, Emilia was swivelling her wedding ring around her finger. 'They look like super-hero gloves, don't they, T?'

'Which they are.' Colette attempted an indulgent smile that the boy didn't return.

He looked like his father and probably always had done, but having gone to great lengths to ensure Adrian would be at work when she came to look at Emilia's phone today, Colette couldn't help but feel that his mini-me had been sent to taunt her.

Children unnerved her generally. Like the horses who could smell your fear, they seemed to be able to sense the fraudulence, feel not only that she wasn't a mum, but that the word had no meaning for her, either practically or emotionally.

When still of an age to be told that 'the clock was ticking', Colette had nodded, smiled in apology – the need for one implicit – and longed for the ticking to be done. Now that as a single fifty-seven-year-old the questions and warnings had mercifully stopped, Colette continued to see them only as vaguely hostile little beings – and a jeering reminder of everything she'd lacked as a child.

'Nope.' Cautiously she brushed the loose fragments of screen into one of the Ziploc bags she kept in her case. 'You're going to need a new phone. The basic functions may still be working but it's possible your logic board's been damaged.' Her client's face was blank. 'Those are the brains of the phone,' she explained. 'And even if it hasn't, the brains of an iPhone 8 are geriatric.'

In Colette's gloved hand, Emilia's phone pinged, a message from the square WhatsApp group appearing at the top of the screen.

Her client groaned. 'Ignore it. It'll be about the party of the decade. The party of the century!' Rolling her eyes, she explained: 'Zoe's spent months planning this "epic" event. We've all been roped in.'

Colette was hyper-aware of the event.

She'd spent the past four months fielding Zoe Mulligan's calls over spreadsheet issues, editing some kind of short historical documentary to be screened on the night, and helping her choreograph the invitations. The visits she charged for, of course, but although the calls were numerous, they were often too short to qualify as a consultation, and Colette had been forced to accept that being there on the night – a welcome member of this tight community – would be her recompense. With less than a month to go, however, Zoe was leaving the sending out of those impeccably designed invitations awfully late. Just that morning Colette had been forced to email her client and ask which of the possible dress codes she'd settled on. There was a navy linen trouser suit on the high street with her name on it: M&S but could be Jaeger.

'I've been helping Zoe out with the party,' she told Emilia now. 'Going to be quite the night, isn't it?'

But her client wasn't listening.

'Wait – if I'm getting WhatsApps, can I really not just get the screen fixed?' Emilia's pleading and increasingly shrill tones brought her back to the present. 'A new phone ... It's such a fag.'

Over the years Colette had adopted the placid tone of a medical professional examining an injury with her clients, finding it helped reduce the disproportionate anxiety she was often greeted by. The impotence she understood. If technology were simple Colette wouldn't be able to charge £100 as a call-out fee. She wouldn't be earning upwards of £150,000 a year making people's lives and jobs run smoothly. But even after all these years she had trouble understanding the rage, this insistence on characterising technology as a hostile force when it was, in fact, the most powerful life-enhancer.

'Emilia.'

'Yeah.'

'A new phone will improve your life, I promise.'

Her client groaned, then nodded. 'Sorry. You know what I'm like with this stuff.'

Colette knew. Although typical of a certain type of technologically illiterate client, Emilia was worse than most in their early forties. Time and time again she'd been forced to caution her on everything from the clapped-out devices she stubbornly refused to replace to the password – Emilia100 – her client had insisted on using on every device, App and site since she'd known her.

In a burst of professional enthusiasm Colette had once sent a round robin email to her least savvy clients – subject header 'Digital Hygiene' – laying down the ground rules for safe and unsafe passwords. No kids' names or birthdays, no anniversary dates, and as for those still using 'password', well, they deserved to have their identities stolen. Not that anyone paid a blind bit of notice.

'I haven't actually told Ade that I smashed this one yet,' Emilia said quietly, picking at the corner of a Peppa Pig plaster across her kneecap. 'This is all the confirmation he needs.'

'I don't follow.'

'Well, that I'm crap.' A shrug. 'Completely fucking useless.' Having forgotten to self-censor, Emilia glanced guiltily over at her son.

For a second Colette thought the half-smile dragging one side of her client's face down was rueful. Then she understood that Emilia was fighting back tears.

The first one fell. 'Ignore me.'

Obviously that wasn't possible, but since Colette was not a tactile person, she sat there beside Emilia, gloved hands crammed between her knees, waiting for the tears to stop.

'It's just one more thing to make me feel like ... like a failure,' the words came out in an angry judder, 'you know?'

Colette didn't.

Drying her eyes roughly with the back of her hand, like a child still holding onto an injustice even after the tantrum had subsided, Emilia turned to face her.

'Are you married? I know you don't wear a ring, but ... '

Colette smiled. All these years working for the Carters, for so many Addison Square residents, and none of them knew a thing about her.

'No.'

The amount of marital fear she encountered in her job – wives fearful of their husbands; husbands fearful of their wives – was just one of the many reasons marriage had never appealed. All that rubbish about 'having each other's backs' really translated into power play and dependency. Over at the Coopers' on the other side of the square it was that lawyer wife, Yasmeen, flexing her muscle over her 'stay-at-home' husband, Hugo.

But where Adrian Carter was concerned it was clear that there was more than a marital imbalance. This man Emilia seemed to believe she was stuck with – he was sick. And like all sickos, clever enough to keep the wife on the back foot even as he secretly binged on smut.

Before her the grey marble fireplace was lined with a jumble of wedding, christening and holiday photographs – the chronology measurable both from Emilia's waistline and her increasing discomfort in front of the camera. Her client could once have been mistaken for that *Titanic* actress. With her high cheekbones and soulful blue eyes she still had an English rose beauty now, but over the years her looks and figure had solidified into something motherly, and the dreaminess in her eyes had clouded into a vague disappointment.

'It's not worth getting into a state.' Colette was no good at this. 'I've got to go to the Apple Store today, so I could pick you up a new phone and drop it back tomorrow. I've got to swing by Yasmeen's anyway.'

'Oh God, really?' Emilia's gratitude was pathetic, and Colette fought the urge to tell her a few home truths. *You are not the disappointment in this marriage – trust me!* 'That would be amazing. But yes, of course Adrian will have to know. He'll see it – you – on the credit card bill.'

'Ah.' Talk about dependency. Just the idea of having her every need and whim logged for another person's judgement made Colette shudder.

'But if you really don't mind?'

'No problem at . . .'

The sound of a key in the lock made Theo jump up and run out of the room. 'Daddy!' Colette swallowed. *No.*

'You're back so early.'

She noted the quick smoothing of hair and clothing Emilia effected before following her son through to the hallway.

'Just for a minute. Thought I'd nip home and change before my drinks.'

'Drinks?'

She could hear the disappointment in Emilia's voice from here. But Colette's heart lifted. 'Just for a minute' meant she might still be able to avoid coming face to face with Adrian Carter.

'I told you last week. Those documentary guys.'

'Right.' A pause. 'I got steak. But it'll keep until tomorrow.'

'I've got that ITV thing tomorrow. 'Fraid I've got work meetings every night this week.'

Footsteps on wooden flooring. Footsteps Colette prayed were leading to the staircase.

Beneath her shirt, her bra felt constrictive, as though someone had moved the hook to its narrowest point. Then suddenly there he was in the doorway, damp-pitted in a Mao-collared linen shirt, a studiously distressed leather satchel wrapped snugly across his paunch.

'If you're here to sort the malware thing, I haven't got time.'

The lack of civilised greeting shouldn't have surprised Colette, yet for a second it was enough to eclipse the revulsion she felt at seeing Adrian again. How many tens of thousands did your parents pay for an education that left you thinking this was acceptable? Then the electrical signals in

Colette's brain kicked in, triggering a series of flashbacks to the last time she'd been standing in front of Adrian. *'Hard to tell what you're into.'*

'Actually, Colette's here for me.' Behind him Emilia hunched with contrition. 'My phone – I smashed it. But she's kindly going to pick me up another. She says I'll be due an upgrade, and I have had that one years.'

'Hmm.'

She had to hand it to Adrian. Conveying so much in that single sound – annoyance, disapproval and the crushing tedium of having a wife who went around smashing up her phone – was a gaslighting masterclass.

Looking past his wife at Colette, Adrian met her eye for the first time.

'Auditioning for a Marvel movie, are we?'

'Sorry?'

'The gloves. Don't get me wrong: they're a good look.'

Colette had forgotten she still had them on.

'They're for handling broken screens.'

'Whatever you say, um ... '

Colette. Not Yvette, Claudette or Odette: Colette. It's not a common name, and yes, people sometimes seem to get confused, but what is it you find so particularly hard to remember about it – about me? Christ, the man hadn't even given her the satisfaction of a flinch when he'd seen her sitting there on his sofa. Did he not remember what he'd done the last time she was here?

Colette opened her mouth to say her name, just once, but loud and with enough attitude to imprint it on Adrian Carter's mind forever, but already her client had turned, slicing through the air with a hand in a 'can I get through?'

gesture of impatience to the wife and child loitering like foot soldiers in the doorway.

'Haven't got time for the other thing now anyway,' he threw back from the hallway, presumably to Colette. 'But if we can get that sorted asap.' Then, without waiting for an answer. 'You're a lifesaver.'

There were 'you' people and 'we' people in the world, Colette decided as she moved slowly along the Hammersmith Road. The 'you' lot saw everyone from IT consultants like her to builders, plumbers and waitresses as people deserving of acknowledgement and Christian names to be addressed by, whereas the 'we' brigade operated with a corporate grandeur that elevated them above others. For them that 'we' was tossed out with faux generosity, like the crumbs from an empty sandwich wrapper to pigeons.

From the passenger seat where it lay in its Ziploc bag, smashed face upturned, Emilia's phone buzzed, and drawing up at a red light Colette leaned over to read the message that had come in.

Hugo:
Fancy another playdate tomorrow? Ollie
keeps asking.

So Hugo Cooper was Emilia's square buddy. Good for her. She was fond of this gentle-mannered house husband. Hugo was kind, considerate, and yes, not unpleasant to look at. This hadn't gone unnoticed by the older residents, who jokingly referred to him as 'the square's George Clooney'. Because of the laughing eyes, the stubbled jaw and the fact that if the square had to have one, well it sure as hell wasn't going to be Adrian Carter. Hugo even had the hot-shot media lawyer wife: a hundred words a minute Yasmeen. No wonder their two better halves had gravitated towards one another.

Ping. Another message.

We could even treat the kids to an early eve picnic?

Ping.

But you and Adrian probably have plans.

Adrian had plans, and Colette was willing to bet they didn't involve work – but Emilia? She'd just be bathing, bedding and bingeing on the kind of unfathomably popular US property reality TV shows that always popped up in her 'recently watched' Sky list whenever Colette was called in to fix the broadband. Unless she took her neighbour up on his offer and allowed herself a moment of carefree companionship? God knows she looked like she could do with the company.

The toot of a horn forced her to drive on, faster now, until, safe in the bowels of Westfield's car park, Colette checked Emilia's phone again. Her client still had her laptop. She might see her neighbour's messages and get back to him from there. But no. Nothing.

Then, as she was waiting for the lift, a muffled 'ping' from her bag. Go on. Say yes to Clooney.

Colette was surprised to find she cared.

Only the message wasn't from Emilia, but Zoe,

spray-gunning her neighbours with more party demands on the square WhatsApp.

> Still in need of volunteers for the morning itself??
> Brawny volunteers.

One tiny tap. An instinctive reaction. A mistake she registered a millisecond too late and was surprised to find had even worked through the plastic baggie. But already Colette was into the square WhatsApp thread, and idly scrolling.

Zoe:
> Heavy lifting will be required! But only for an
> hour – tops 🙏.
> Poor Hugo's on his lonesome at the mo.

A flurry of responses were coming in. Promises to ask husbands and sons. A flexed bicep from Hugo. But Colette's eyes were fixed on the PS from Zoe that had appeared beneath.

> #awks, but tech lady seems to think she's invited.
> We're already at capacity. Does anyone feel strongly
> that she should be there?

In front of her, the lift door opened and closed. Still Colette didn't move.

Guy:

Yasmeen:
Long as I'm not seated next to her 🙏

Hugo:
Poor thing. Can't imagine her diary's packed.

Adrian:
The geek would need a plus one for the
rolling Tumi 🛞

Colette sucked in a breath and held it, waiting, as with a stubbed toe, for the pain to hit. When it did, she found that it was focussed around the 'poor thing', the Tumi comment, and a joke that was all the more humiliating because she didn't understand what was funny.

In a daze she made her way up to the Apple store and waited patiently as a young man named Najid with a man-bun and the slender, hairless forearms of a teenage girl worked his way through her list of requirements. When he went off to get Emilia's upgrade, Colette couldn't help herself. Pulling up the thread again, she felt the sting of the words anew. Only one person had come to her defence while she and Najid had been talking: Sylvia.

Definitely invite Colette! Think of the holes she's dug
us out of over the years.

Hugo's Go on. Throw her a bone hardly counted.

Colette flashed back to Leila's smirk, the day before. Her own: *I'm as loyal to my clients as they are to me.'* What a fool she'd been. A self-important, misguided fool. It didn't matter how many years she'd looked after them, or how many holes she'd dug them out of; they weren't going to stick their necks out for her. God forbid any of them should actually be forced to socialise with her for a couple of hours.

Man-bun was back with Emilia's new phone, and as he removed the protective packaging strip by strip, Colette stared down at the smashed screen in her open palm.

The words of a headteacher in a *Wired* op-ed she'd read a few months ago – THE PROBLEM WITH KIDS AND WHATSAPP GROUPS – floated back to her. 'Like any kind of defined group or clique, it's all too easy for the tone to descend into bitching or bullying. Especially when people believe they're in a private and therefore "safe" space.'

What else had this lot said about her over the months, years? What more could Emilia's phone tell her? In this instance she'd been Zoe's 'PS', but before that, had she been a running gag – a punchline?

That one tap had revealed the truth about her clients. Had she not glanced at the square WhatsApp thread, she might never have known who these people really were, that they were weak, frivolous, disloyal . . . and worse. Because one of them was a stalker, a predator, a criminal. And how hard would it be, with this keyhole into Addison Square in her possession, to work out who that was?

Leila's suggestion had seemed so outrageous in the moment. But she was a young, foreign, single woman, and she was being preyed upon by someone in her own community.

That thing she'd said, about it feeling 'like an assault'? It was neither 'hysterical' nor 'hyperbolic': two of the choice adjectives for entirely legitimate female reactions to intimidation or aggression. After that night in Adrian's study, Colette understood this more than ever. Humiliation was the objective: Mr Carter's specialty, as it happened. And if she were to look into Leila's stalker, she knew exactly where she'd start: who her number one suspect would be.

'Right.' Najid held out a hand for Emilia's phone. 'Now I'll just transfer the data.'

She looked from him to the slim rectangle pulsating with possibility in her palm, and back again. Then, after a moment's pause, she handed it over. 'Once you've done that transferral,' she asked with a smile, 'how long would it take you to fix the screen? I might actually keep the old device.'

CHAPTER 8

HAMMERSMITH POLICE STATION
EXTRACT OF RECORDED INTERVIEW
WITH MRS EMILIA CARTER

Date: 16 July
Duration: 106 minutes
No. of pages: 51
Conducted by Officers of the
Metropolitan Police

EC: Do I need a lawyer?

DC HARRIS: Do you think you need a lawyer, Mrs Carter?

EC: Yes. No. I don't know.

DC BAXTER: Tell you what, let's put what happened between your husband and Ms Mercheri to one side, for a moment. The victim had only moved to Addison Square in May. You lot are, by all accounts, a 'tight knit' group. Did she get on with everyone? Or was there maybe someone she rubbed up the wrong way?

DC BAXTER: For the benefit of the tape, Mrs Carter is smiling.

EC: I'm not smiling. It's just the way you put it. I mean, I can't think of anyone Leila *hadn't* 'rubbed up the wrong way'.

DC HARRIS: One of your neighbours was particularly riled by Ms Mercheri, though. She'd spoken to you about it, hadn't she?

CHAPTER 9

ZOE

'Timer's telling me you've got exactly nine minutes left, Felix.'

Eyes fixed to the fiery red figure on the screen, thumbs twitching on his console, her son didn't answer. In his ears Zoe spotted the white stems of his AirPods.

They'd seemed like such a good idea when she'd bought them for him last year. Worth every pound for the peace they'd given them. Now that Felix had taken to wearing them constantly, like tiny prosthetic limbs, she regretted her decision. They reminded her of that rag of a T-shirt her son had carried around with him everywhere, long after it was socially acceptable for a child to have a comfort toy.

Her dislike for his 'fiddlything', as he'd called it, had grown so violent that Zoe had taken a cruel pleasure in stuffing it into the mouth of a street bin on Felix's tenth birthday. Like his 'fiddlything', he was using those pods to seal himself off from the world. From her.

'Felix?'

As her son turned off the pods, the sound erupted, rifle shots crackling out through the flat. 'Jesus. How loud have you got that thing? You'll damage your hearing.'

'Mum.'

'Eight minutes, got it? Then homework while I get supper ready.'

In the corner of the sitting room that doubled up as her husband's office, Guy was at his desk, tapping away on his keyboard, and for a moment Zoe stood there unseen in the doorway, watching him.

'Did you hear how loud that was?'

Glancing up, her husband shut his laptop in a swift movement.

'I told him to wear his pods.'

Zoe's stomach tightened.

'So he can damage his eardrums as well as his brain? I'd rather he came off that thing.'

'O-kay.'

She softened her voice.

'We agreed to half an hour's gaming MWF.'

'I don't know what that means.'

'Monday, Wednesday, Friday.'

'Right. Well, he's literally just got back from school, so I think he's allowed a moment to chill.'

'I just think he should,' *could*, she reminded herself too late, 'find other ways of doing that. He breaks up next week and I'm not having him on that thing all summer.' She resented that nagging note in her voice. Why was everything always left up to her? Why was she always forced to be the fishwife?

'You definitely put all the safety locks on when you first set him up on the XBox?'

'We've been through this.'

'I know, but everyone says the privacy settings are crucial. I don't want him talking to random strangers and so on.'

'Pretty sure I did all that.'

That's a 'no' then.

'I think we should get tech lady back in, just to double check.'

That after all this time – and all the help she'd given her with the party – Zoe still had occasional mind blanks about the IT lady's name was something she irrationally held against Colette. Of course: Colette.

'We really don't need to spend a hundred odd quid on it.' Guy grumbled.

'All the other stuff she's been doing has gone on the committee's tab,' she reminded her husband. 'And she could check out those two-step verification alerts you were worried about – tell you if you've got to set that up.'

'I don't want her touching my stuff.' It was so abrupt that Zoe laughed. 'She always messes with the settings ... ' He reached for a file from his in-tray. 'It's a pain.'

'OK fine.' What on earth was he on about? 'We'll leave it. God forbid anyone should touch your precious "stuff".'

She thought back to the translucent pallor of her son's neck against that angry red screen, a pallor she couldn't help but resent because it was a constant reminder of Felix's father. There had been a yellow pustule pushing through the fuzz at the base of his hairline. She'd have to squeeze that later.

'But listen: with the next few weeks so full on with party prep, I just want to be sure Felix is being held to his time limits when I'm not here.'

'Being held.' She'd turned down the page in *The Argument Free Marriage* where the psychotherapist had explained how 'removing that accusatory "you"' could diffuse a situation before it 'threatened to become explosive'. In fairness to Guy, Zoe had never felt that he treated Felix like anything but his own flesh and blood. But with that threat implicit in so many of their conversations now, even the most banal, and the balance of their relationship more precarious than ever, Zoe had been trying to use that tip to steady their interactions. As though their marriage were like an uneven-legged table, needing a wedge. As though without the wedge *she* was constantly providing, everything could at any moment go flying.

'I don't know why you had to take on that party,' Guy muttered. 'On top of everything else. On top of all the croquet tournaments and the film nights you've laid on this year ...'

'I'm the committee chairwoman. How could I not be involved in the biggest event the square's had in fifty years?'

He gave a tight-lipped smile. 'I just don't want you to get stressed out, that's all.'

A look passed between them that was layered with so many emotions: recognition, blame, challenge. But the top note was caution.

'It's a lot, I know.' Dial it down, dial it down. 'But I'm delegating. Trying to, anyway.'

The cleaner had been while she was out. Zoe knew this

from the way the two wingback chairs on either side of the fireplace were squarely facing the sofa and not at the forty-five-degree inward angles she always positioned them at. Crossing the room, she shifted the left one, then the right, and stood back, admiring the chairs' perfect symmetry on either side of the personalised 'family photo dome' that sat in the middle of the mantelpiece – all four family members frozen within it clearly visible.

The day Guy had given it to her – on her birthday two years ago – had been a good day. He'd insisted she have a lie in, even though Zoe had never enjoyed them. Too many years catching that 6 a.m. train into the city. The kids had made her breakfast in bed. And as everyone had piled onto it with their presents, tearing open the packages they'd only just wrapped for her and eating her crumpets, Zoe had felt the wholeness of their family. She'd shaken up that delight-fully tacky 'non-seasonal snow globe', watched the flakes of glitter shower down over their tiny 3D portraits and thought: We're safe. I'm safe. This marriage is different. This year is going to be different.

'Oh, and good news.' She turned back towards Guy. 'The landlord of the empty flat downstairs has said we can stash all the party gear and the booze in there.'

'Aren't the builders still working on it?'

'There's been some hold-up, so they won't start up again until August now. He agreed that since it's just sitting there unused and nearest to the garden entrance, we might as well make the most of it.'

'Great.'

'Also, I've asked Adrian to get us a new host. One of his clients.'

'You've done what?'

'Well, I've asked Emilia, and she doesn't think it'll be a problem, so I emailed a wish list over . . .'

'A wish list?'

'Can you imagine if he managed to get us that *BBC Breakfast* guy he looks after? Wouldn't he be fab?'

'Zo,' closing his eyes, her husband pinched the bridge of his nose. 'Why on earth would Charlie Stayt want to host a garden party?'

Above them a single muffled beat thudded through the ceiling. Then another. She and Guy locked eyes as they waited for the remorseless single-note sub-bass drone of the intro to stop. Then again, that was when the singing, if you could call that snarling singing, would start.

Zoe had heard this song so many times that she often found herself humming or singing the refrain. *'I'm coming in quick, quick, quick. Coming in slick, aye, aye.'* But her irritation levels paled in comparison to Guy's.

'Please, God, no.' Her husband flicked his eyes to the ceiling – then back to her. 'You haven't spoken to her, have you?'

'I was going to the other day, but . . .'

Jerking his chair back, he cut in: 'D'you know what? I think I've had about enough of this.'

'Wait.' Zoe held up a hand. 'You'll only make things worse.' She smoothed her hair. 'I'll do it.'

As she climbed the stairs, a strategy formed. She would ignore what had happened in the garden (if the woman had been meditating, Zoe probably shouldn't have bothered her), and give Ms Mercheri the benefit of the doubt on the noise levels too.

They would start from scratch. Zoe would get a date in the diary for their drink, and then, as a slightly embarrassed 'by the way', mention the music. After that, she would broach the subject of the square party.

A rap on the door yielded nothing. Of course. Leila couldn't hear it. Zoe knocked again, harder and longer. Still nothing. Was it possible the young woman wasn't in? That the music had come on by mistake in some way? Peering pointlessly in through the spyhole, Zoe remembered the spare key Mr Bevan had given them before he moved out. The one that had been sitting in a bowl on their hall table ever since. The previous occupant certainly hadn't been as loud as Leila, but he had locked himself out on average once a fortnight – hence the spare key. If the locks hadn't been changed . . .

A noise inside made her rear back from the door. Then the music cut out and she heard footsteps approach.

'Hi.'

It takes people a millisecond to rearrange their faces when they answer their front doors. Which is why you'll occasionally glimpse a 'why the hell are you bothering me?' scowl before it morphs into the requisite 'what can I do for you?' smile. Only Leila's scowl didn't morph into anything even vaguely civil. No, their upstairs neighbour just looked very pissed off.

For a moment Zoe was so flummoxed by the sight of this antagonistic-faced, damp-skinned woman in her steel blue corset-style tank top and matching leggings, that she forgot the bubbly opener she'd rehearsed on her way up.

'Sorry!' Leila offered, looking anything but. 'Music too loud?'

This only threw Zoe further off balance. She hadn't wanted to go in on that.

'It is a *little* loud.' She softened this with a small shrug. 'But that wasn't why I came up.'

'Oh.' Placing her palms flat against the hall wall, Leila embarked on a small series of stretches that defined every sinew in her long legs, distending the thin shiny fabric around her thighs and buttocks to near transparency, so that Zoe found herself looking away. 'I can get carried away when I'm doing my Tabatas.'

'Your . . .'

'You never tried Tabata's HIIT workouts? Literally torches calories. And the tracks are a-mazing.' Leila's mouth stretched out into a smile so wide you could see her molars, and Zoe couldn't help but feel relieved at this gaping imperfection in an otherwise flawless physique. 'Don't you just love Sho V?'

If Sho V is the rapper, then no – not a massive fan. But he's the bane of my husband's life.

'Not as much as you, clearly.'

It was supposed to be jokey, but from the way Leila had pulled her chin into her neck, this didn't come across.

'I mean that song's obviously . . . a favourite.'

For a moment both women stood on either side of the threshold, scrutinising one another. Then Zoe pushed on, 'Actually we wanted to get a date in the diary for those drinks?' She was back on an even keel now. 'We feel terrible that we haven't managed to yet. Maybe Wednesday or Thursday next week?'

Don't offer up any more. Makes you sound desperate.

'Actually, next week is kind of tricky.' Leila had placed

her hand on the door frame, as though about to close it, and Zoe glanced at the smartwatch on her wrist. She'd bought one for Guy last year, thinking it might help get her husband moving more, trim him down. He'd ditched it after a month. 'But soon, yeah?'

That this woman hadn't even bothered to dress up her brush-off made Zoe double down. So what if it made her neighbour uncomfortable? She *should* feel uncomfortable.

'You just let us know when works. Oh, and you got an invitation to the party, didn't you?' *I know you did; I slid it under your door myself.* 'It's going to be a fabulous night. Everyone's been so generous with their time. But I'm still short on volunteers for the night itself. You might have seen my notes on the square WhatsApp group? I've got a spreadsheet downstairs. I can nip down and get it.'

At the word 'spreadsheet' the twitch of a smile started up at the corners of Leila's mouth. Without bothering to suppress it, she threw out casually: 'Oh, I don't get involved in that stuff.'

Zoe walked back downstairs in a stupor.

'How did it go?'

Guy looked up from his computer.

'Well, I told her.'

'Great.'

'But I don't think she'll be coming for a drink anytime soon. And she made it pretty clear she wasn't interested in pitching in with the party.'

Zoe thought about the way Leila had said 'that stuff'. About the irritating fluency of her English – with its American-style up-notes at the end of every sentence, as though she'd learned the language watching *America's Next Top Model* – and experienced the same peculiar mix of awe and offence that she'd felt that day in the garden.

'Still, overall a success.'

For a second, she thought her husband was being sarcastic. But he was pointing at the ceiling. 'She's not just turned it down: she's turned it off. Nice one.'

Right on cue, the familiar beats buzzed from above, as loud as before. Seconds later: *I'm coming in quick, quick, quick. Coming in slick, aye, aye'* rang out.

'You've got to be fucking joking.' Guy's hands were on his cheeks. 'This is deliberate. Has to be.'

''Course it's not. She's just thoughtless, like everyone her age. I'll talk to her again. For now, let me get you a glass of wine. I could definitely do with one.'

As Zoe sipped her rosé and started on supper, she found herself soothed by the small, repetitive tasks: the tossing of the salad, turning of the lamb chops in their Le Creuset and laying of the table, always with the right condiments, because Guy was a stickler for those. Everything is under control.

'Freya, Felix: hands please,' she called out. 'Dinner's ready.'

But it was always after supper had been eaten and the table cleared away, after the kids were bathed and in bed, Freya's 'doodoo' tucked tightly beneath one limp arm, that the balance Zoe worked so hard to maintain was lost.

She had learned to spot the signs. The build-up of frustration from the day. The charge in the air between her and Guy just seconds before. The circling and curious formality. Which was why she always checked that Felix and Freya's doors were closed first. It was why she was careful to put the TV on beforehand – something rowdy enough to drown out what was to come. Because there was no mistaking the crash of a body against a wall, a side table, a lamp. The splintering of glass and china and dull thump of skin against skin. The rawness of human pain: too raw, sometimes, to be held in. And she couldn't have the children hearing that.

CHAPTER 10

HUGO

The table was laid, the aubergine parmigiana warming in the oven, and Hugo had just finished sellotaping Ollie's WELCOME HOME sign to the front door when Yasmeen's call came in.

'ETA?'

Noticing a set of sticky prints on the door frame, he gave them a rub with his sleeve. 'Oh God.' His grin faded. 'You only just landed?'

Careful to keep the dip of despondency from his voice, Hugo wandered back through into the kitchen and turned off the oven. 'Yeah, I bet. Well, we're . . . here, so I guess we'll see you when we see you.'

'Is it Mum?'

In a set of outsized pyjamas that pooled around his feet,

Ollie bounded up. Daddy might be the one doing the daily graft, but Mummy would always be the VIP. In fact, it sometimes seemed as though the more time his wife spent away on work trips, the greater their son's love for her grew. Which he shouldn't resent.

'Give me a sec, bean. Trying to hear what Mum's saying. She's running a bit late.'

It was overly dramatic, as always, but the collapse of his son's face mirrored Hugo's own feelings, and he did the quick flash forward every parent effects in the face of childish disappointment. It would take Yas at least an hour and a half to get home from Gatwick. Too late for Ollie to stay up. Which meant the inevitable pleading and sulking before bed, and his son hadn't been his usual bouncy self today anyway. He'd been slightly moody and withdrawn all week, and Hugo couldn't work out whether it was simply a case of him missing his mum or something else.

Eyeing the bottle of Malbec he'd uncorked in preparation for Yas's 'welcome home' supper (Christ, he'd built this up like a child himself), Hugo had the peevish thought that he might make a start on it now, before deciding against it and putting Ollie on the phone. At least that way Yas could break the news herself.

She hadn't, of course, ringing off shortly afterwards. And the next hour was spent as predicted, before exhausted from the pleading Ollie had finally climbed into bed.

'Now what are we going to go for tonight . . . '

Running his finger along the spines on the bookshelf, Hugo wondered how much longer they would have their precious ritual. Already he was steeling himself for the day Ollie declared himself 'too old for bedtime stories'.

'*Mr Penguin and the Fortress of Secrets*? *Dragon Slayers' Academy*? Oh, I know: we have a winner.'

Ollie really was too old for *Burglar Bill* now, but children tended to regress when upset and they'd read the story of a burglar who gives up thievery after almost being burgled himself so many times over the years that Hugo felt sure his son would find it comforting.

Perched on the side of his bed, stroking the back turned to him with one hand, Hugo began to read. Rather than grow limp with the lull of his voice, as they usually did, he felt his son's limbs stiffen. Abruptly, Ollie sat up.

'I don't want this book.' His voice wavered; his eyes were glossy with tears. 'I don't want it!'

To his astonishment, Ollie then reached over, snatched the book from Hugo's lap and flung it across the room.

'Hey!'

His son buried his face in his pillow, sobbing silently.

'What was that, bean? What's going on?'

Whatever it was, Ollie wasn't ready to talk about it, and for what felt like forever Hugo just sat there, watching the floating nebula projected against the walls by his son's night light – a birthday gift from Sylvia, who sweetly always remembered – waiting for his shaking shoulders to still and his breathing to even out. Then, the buzz of Hugo's phone snapped him out of his weary trance and he crept out of the room.

His back and forth with Emilia, earlier, had been cut short. Perhaps this was her now, picking up where they'd left off. But it was only Amazon Fresh: a reminder of tomorrow's delivery. And for some reason that settled it.

Pouring himself a large glass of wine he leaned against

the kitchen counter and started composing a WhatsApp to Emilia before deleting it. Putting the phone down, he thought about what those deletions meant.

They were new. Everything about this connection he'd formed with a woman who until recently had been more neighbour than friend was new.

It seemed unfathomable now that for all those years before their three-year stint in Copenhagen Emilia had been right there over the road, without really existing for him. Over the first two months of this year they must have exchanged, what, half a dozen text messages? Spent a couple of hours together in total. Always running into one another by chance in the garden and never quite breaking through the 'neighbourly' plateau.

Hugo avoided friendships born of circumstance. Just as he had never been one of the troop of hacks filing into the nearest pub after work before being made redundant, he had always found the idea of spending time with the school mums and dads shuddersome.

Emilia was different. He'd realised that the night of their return to London, just before Christmas, when he and Yas had celebrated with a 'date night' at the square pub.

He'd spotted his neighbour immediately, sinking a pint of Guinness at a table outside, wrapped up in a bright scarf and beanie while Adrian, beside her, barked into his phone.

As they'd hopped from one leg to another in a vain attempt to keep warm, Yas had leaned in and whispered, 'The Carters – four o'clock.'

'I know.'

'Should we go over and say hello? Tell them we're back?'

'Let's wait until he's off the phone.'

'Not become less of a twat while we were gone, has he? Put your phone down, mate. It's rude.'

Hugo had found it hard to keep a straight face at that.

'Shut up.' His wife had pinched his arm. 'I always take my calls somewhere private. And I would never leave you sitting there for everyone to feel sorry for.'

Adrian had. Through their first round and the second. And actually 'twat' was too kind for their neighbour. Those stupid braided leather bracelets Adrian insisted on wearing, as though he were just back from a gap year. The constant facial hair experimentation that had taken him from mutton chops to a Van Dyke goatee in the years they'd known him, the chin-strap style he'd sported the Christmas before they moved away a whimsical low-point.

But while his wife was feeling sorry for Emilia that night, Hugo had felt intrigued by this woman he'd never got to know. This slightly frazzled blonde who drank pints of Guinness and was so bored by her own husband that she'd started dipping her face down into the froth and sucking it off her top lip, like a child forced to create her own fun.

When they'd crossed paths again in the garden the following week with the boys it had been as fleeting as all their encounters, and Hugo had forgotten about his neighbour until Theo's sixth birthday party, that February. *Feel free to drop off,* the invitation had said. Only he hadn't done that. Because by the time he and Ollie had let themselves into the square gardens, Adrian had already bunked off his own son's birthday party 'to deal with a work crisis', leaving Emilia the only adult there.

Hugo hadn't had the heart to leave his neighbour sitting on a bench alone, watching a semi-circle of kids be entertained by a man in a Captain America suit, so he'd stayed until the very end, even helping with the clean-up, for the single selfish reason that he was enjoying this woman's company.

As Hugo picked up his phone again and took in Emilia's smiling WhatsApp profile picture, another memory surprised him. The night of Theo's birthday, after Ollie had passed out, he'd used the image of Emilia in the shower. He'd used the curves of her cupid's bow and the slightly hoisted upper lip that revealed a row of white teeth when she laughed, the milky nape of her neck and the fullness of her thighs beneath the jeans she'd worn that afternoon – and it had only taken seconds.

Hugo hadn't thought about where that urge had come from until today, at the end of this fortnight in which they'd seen more of each other than ever before.

A burst of Tamil outside the front door made him look up. For some inexplicable reason Yasmeen always spoke to her Sri Lankan father at a decibel audible from outer space. Registering his guilt – *why do I feel guilty?* – he slipped the phone back in his pocket.

'Got to go, Dad. Love you.' Letting herself in, his wife kicked the door shut behind her. 'Oh. My. God.'

Hugo couldn't help but feel the significance of that kick: only someone who hadn't spent a torturous hour putting their child to sleep could be so oblivious to the perils of a slammed door. 'So the mytaxi app wasn't working, and the queue at the rank was ridiculous. Then the idiot driver only decides to go via—'

'Yas,' Hugo cut in, holding out his arms and pointedly lowering his voice in a way he hoped his wife would emulate. 'I don't care about your driver's idiotic route. Get in here.'

For a minute they just held one another, rocking gently from side to side. Then Yas disengaged herself – the first to do so, as always.

She was like a squirrel, his wife: her movements small but constant. 'What are you like? I've only been gone three days.'

Was Yas aware that she did that? Shaved a couple of days off trips? Was it a way of playing down how much time she spent away, both to him and herself?

'Five. Not that I've been counting.'

She leaned in again and kissed him lightly on the mouth. 'So annoyed I missed Ollie. Let me go and have a peek. Then I need a shower.'

As Hugo reheated the aubergine, poured the wine and put some nuts and olives out on the kitchen table, he tried to quash a niggle of resentment at the special treatment Yas always got when she came back from a trip. Given he was the one who laid it on thickest, it made no sense to feel that way. Maybe it wasn't resentment but envy. She didn't seem to appreciate the independence those business trips gave her. Little things he'd once taken for granted, like being able to pop out for a nightcap alone or go for an early morning jog. Christ, Hugo hadn't been to the gym in so long that he'd had to remove his membership card from his wallet just to give himself a break from the guilt pangs.

'Smells amazing.'

In a navy silk kimono and a towel turban, Yas flopped down into a chair and started tapping at her phone.

'Now none of my Apps are working.'

'It's that Carluccio recipe you love.'

'I thought it was just the Gatwick WiFi.'

'Yas.'

She looked up, exhaled a 'sorry' and placed the phone face down on the kitchen table: a sacrificial offering.

'I'll call the geek tomorrow. Maybe it needs a factory reset or whatever they're called. Anyway, tell me everything,' she ordered. 'About your week, Ollie. He looked different, older? How is that even possible?' Reaching for the almonds, she began to work her way through them in a series of darting hand-to-mouth movements.

His wife ate with the same kinetic energy she injected into everything, from talking, laughing and working to sex. How she stayed so skinny had baffled him when they first got together. Now he understood that the furnace inside Yas needed constant refuelling for her to blaze as brightly she did.

'Enough.' He took what was left of the nuts and olives away. 'It's ready.'

Ordinarily this was the part Hugo loved most: filling his wife in on all the latest changes in their son, whether at the end of a day or a week. Telling her about Ollie's new obsession with magnets, his new phrases and friendships. But tonight he felt as though he were having to provide yet another service on top of the ones he'd been struggling to carry out all week. And Hugo wasn't sure he could explain what had just happened – how uncharacteristic Ollie's little fit had been just now, how out of sorts he'd seemed generally of late – so he didn't.

'Not much to tell, really. We swung by Sylvia's briefly for a cuppa earlier in the week, and he's had a kick about with Felix.'

'Sweet that he plays with Ollie.'

'Yeah.'

Was it? Hugo wasn't sure. Yet Felix seemed to have taken

Ollie under his wing, and it was good for him to have someone other than Theo to play with in the square.

'He and Theo have had a couple of playdates too actually.'

Reaching over, Yas speared a piece of aubergine from his
plate. 'So you were stuck with the mum.'

'Emilia? She's fine. She's not . . . '

'Not what?'

'I don't know. Dull.'

His wife gave a low laugh.

'If that's the nicest thing that can be said about her . . . '

'You know what I mean. Obviously her husband's a . . . '

' . . . prize cock.'

'Right. A bit of letch too, I reckon. Seems to have honed
in on that new French girl. I saw them heading into the
Addison together last night.'

'She's a dancer, isn't she? He'll be giving her "career advice".'

''Course he will. But Emilia's good company.'

'Doesn't actually do anything though, does she?'

Yas could be disparaging like that – casually writing off
anyone who didn't match her achievements with a single
judgement. Sometimes Hugo wondered whether secretly his
wife looked down on him in the same way.

'Bit harsh.' Then, to diffuse this. 'Can't imagine how they
ended up together, can you?'

'Haven't given it much thought.' She reached for a school
letter Ollie had brought home earlier that week. 'What's this?'

'End of year Sports Day. I've said I'll help out with
the relays.'

A flinch of something like embarrassment crossed
Yasmeen's face. So tiny and brief that anyone else would have
missed it. But Hugo knew what it meant.

'Tell me you're not . . .'

'I've got the Dubai forum.' Her eyes were pleading. *Don't make me feel bad about this.* But why shouldn't he?

'All week?' He tried to keep his tone neutral.

'It's only a three-day thing, but I'm pretty sure it doesn't wrap up until that day.'

'So you'll miss the end of it. You'll tell them you've got a prior commitment.'

'Not sure I can really . . . But I'll look into it.'

'OK.' He didn't have the energy to argue.

'I've missed you, you know.' Loosening the tie around her waist, she let her kimono fall open.

Underneath, his wife was naked, and Hugo took in the graceful symmetry of her clavicle and the matte sheen of her brown skin all the way down, past the perfect scoops of her small breasts, to the belly button that had remained tightly tucked, even after Ollie.

'Look at you.'

Angling her head to one side in a pastiche of seduction, Yas pushed her lips out. 'You can do more than look. I mean, if you like.'

The conference must have gone well. Professional success had always been an aphrodisiac for his wife. In the early days she could scarcely make it through the front door after a great day in court before fumbling with his jeans and hitching up her skirt, desperate to celebrate. It had become an in-joke that only as they lay there panting afterwards would he ask, 'You won the case, then?'

Now, although the beauty of Yas's body and the directness of her desire still filled him with wonder, Hugo no longer felt able to reciprocate with the same immediacy. It took him a while after he dropped Ollie off at school in the morning and put him to bed at night to go from parent to man again, and although the triumphs he experienced on a daily basis with his son were intensely rewarding, they sent a rush of blood to the heart, not the ego. They definitely didn't send you home yearning to bend your wife over the dining table.

'Getting chilly here,' murmured Yas, crossing her hands over her breasts, and as Hugo stood to join his wife on the other side of the kitchen table, his limbs felt heavy with conflicting emotion. He did want her. Who wouldn't want ... that? But he was also aware of the plates still being there, and a need to clear them away before all that cheese congealed and he had to chip it off with a knife.

He was tired. But there was something else too. Something he tried to ignore. An itch of irritation. A defiance. Because as sexy as it was, the way Yas expressed her desire was so very masculine. She wanted sex when she wanted it and always, always on her terms. Although Hugo knew that he should feel smug about how good that part of their marriage was compared to friends of theirs who 'worked at it' – some even admitting they included sex on 'To Do' lists – he often felt as though Yas's dominance was a part of the kick for her. That he was a prop in the queen bee role she was playing.

He sat down a little too heavily beside her, knowing what she wanted, how she liked to clamber on top of him, guide him inside her, and – in the words of some crap bonkbuster, 'take her pleasure'. Because that was exactly what Yas did: she took what she wanted ... from him. Well, tonight, Hugo was going to take his own pleasure.

'Get off a second.'

'What?' She looked down at him in confusion.

'Get off and turn around.'

If it was possible, Yas was even more beautiful from behind, the clear sweep of flesh marked by two shady indentations just above the cleft of her buttocks – the dimples of Venus – and as she began to move again he stilled his wife with a hand on her neck, bucking deeper and deeper. Only when he closed his eyes the body in front of him turned paler, fuller, and suddenly it was no longer Yas that he was driving into. The thought was enough, and when his wife righted herself, the ribbons of her kimono hanging by her sides, she tried to mask her irritation.

'You beat me to it.'

'Sorry. I wanted to try . . . '

' . . . something different. Sure.'

Wrapping the blue silk back around herself, she gave him a quick 'don't worry about it' peck on the mouth.

'Going to dry my hair. Then we can finish watching that Sky thing if you fancy,' she threw back from the hallway.

After promising he wouldn't 'cheat', Hugo had finished watching the drama while Yas was away. But he wouldn't tell her. Which meant watching it again, and it hadn't been great the first time.

Zipping up his jeans he stared at the plates on the table, at the congealing cheese. I'll deal with this lot, shall I? Then he reached for his phone again, for Emilia, and when he saw that there was a new message from her he felt a zing of excitement.

Sorry I couldn't do our picnic this week. Lovely idea though. Raincheck?

Our.

There was no need to feel guilty. That was the beauty of fantasies: if they stayed inside your head, nobody would ever find out, and nobody could ever get hurt.

CHAPTER 11

COLETTE

Entangled in her damp sheets, the fan doing no more than circulating hot air, Colette pushed up her sleep mask and peered at the luminous geometric digits on her alarm clock.

12.04 a.m. Which meant she'd been lying there for almost two hours, kept awake by a dozen variants of the same question: am I really going to do this?

Leila's voice in her head: 'You're inside their homes, their devices, their heads. If one of them was stalking me, you would know, wouldn't you? Or could know.'

It would be deeply unethical. Against everything she stood for. But given the circumstances, would it really be wrong?

Switching on the light, Colette sat up and reached for the phone lying beside hers on the bedside table. The one with the brand new screen, the one she'd walked out of that Apple store holding, her heart beating fast. Emilia's phone.

She'd been so sure of her decision in the moment, the immediate shock of those square chat WhatsApps giving way to a rage she hadn't felt since that fire drill over ten years ago. But two days had now passed, and still Colette hadn't contacted Leila to tell her that she'd changed her mind: that she was ready to ditch her principles and abuse her privileged position to find out who was persecuting this young woman. Still, she hadn't so much as switched Emilia's phone on.

Pressing down hard on the side key now, she held her breath until the Apple icon appeared.

Wipe it clean before you bin it. Wasn't that what she always told her clients? Yet she'd seen people chuck out everything from laptops to old hard drives along with the household waste over the years, blissfully oblivious to how much information could be retrieved. They had no idea, for example, that an old phone could easily be cloned, 'mirrored', if it fell into the wrong hands; that even without the SIM, it was possible to access a person's iMessages, emails, photos and more on an old device. WhatsApps were also accessible: all you had to do was activate them by pointing that phone at a QR code on your desktop or laptop screen, and the chats would appear there. Only in this case, surely Colette's were the right hands?

In a second she was out of bed and in her darkened study. Sitting down at her desk, blinking at the brightness of her screen, Colette logged into Emilia's WhatsApp. Going straight to the square chat, she scrolled through the exchanges of the past forty-eight hours. After Sylvia's valiant defence – her insistence that Colette should be invited to the party – there had been no further mention of her, the 'geek' with the empty calendar, the 'dog' hankering for that bone. Although she was still smarting at those words, still angry, that wasn't the only reason she was breaking a code of ethics scrupulously upheld for decades. No.

She was doing that because Leila had been right. Colette was and always had been an outsider, just like her. Because she wasn't valued. Because for all these years her loyalty had been one-sided and because she was pretty sure that the person stalking Leila was the same one who had humiliated her: a man who liked to intimidate women for fun.

Twenty minutes later, having scoured the thread – paying special attention to Adrian's messages – and found nothing, Colette took off her glasses and massaged the bridge of her nose. If it was indeed Mr Carter doing this, it was unlikely he'd drop any clues on something as public as the square chat.

Again, she replayed that evening in his study, his impatience with her, with his wife. Click. Another memory landed, this time Colette calling out a final word of caution to Adrian: 'You'll remember to log out of TeamViewer ...' and getting only a slammed door in response.

She typed out a few words. Double-clicked. Adrian hadn't bothered to switch off his TeamViewer. Of course he hadn't. In a world of uncertainties her clients' laxity with their own personal security was one thing she could count on. And powered by an instinct she had never felt before, by an overwhelming sense of purpose, Colette logged on to her client's computer. Bingo. Thanks to Adrian's carelessness Colette now had access to everything inside his warped little head.

She was tentative at first. It was late, but she had to be

sure that her client wasn't sitting there in the middle of the night, watching that rogue arrow moving around his screen in real time. Then brisk, business-like, as she flitted about his computer, dipping into the different pockets of his work and life. Because this man was hiding things, that she was sure of – darker things than an idle porn habit.

Open, again, at the bottom of Adrian's screen was his stash. This wasn't the Ocado-style porn but a different kind. Not quite illegal, although it should have been.

A quick browse of the 'KaoticKink' site confirmed that her client liked his women Eastern European, tied-up and outnumbered. But it wasn't until she uncovered the thirty-eight 'favourites' he'd accumulated over the past four years – bravo Adrian! Bravo! – that Colette felt her decision had been validated. Drunk American Teens. No Don't Mean No. Comatose Teens. Crying Teens? This guy got off on degradation. He was a shame junkie, a deviant – a stalker?

As she moved from the open tabs and documents on his desktop to his iMessages and his photos, Colette found herself smiling in anticipation. Any minute now there would be a stash of stolen shots: Leila sunbathing in the square garden, Leila shopping, walking, blithely going about her life, unaware of the predatory neighbour logging her every move.

'Come on, Adrian. Where have you hidden them?' Moving through the early weeks of June back to May, through happy family snaps on a half-term break in Aix and a whole load of Adrian giving some kind of speech at a media forum, Colette felt the annoyance building. Her client wasn't tech savvy enough to know how to conceal evidence: she knew that for a fact. But there was nothing here connecting him to Leila.

Outside, a burst of raucous laughter drifted up from the

riverside beneath. Someone kicked a can along the pavement, and vaguely Colette registered how late it was, how long she'd been sitting here. Maybe it was time to call it a day. But there was still Adrian's Inbox.

As soon as she opened it, the name shone out at her: Lmercheri@gmail.com. There were two, from that day alone. The first thanking Adrian for their drink at the pub the night before – the night of one of his 'work meetings'.

> You are naughty, making me have that third
> vodka tonic!

The second a series of questions about what you need from me to make this happen?

'Think I know what Mr Carter's going to need from you,' Colette muttered, as she read through the promises her loathsome client had been making his gullible new neighbour.

> Told you: call me Ade!

Because having zoned in on Leila's TV ambitions, it seemed Adrian had decided to dangle a large carrot.

> OMG I still can't believe you're going to give my
> showreel to *the* Chloe Hartnell.

Colette didn't watch morning telly, but no one could escape the pint-sized, caffeinated 'lifestyle guru' urging Brits to 'Supercharge your life!' from every billboard and bus stop in town – and according to Adrian, who looked after the TV star, Chloe was on the hunt for a fresh face to host a Sunday morning dance segment on her show.

How kind of her client to go to such lengths for a neighbour; how selfless of him to have had – Colette scrolled down the email thread – at least two separate meetings with Leila about her 'transitioning into telly'. Did Adrian's wife Emilia know about this mentorship? It seemed unlikely. Perhaps someone should tell her. Perhaps someone would be doing her a favour.

Calling up their email thread, Colette selected 'forward', typed in Emilia's email, and pressed 'send'. Because life didn't even the score. Anyone over the age of twenty knew that. But on this occasion, maybe Colette could.

Closing her eyes, she raised her arms above her head in a long stretch, jolting in alarm when she opened them again. Because that little cursor was moving about the screen. Back home at number 46 Addison Square, at 2.43 a.m., with Emilia asleep upstairs, Adrian had just opened up his Inbox and was typing out an email to greeves@gmail.com. If it weren't for that stretch, he might have seen that little arrow moving about. He might have busted her, and Colette closed her eyes for a second, waiting for the hammering in her chest to subside.

You need to stop calling, love, her client was typing now, the tone unmistakably similar to the one he'd used on the phone that evening in his study, when she'd watched the colour drain from his face. And you really need to stop threatening me. No one's going to believe ...

For a moment the cursor flashed indecisively. Then it backtracked, wiping out that second sentence letter by letter. Whoosh. Off went the email and Colette leaned forward.

'No one's going to believe what, Adrian?'

Immediately, a reply pinged in.

> Maybe I'll just go ahead and do it then. Maybe I'll tell
> people exactly what you are.

What are you, Ade? A porn-addict with a weakness for pretty young women? An opportunist using the oldest trick in the book to lure Leila in? Or are you a predator, a violator, a stalker?

Even as she asked herself these questions, Colette was pretty sure she knew the answer. This guy didn't operate invisibly, in the shadows; he was an out-in-the-open fully paid-up sleazebag who couldn't even be bothered to delete his emails to and from Leila, or indeed this 'greeves' – whoever she was. And that negligence he would now pay for. But if Adrian hadn't been taking those photos of Leila, threatening and intimidating her by posting them on that fake Instagram account – who was?

CHAPTER 12

HAMMERSMITH POLICE STATION
EXTRACT OF RECORDED INTERVIEW
WITH MRS SYLVIA RYAN

Date: 16 July
Duration: 58 minutes
No. of pages: 30
Conducted by Officers of the
Metropolitan Police

DC BAXTER: You've lived in the square a long time, Mrs Ryan.

SR: Not as long as some.

DC BAXTER: But you've always been very involved – with the goings-on, with your neighbours.

SR: I'm not a gossip, if that's what you're getting at, Detective Constable.

DC HARRIS: Our point is that you'd see things, hear things.

SR: I suppose so.

DC BAXTER: Did you notice anything unusual about Oliver Cooper?

SR: Yas and Hugo's son? I mean, I know he was spending quite a bit of time with the Mulligan boy. That was new. Why do you ask?

DC HARRIS: Nothing else?

SR: No.

DC BAXTER: Then again your focus has been elsewhere.

DC HARRIS: You've had problems of your own, haven't you?

CHAPTER 13

LEILA

She saw her as she turned into the lane. The IT woman: Odette. Was that her name? No. Yvette? Something similar. She was standing outside Addison Mansions, frowning down at her watch, as though Leila was late. Glancing at the phone in her hand she realised that she was, but only by six minutes.

'Hi!' She wasn't going to apologise. Not for six minutes. Not when she wasn't even sure why the woman had asked if she could 'pop round'. There was only one thing Leila needed from Odette – Colette! – and the IT lady had made it very clear on their last meeting, three days earlier, that she wasn't prepared to help her with that.

Striding towards her, Leila raised a hand in greeting, and took in the slight double take her appearance tended to prompt.

Mostly, she enjoyed watching people drink in her looks, try to break them down into something digestible. Once they had, the men would imagine what it was like to fuck her; the women what it was like to be her. That moment was as undiluted as power got.

'Hi there.' Colette smiled and Leila wondered how anyone could have reached this woman's age without being introduced to Invisalign. Maybe they thought it was too late. It was never too late to sort that stuff out.

'Shall we, um, go on up?'

To be fair to her, Colette seemed in pretty good shape. She'd noticed that the last time. As they climbed the stairs there was none of the exaggerated puffing Leila had got from the plumber yesterday, and she was about to toss out the compliment when a door above slammed. The pounding of feet echoed down the stairwell, and the ginger kid from the flat beneath appeared on the upstairs landing.

A school tie dangled from his neck and his shirt was untucked on one side. He was clearly late for school and only managed to break his momentum by grabbing onto the banister.

For a second Leila thought he was waiting to let them pass. 'Morning.'

Blinking at her through his fringe (something about those fair lashes gave her the chills) the boy waited a beat before tearing past them both, his rucksack swinging into her ribs.

'"Sorry" would be nice!' Leila called after him. Not that he could hear her with those buds jammed into his ears.

'Jesus.' She waited until she'd let Colette into the flat and shut the door. 'That family.'

Colette, who was taking off a hideous pair of sandals, looked up.

'Because of the arguments you mentioned?'

Remembering that they were her clients – and the absurd little speech she'd made about loyalty – Leila shrugged. 'I mean, I really don't know them. I'm sure they're fine. Very uncool about my music, though. Seem to want me to live like *une bonne soeur*. You know: a nun. And it's like: *sorry, guys, not going to happen.* Right?'

Colette just stared. Conversation didn't work with this woman. She didn't fill in gaps in the normal way, or even hold herself in a normal way. Right now she was standing there in Leila's sitting room, arms hanging limply by her sides, her rolling briefcase between her feet. Then again maybe Colette didn't do humans. Maybe she could only do tech.

As if to confirm this the IT woman gestured at the boxes of brand-new video equipment piled up in the corner. 'That's some top-of-the-range gear you've got there.'

'Yeah.'

All that money. Leila had felt giddy when the guy in the shop had read out the figure. But it was going to be worth every penny. Her showreel was going to be sick. She had until July first – two more days – to get it right. Adrian Carter had revealed himself to be a bit of perv the other night, when he'd taken her to the pub to run through what she needed to get across in what was essentially an audition tape, but he was a top agent: he knew his industry. He knew when people had 'it'. 'And trust me, Leila,' he'd said, with a nod and a smile, 'you do.' Most importantly, he knew Chloe Hartnell. She'd been his client for years. So although he'd still need her to go through the motions, Leila was 'the only one they're looking at', he'd assured her. It was 'basically in the bag'.

'I'm transitioning to TV,' she said now, enjoying the way it sounded. As though it were as simple as her having made the decision. 'I mean, I love dancing, but for me it's all about combining it with workouts – getting people up and moving but in a fun way, you know?'

Colette nodded.

A silence. One Leila couldn't help but fill.

'You know Adrian Carter?'

Another nod. 'I've worked with him and Emilia for years.'

'Right. Well, he's sort of taken me on, and he's put me up for this amazing job.'

'That was nice of him.'

Sometimes, when she replayed the moment Adrian had told her what he did for a living, Leila laughed out loud. All those years chasing contacts. She'd planned days, nights and trips around 'chance' encounters with the right people; bought outfits, tickets to galas and restaurant meals she couldn't afford as part of her 'right place, right time' crusade. But moving to a London square only to discover that a legit major telly agent lived across the way? That was fate telling Leila she deserved this.

'Anyway, Adrian said to keep it on the down low. Obviously most of his female clients would kill for a chance like this, and since I'm not formally a client yet.' She probably shouldn't have mentioned his involvement, but it was all too exciting. 'You won't say anything . . .'

''Course not.'

Wandering over to the mirror above the fireplace, Leila examined a faint crease at the corner of her mouth. She needed to be more rigorous with her daily face gym exercises. She needed things to start moving forward fast. All that crap she spouted to her Instagram followers about finding self-worth within, when she was in no doubt as to where her value lay: in her face, her body – and decreasing daily.

Turning, Leila motioned at the sofa. 'Do you want to? I should say that I've only got a few minutes,' she lied. 'Got a rehearsal in town at five.'

'No, no. I won't keep you.' Pushing down on the handle of her briefcase, Colette slotted it back into place. 'I just wanted to say that I've been thinking about what you said. About your . . . situation.'

'OK.'

That 'situation' had been getting steadily worse, making it impossible to enjoy the rest. Leila felt a flutter of hope in her chest.

'Tell me you've changed your mind?'

Colette nodded. 'I think I can help you. Because what's happening isn't right.' She spoke fast now, the sentences running together. 'As I said before, these photos that are being taken of you without your consent, these Instagram posts going up on RealLeila, they're not just scary but illegal. Doxing – the disclosure of personally identifiable data against the target's will – is a criminal offence. They passed a law a few years back. As is stalking, obviously. And if you're really not willing to get the police involved, then I think we need to find out who's doing this. Make them stop.' She paused. 'But this is going to have to stay between us.' Colette's face was grave, almost scared. 'I need you to understand the risks I'm taking . . .'

Leila sank down on an armchair.

'I'm so relieved you said that. You have no idea – and it will. I do.'

The IT lady moistened her lips, took a breath.

'You really have no clue who might be doing this? You can't think of anyone in the square who's – I don't know – showing a bit too much interest?'

It was hard not to smile at that. Everywhere Leila had gone since the age of thirteen people had shown a little too much interest.

'No one capable of this.'

Colette seemed to be debating whether to say something more. Then: 'You mentioned Adrian helping you out. There's no way he . . . ?'

'Ade? God, no.' She knew exactly what Adrian Carter was, and it wasn't *this*. 'But have a look at these . . .' Pulling up the page she'd spent the previous night poring over in a horrified trance, she handed her phone to Colette, watching her face closely as the woman scrolled through the comments made beneath the last post – a close-up of her dancing at a Keisha concert last year in a particularly revealing cutaway leather one-piece with chain embellishments.

The words beneath were printed on her mind.

> Loved your Kink profile, slut.
> If you like it hard, I'll be your master, RealLeila.
> Sex cages my thing too. DM me for pics.
> Wanna try throttling with me?

'Jesus Christ.' Colette swallowed hard. 'When did these start?'

'Yesterday. There are hundreds of them. Whoever's doing this seems to have put my profile up on some BDSM website. I mean, what kind of man would do that?'

'Why do you think it's a man?'

'It has to be, doesn't it?'

'Not necessarily. Cyberstalking's like harassment, remember. It's about power: the power to make you feel scared in your own environment.' Eyes back on Leila's phone, Colette sighed. 'People think it's as easy as tracking down an IP address; sadly, it's not. Even the police have drawn blanks trying to track down these people.'

Leila's shoulders sagged. Google had warned as much, but she'd hoped Colette would tell her different.

'But listen, the BDSM profile is easy to take down. I'll have that sorted by tonight. And I am going to try and help you. Do some digging. That's all I came to say.'

Leila felt a rush of gratitude. She could have hugged this weird woman. Instead, she offered Colette one of her broadest smiles, the ones reserved for people who gave her what she wanted. 'Honestly, I can't thank you enough.' This was probably about more than the money for Colette. She had the look of an old-school man-hater about her. But Leila added, 'I'll pay, obviously, whatever it costs.'

Only Colette wasn't smiling back. She was holding out Leila's phone, showing her something: 'They've just put up another post. Three minutes ago ... '

Leila scrutinised the image. It was a close-up of some kind of dresser, and it took her brain a moment to register the familiar patina of the white painted drawer that had been pulled open; the hexagonal marble knob. In the foreground, the contents were clearly visible: a jumble of multicoloured underwear – her underwear.

'Leila,' Colette was blinking over at her, 'has this been taken from *inside* your flat?'

CHAPTER 14

SYLVIA

This morning's walk with Reggie had been a dud. Two loops of the square they'd done, but that green door had remained closed. No sign of life. *No sign of you.* Then Sylvia had remembered that it was Thursday. Sometimes she got a sighting late afternoon in the garden on a Wednesday or a Thursday, but now here she was, sitting on the bench with the clearest view of all four corners – and the place was empty. If only the square allowed dogs, she might at least look more purposeful.

Where are you? If she tilted her head back and squinted up above the towering plane trees at the far end, she could see the bedroom window.

A rustle in the bushes obscuring the south entrance

brought her eyes back down to ground level, but it was only a bird. Then she heard the whine of the gate.

Sylvia sat up straight, eyes fixed to the narrow opening in the hedge that had formed organically over the years, thanks to dozens of impatient children trampling through it, season after season. For a moment no one appeared, and Sylvia wondered if she might have imagined the noise. Then a silhouette filled the space: tall, lean, unmistakable.

Spotting her immediately, Leila curved a hand around her mouth and shouted out across the lawn, 'You waiting for someone?'

Sylvia shook her head. There was always tomorrow. Patting the space on the bench beside her she called out, 'Come!'

As Leila crossed the lawn with springy steps, she took in the smiling face, the aureole of tight curls, and the seafoam green cropped leggings that wouldn't work on anyone but this racehorse of a woman.

She'd been transfixed by that smile the first time they'd met, in the 'Ten Items or Fewer' queue at Waitrose on a May Sunday. Sylvia had felt a light touch on her arm and turned to find this marvellous-looking creature ... who apparently knew her.

'I think we're neighbours.'

Then, as now, that smile had been so outsized, so goofy. There were too many teeth, and definitely too much gum. Had she been a celebrity, Leila would have been instructed early on never to laugh in public. But it was one of those smiles that felt like a gift, and when Leila had laughed – possibly at the look on Sylvia's face – it had been one of the most life-affirming laughs she'd ever heard. A promise of good things to come.

That she'd done something as uncharacteristic as inviting her back for tea had been the first surprise. That Leila had accepted, the second. But her heart had sunk as she'd shown the young woman into the kitchen still littered with cards and flowers. A kitchen decked out with death.

'My husband recently passed,' she heard herself blurt out. And how she hated that expression. Why bother downplaying death? He died. He's dead.

As soon as the words were out, she had braced herself for the inevitable 'I'm so sorry's, 'how awful, you must be devastated'. Please, God, no more pity.

Only Leila had just nodded. Folding her long limbs onto one of her kitchen chairs, she'd looked around not with the queasiness most people her age seemed to feel about the recently departed – as though death were somehow catching – but with awe: 'What a gorgeous house. How long have you lived here?'

Approaching the bench now, Leila pulled a vast water bottle with the words BOTTLED JOY printed along the side out of her sports bag and sat.

'Twenty-seven degrees,' she said, tilting her head back and taking a long slug.

'Feels like thirty. I tried to buy a fan yesterday and the guy almost laughed in my face. Said they could put my name on a waiting list. A waiting list!'

Sylvia watched the muscles of her smooth brown throat contract. There was something so pure about her; something that made you want to be better. No wonder she had all those online disciples.

'You know the other day, when you mentioned your classes down the road?'

Leila's eyes widened.

'Sylvia Ryan, are you thinking about entering the world of physical fitness?'

Sylvia laughed. It was high-pitched, almost girly. It sounded like what she was: flattered by Leila's attentions.

'Is that bonkers?'

'What? You're in good shape. Better shape than some of my ladies half your age, let me tell you.'

Sylvia didn't need to be told. She'd always looked after herself, and rather than feel guilty for her strength and vitality as Archie's had faded, she'd secretly enjoyed the growing disparity.

'D'you know what? I thought I might. But only if you're sure they allow oldies.'

'Sylvia . . .' Leila leaned in towards her. 'Have you looked at yourself in the mirror? You're probably one of the healthiest, strongest-looking seventy . . .'

' . . . four . . .'

' . . . seventy-whatever-year-olds I've ever met. And they do a whole heart, strength and dexterity test beforehand, so . . .'

'So?'

'So when do you want to start?'

'Gosh. I don't know . . .'

'How about now?'

'Now?' Sylvia balked.

'I've got to go and give a class in thirty, so we could at least book you in for your assessment.' Leila paused, tipped her head to one side. 'You know, this is your moment.'

'My . . . ?'

The young woman shrugged. As though it were obvious. 'To be whoever you want to be.'

Of all the many takes people had offered up to Sylvia over the past few months, all the condolence philosophies that managed to be both trite and dour, there had been nothing like that. Nothing suggesting that far from Archie's loss being a kind of painful endurance test to be 'taken one day at a time', this was a chance to start afresh.

'Alright then.'

Leila laughed, delighted, but also disbelieving: 'Really?'

'Yes.' She felt happy, and a little silly. 'Let's go and see what they make of me.'

'Cool. Do you mind waiting while I run up and change my trainers?'

'You go.'

'Oh, and Sylvia?' Leila was peering down at her feet, shamefully exposed in their open-toed wedge espadrilles. 'You really need to do something about those. When was your last pedicure?'

She debated whether to lie, before coming out with it. 'Never had one. Or a manicure. Just not the kind of thing I would do, I suppose.'

As they made their way towards the gate, Leila muttering, 'OMG do we have work to do,' a neon green frisbee cut through the sky and landed on the lawn a little way off. Two boys followed, panting and shouting: Theo and Ollie.

Sylvia slowed to a halt.

'Not a bad place to grow up,' Leila commented. 'The taller one's . . . '

' . . . Hugo and Yasmeen's boy. You've met Hugo?' There he was with Emilia over by the gazebo. Whatever he was saying had her creased up with laughter, and him repeating the punchline, one hand on her arm.

'They look very cosy.'

The way she said it made Sylvia's neck spin around. To check her expression; check she was joking. But Leila looked perfectly serious.

Nodding at the pair – neither of whom had spotted them – she added, 'I mean, get a room, right?'

'No, no ...' Sylvia followed her towards the west gate, pausing every two steps to look back at the scene behind her. 'Their boys are friends, that's all.'

'Whatever you say.' Leila threw back as she locked the gate behind them, jogging up to the mansion block's front door. 'Back in a sec.'

For a second Sylvia felt tempted to retrace her steps or see if she could get another visual of Emilia and Hugo through the railings. Then she shook her head, smiled to herself. It was funny, the way young people saw sex in even the most banal situations. What could be less sexy than a playdate?

A digital chirrup from her handbag broke her train of thought. It would be Colette: she'd forgotten to fix a time for their appointment. Only it wasn't, and without thinking she tapped on the message – number withheld – remembering too late the vow she'd made the week before.

If there is another message, a third message, don't open it. You've done what was asked the first and the second time. Ignore it and this person – whoever they are – might go away.

As Sylvia read the message, a wave of acid rose up her oesophagus and she reached out to steady herself against the railings. How could they know? How much did they know?

114

It was as short as the previous ones – just one line:

More of the same or I tell.

CHAPTER 15

HUGO

'Anything good in there?'

He'd spotted Emilia from the end of the lane, standing there in a pretty yellow sundress before the Little Free Library, one child on her hip, another trying to prise open the picnic basket at her feet.

So engrossed had Emilia been in sifting through the donations that she hadn't heard him approach, looking up in surprise as he called out.

'Might have to nab this Danielle Steel.' She held up a thick paperback with an embossed gold title. 'If you promise not to tell anyone.'

There was a suppressed excitement in her smile that mirrored his. From the moment her WhatsApp had come

in – Can I cash in that raincheck? How about this Friday for our picnic? *Could really do with a chat* – **Hugo had been anticipating this casual neighbourly supper more than he should.**

As he held open the garden gate for Emilia he saw that there was something different about her. Several things.

Her hair had been released from its usual messy ponytail, her lips smudged with something matte and poppy-coloured, and was she wearing eye make-up?

'I'm hungry, Mummy,' whined Theo, as they looked around for the perfect spot.

'Me too,' chimed in Ollie.

They both laughed, relieved to have the children there to break the tension. Because there was tension; he wasn't imagining it.

'Leave that, darling. Hugo and I are going to get it all set up while you two have a run around, OK?'

As he'd put the Sauvignon in the fridge that morning, Hugo had quashed another niggle of guilt, as though the foresight alone was wrong. As though simply by thinking ahead to the picnic that had gathered such weight in his mind, he was being disloyal to Yasmeen. Which was silly. He and Emilia were both adults who were fully entitled to enjoy one another's company, he reasoned. It was another insanely hot evening – too hot to stay indoors – and had his wife been there and not working, as usual, she would have joined them. In which case why hadn't he mentioned it to her?

'Where shall we . . . ?'

Forgetting their hunger, the boys had already run off to climb their favourite plane tree, a vast bole rising up into two curling limbs that fused together in a central arch before spiralling off in every direction.

Other than them, the garden was deserted, and they walked slowly along the path, taking in the rose pergola and Grecian-style gardener's lodge in the distance. Tonight that beauty seemed excessive, contrived to the point of pressurising – like a romantic restaurant crooner bearing down on two friends he'd mistaken for lovers.

'There?'

Hugo pointed to a flat, green expanse beneath a horse chestnut, where the frazzled lawn had been shielded from the violence of the sun.

'Perfect.'

In silence, he and Emilia spread out their blankets, and when that silence was broken there was a tentative quality to their exchanges that was new. As Emilia gently laid down her daughter on the rug and began to unpack Tupperware containers filled with cold meats and salads, he wondered whether that cryptic 'could really do with a chat' was at the root of it.

'Everything OK? Sounded like you . . .'

Emilia stopped jiggling the *Hungry Caterpillar* over her daughter and glanced up.

'Oh.' A flash of awareness. 'Yeah. Sorry. I sent that message when I . . . It's been a weird few days.' An inner wrangle played out across her features before a smile wiped it clear. 'Still, nothing a glass of wine won't fix.'

It was unconvincing. But Hugo wasn't going to push, and after they'd downed their first glasses, after they'd shouted out too many 'be careful's to the boys and chuckled through full mouths at Ollie's 'We are being careful!', their usual easy banter resumed, and it was Hugo who was the first to open up, midway through an anecdote about the parents' evening he'd attended, alone, the previous night.

'I try not to let it bother me, but Jesus, there I am: the only dad there alone in the whole damn queue. And I know what all those couples are thinking to themselves.' He paused. 'Thing is, I'll do the drop-off and pick-up every day, and I don't mind it – I don't. But when Yas can't make those key events … I mean, people must be wondering if I've made her up.'

He was conscious none of this was showing him in the most appealing light, but it felt too good to be saying it out loud. 'Anyway, Yas had promised to join us on FaceTime yesterday. Sit in on the chat with his teacher remotely. But when the moment comes she's unreachable. So there I am asking Mrs bloody Heller to hold on while I try my wife again, feeling like such a twat.' He shrugs. 'Yas blamed her phone, but I'm not sure I buy it. Our IT lady had only just reset the damn thing.'

'Colette?'

'Yeah.' He shook his head. ''Course. You were the one who recommended her.'

He liked that Emilia didn't try to reassure him here, tell him his wife couldn't possibly have forgotten. Instead, she just nodded as he went deeper, into the job he missed and the colleagues he'd deliberately lost touch with, finding the inevitable 'So what are you up to these days?' too demeaning to answer.

'It's about the power dynamic,' she said eventually, adjusting her position on the rug so that she wasn't squinting into a shaft of evening sunlight. As she did so, the slit at the side of her dress rode up, exposing a deep slash of thigh. 'I feel that all the time with Adrian. When he couldn't make Theo's nativity play . . . '

'He didn't make the nativity play?'

'Stuck in a meeting. Apparently.'

The sarcastic lilt was new. Emilia was usually quick to defend her husband.

'The other day Yas casually let me know she wasn't going to make Sports Day. She'll "try to", but she won't. So Ollie'll be gutted, and he's been . . . '

'What?'

She'd picked up on his pause.

'Going through something?'

Beneath the tree where the boys were amassing a pile of twigs for their imaginary campfire, Ollie was laughing: a full-faced laugh that went right up to his eyes. How long since he'd seen his son laugh like that? 'He's definitely not been himself. Sort of quiet and cranky, and then the other night he had this tantrum when I was reading to him. Out of nowhere, threw a book across the room.'

'Really?'

'I'm convinced it's about Yas being away so much. What else could it be?'

Emilia shrugged. 'Any number of things. Something at school. Could someone be bullying him?'

'I asked his teacher about that yesterday, and she was adamant that she would have spotted it. Said they have a "zero-tolerance policy" etc . . . But what worried me is that she'd noticed it too. Even asked me if there was anything going on at home.'

They glanced at the boys again.

'He looks perfectly happy to me,' Emilia ventured, and the two deep parallel lines scoring her brow were so touching to him. This woman who had been made to feel unimportant didn't realise how special she was, how infinitely superior to the mums at Ollie's school – the ones who had had their sense of humour zapped along with their laughter lines.

'I . . .' She started in a low voice, tracing the rim of her glass with a forefinger. 'Adrian and I aren't in a great place either. After Hattie arrived . . . well, I sort of thought it was normal that he didn't – doesn't – find me as attractive as he did.' She winced at the admission. 'And who can blame him? My mum always warned me about "letting myself go".' She smiled, and there was a watery quality to it, a loosening around the lips. Not drunken, but definitely tipsy. Definitely in the 'saying things that make you wince the next day zone'.

Swallowing his initial response, Hugo opted instead to go with a humorous one.

'How very Stepford Wife of you. My mum's the same, always going on about Yas not cooking for me, apparently forgetting that I'm the house husband.'

'The "never let your husband see you without lipstick on" generation.' She smiled. 'But what if they were right all along? Because Adrian . . .'

'Oh Jesus. He's not . . . ?'

'Fucking someone else? You'd think that would be the worst thing, wouldn't you, but shall I tell you what's worse?'

'Go on.'

'Having a husband who is actively trying to fuck someone else.'

'Shit.' Hugo had never been less surprised by anything in his life. Of course Adrian Carter was trying to shag another woman. An honest response would have been: 'Just the one?' To conceal this he began asking a series of quick-fire questions. 'Wait: how do you know? When did you find this out?'

'Someone helpfully forwarded some emails between them earlier this week.'

'What? Who?'

'No idea. But it's his work email so my guess is someone from his office. A disgruntled junior, maybe.' She took another sip of wine. 'Don't you want to know who the woman is?'

She sounded almost triumphant. Again, how could he tell her that he had a pretty good idea? That when he'd seen her husband guiding Leila Mercheri through the doors of the Addison, one hand on the small of her back, Adrian had had the smile of a man about to tuck into a freshly carved ribeye.

Emilia waited a beat.

'It's our new neighbour. It's bloody Leila.'

Caught between a vehement desire to comfort Emilia and the fear of saying something inappropriate – 'I think you're beautiful. I think you're soft and real and do you have any idea how much more appealing you are than the Leilas of the world?' – Hugo heard himself blurt out, 'Well, then Adrian's a dickhead.'

For an awful moment Emilia just stared at him, wide-eyed. Then she burst out laughing.

Embarrassed, Hugo rubbed his jaw. 'Sorry, but he must be if he ... '

That only made her laugh harder. And he joined in – until he saw that there were tears in her eyes, caught in her lash line, tipping over and running in sleek tracks down to her jaw.

'Hey . . .' Instinctively, he leaned forward and reached over to the hand that lay upturned in her lap.

CHAPTER 16

EMILIA

T hrough the blur of tears she watched Hugo's hand stop inches away from her own – and pull back.

For a few seconds neither one of them spoke or moved, both acutely aware of the force field encircling them. From the other side of the square Emilia heard Theo whoop and Ollie cackle. And suddenly she wasn't sad anymore; she was angry. Angry with herself for having ruined this perfect evening by crying in front of Hugo, angry at Adrian for having made her cry. But what she'd felt towards Leila when she'd read those emails? That went beyond anger to a cold, clinical place inside her that Emilia hadn't known existed.

One minute she'd been tearing through a box of Jaffa Cakes in front of *Selling Sunset* – halfway to the desired oblivion – and the next clicking on an email forwarded by Adrian, with the odd subject header: Your next chapter.

The heart lift she'd felt when she saw those words and actually thought, for a second, that they were meant for her. That the husband asleep upstairs had noticed how down she'd been and gone to the trouble of thinking up a way to get her out of this slump. That moment's hope had made her feel so very stupid in the minutes that followed. Because it had never even occurred to Adrian that she wanted, needed a 'next chapter', but he'd dedicated an awful lot of time to their new neighbour's. And from the smarmy tone – I know without ever having seen you on screen that you're a natu-ral – her husband would very much like his next chapter to involve Leila.

People talk about women 'misdirecting' their anger in moments like these, but that wasn't the case for Emilia. The rage she'd felt towards the young Frenchwoman when she'd read that email was directed at the right person: legitimate. Adrian was what he was (even if trying it on with a neigh-bour was taking things to another level). But there was a special place in hell for the women who played along with men like her husband, not because they were remotely inter-ested – just to get what they want.

'When you say that Adrian's been "trying" . . . with Leila,' Hugo said now, 'I mean, a bit of flirting doesn't mean that . . . ' His sentence died out and Emilia realised that there was something wrong with Hugo's reaction, generally. It took her a second to understand what: the surprise – it was phoney. Oh God. Because Adrian was that guy, wasn't he? To everyone in Addison Square, she'd long been an object of pity.

'Here.' She pulled out her phone, called up the emails. 'Have a read. Decide for yourself.'

Hugo did, in a silence broken up only by the occasional headshake and a muttered 'don't eat and run' when Ollie ran over to grab two sausage rolls before scampering off again.

'So what did he say?'

'Say?'

'Adrian – when you told him about the emails.'

'Oh.' Playing for time, she scooped up Hattie, gave her a bottle and lost herself in her daughter's blissed-out face for a moment. 'I haven't actually said anything yet.'

'But you're going to?'

Emilia had thought about it every day since, about all the things she had long suspected and might find out for sure if she started that conversation. But then what? 'I know I should. It would be a hell of a lot healthier than checking his emails whenever I get the chance. But . . . '

'You've been reading his emails?'

'When he goes downstairs for a coffee or takes a quick shower.' She wasn't going to apologise for doing this; she didn't feel guilty. 'His laptop asks for a password if I leave it any longer than that.'

'And?'

'And they're pretty frequent, between him and Leila. She seems to be convinced he's going to get her this gig on telly. Presumably he'll say anything to get her into . . . '

Hugo was nodding at a space behind her right ear. Swivelling her neck she saw Theo running towards them and stopped short.

'Water,' he wheezed.

She handed him his flask.

'Where's Ollie?'

'Dunno.'

'What do you mean you don't know?'

'He went off a while ago – behind there.'

Hugo was already up, striding across the lawn in the direction of Theo's finger.

'Come on.' Scooping up Hattie, Emilia followed. 'Could he be hiding?' But she could tell from her son's face that he wasn't. 'You were both under here,' she prompted when they reached their tree.

'Yeah, but then Felix came along.'

'Felix?' Ahead of them Hugo turned off down the narrow pathway leading towards the south gate. Emilia was right behind. As they cornered the hedge, however, she slowed to a stop.

Ollie was there with Felix, in the darkest, most overgrown section of the pathway, Hugo standing over them both.

'Everything alright?'

Out of nowhere, Ollie burst into tears and ran past them, back across the lawn.

'Hey,' Hugo went after him. 'Ols – hey! Can you slow down, please. What's going on?'

'I want to go home.'

Father and son were back by the picnic blankets at this point, Hugo gathering up their things, and Emilia realised that the evening, with all its revelations and its promise, was over.

'I think maybe it's bedtime.'

Oblivious to the drama, Hattie had already fallen asleep on her chest, but Theo was looking up at her with concern.

'What's wrong with Ollie?'

'I think he's just overtired, my love. He'll be fine in the morning.'

Emilia wasn't sure she believed that. Hugo was right: something was up with his son, and she had a pretty good idea what it was.

CHAPTER 17

HAMMERSMITH POLICE STATION
EXTRACT OF RECORDED INTERVIEW
WITH MR HUGO COOPER

Date: 17 July
Duration: 78 minutes
No. of pages: 39
Conducted by Officers of the
Metropolitan Police

DC HARRIS: So you had good reason to worry about your son.

HC: If only I'd known, worked it out.

DC HARRIS: I doubt any parent could've guessed, to be fair. And it can't have been easy, being in sole charge, what with your wife away so much.

HC: I never resented looking after Ollie. Not for a second.

DC BAXTER: We still allowed to call you lot 'stay-at-home-dads'? I know 'house husbands' are out.

HC: I think the preferred term is 'primary caregiver'.

DC BAXTER: Still. Must have made you feel like you had little in common with the other square dads?

HC: Not sure I'd want to have much in common with the likes of Adrian Carter, to be honest.

DC HARRIS: What about Guy Mulligan? How well do you know him?

HC: Pretty well. Least that's what I thought. Turns out none of us knew him at all.

CHAPTER 18

COLETTE

From the moment Colette pulled into Carmel House's car park to the moment she rang the nursing home bell, there was always a fifteen-minute gap. Over the years, she'd started to factor that ritualistic pause into her schedule, arriving twice weekly at 2.45 p.m., knowing that inside the unlovely imitation period red brick building Gillian wouldn't yet have woken from her nap.

What did she use that slice of time for? Nothing. Which was curious in itself for someone who loathed idleness in any form, worked weekends, and only ever took a holiday if one of the tech courses she signed up to twice a year was too intensive to fit around her work commitments. Yet for that quarter of an hour she would sit there, watching the relatives who didn't want to be there any more than she did come and go, resignation on their faces as they rang the doorbell; relief lifting them as they left. Duty done.

That Monday, the car park was empty but for her Fiat, and Colette relaxed back into the seat and thought about Leila.

The deeper she delved into Adrian's computer, the more convinced she was that he wasn't behind RealLeila, the fetish profile set up in the young woman's name – any of it. As for who had managed to get into Leila's flat and take those photos of her underwear drawer, Colette was drawing a blank. Asked which of her neighbours had been inside the property, her client had been adamant: 'No one.' There were the flat viewings, Leila had added, and she was never there for those, 'but they're supervised by the estate agent, so . . . '

A thought had occurred to Colette the night before: what if 'Call Me Ade's involvement with Leila hadn't been news to his wife? What if she'd already read those emails or found out about his 'mentorship' in another way?

That thought had given Colette permission to rummage through areas of Emilia's 'mirror' phone she'd denied herself previously, and as the evening had turned into night the picture she'd formed of her client had become sharper than anything even the most insightful therapist could have put together.

She hadn't exaggerated Emilia's unhappiness in her mind. If anything, Colette had underestimated it. The emails to her best friend Caroline were shockingly bleak. She wrote honestly about her 'disillusionment' with life and motherhood, but most of all with marriage, and described the 'invisibility' that had cloaked her from the moment she hit forty as feeling like 'a kind of bereavement'. Then there was the baby weight she still hadn't lost after Hattie, which left her feeling 'repulsive – not just to Adrian but myself'.

Any mention of Hugo to Caroline had instantly lightened the tone. They were fleeting, at first:

> I told you about Theo's friend Ollie, from across the square? The one with The Dad?

But over the past few months Hugo's name had crept in regularly and superfluously. To the point that Caroline had eventually joked, 'Someone got a crush on their neighbour?'

Here and there in these long, shambolic diary-like confidences, Colette had found hints that Emilia suspected her husband of, if not playing around, then coming close. A twenty-eight-year-old 'weather bimbo' on his official client list had been mentioned a few times. Back in March a new actress Adrian had just taken on, Gemma, was described as 'the flavour of the month', and just two months later, when Emilia found out that the twenty-two-year-old had left the agency, she'd expressed her relief alongside a photo of a wide-eyed, snub-nosed brunette, cut and pasted from Facebook. 'Could hardly compete with that.'

Sometimes the emails were a couple of despondent lines. Once or twice Emilia had mentioned wanting to get a job.

> But Adrian's right: who would want me? Plus the money I'd bring in wouldn't even cover the cost of a nanny. I told you he wants another? I mean: hole in the head, right?

Colette had read that part twice. Lying, cheating Adrian wanted another child? Why? She'd gone back four months to find the answer:

> Ade keeps saying that he was one of three, that all his mates have three.

So it was a status thing. Of course.

The previous week another late-night takeaway binge had been dutifully logged in her Notes.

Two slices of leftover kids' pizza. One chicken korma with rice and naan bread. Seven and a half chocolate-chip cookies.

God, that half cookie was pathetic. This woman wasn't living, she was plummeting through life, grasping at things to slow the fall.

In amongst the photos there had been another eye-opener. Scrolling through the endless images of the children sleeping, laughing and playing was a series of selfies Colette had been deeply saddened by. Taken in front of her bedroom mirror, where Emilia was standing in mismatched underwear, legs planted firmly apart, stomach pushed out as far as it would go, these were the kind of self-shaming shots women stuck to fridges in an effort to remind themselves of their shortcomings. But it was the look on her client's face that was so devastating: a look of pure self-hatred. As though she hated that woman in the mirror enough to punish her, hurt her.

All of this Colette had taken in before finally switching off the phone, slightly sickened by her own binge.

Steeling herself for the hour to come, she grabbed the Bakewell tart she'd picked up earlier from the passenger seat and opened the car door. A sweaty overlay of icing had stuck to the clear cellophane wrapper, and briefly Colette hung her head in annoyance – at this and at the prospect of the next hour. Then, because this was always the worst part, Colette strode up to the front door and rang the bell.

Despite the closed curtains, her mum's chair was in its usual position, facing the French windows that opened out onto the nursing home's trellised courtyard. Beneath the thinning muss of her hair – pulled back into a low ponytail today – a few inches of skull were visible. Like the old woman's face, there was something stubborn about that pale, hard skull. An absurd thought that was nonetheless true.

'You still not dressed?' In two brisk sideswipes, Colette let the light back into the room and pulled up a chair beside her. 'You must be boiling in that thing. Shall we get you into something airier?'

Her mother's eyes settled on her – cool, detached, bored. The look of a woman for whom life no longer held many pleasures, if it ever did; a woman who was ready to go.

'I brought you a tart.' Colette held out the Bakewell, conscious of how unappetising it looked, how she would have to force every mouthful down. 'Thought we could have it with our tea.' Nothing. 'But we don't have to. We can just ... sit.'

For what seemed like an age they did, staring out at the sun-glazed courtyard – a space from which life and movement always seemed conspicuously absent to Colette. As though even the birds and insects were aware that if you spent too long in this place, you might catch death.

Then, a low murmur from beside her. 'Will you ...?'

''Course. It's ...?'

'In the desk drawer.'

The old Mason Pearson hairbrush was thick with silver down and Colette dropped a dense cloud of it in the bin before releasing her mum's ponytail from its brown rubber band.

'These'll rip your hair out. I'll get you some nice ones. I'll get you a scrunchie.' The artificiality of her own laugh made her wince. 'How about that?'

Gillian didn't reply, but as Colette began to run the brush in slow rhythmic strokes through her hair, she felt some of the dissatisfaction ebb away.

'I've been busy at work,' she murmured when the silence became oppressive. 'Lots of troubleshooting.'

'What sort of trouble?'

How aware her mother was of what Colette did for a living seemed to vary week to week. There were moments of surprising lucidity, then total blanks drawn. Which was why generalities were usually the safest option. But today Colette found herself hoping not for lucidity but the blankness that might allow confidences on her part. Confidences that would instantly be forgotten.

'People getting themselves into tangles, Mum.'

'Tangles?'

She reached up to her head with a speckled hand.

'Tech tangles. But also life tangles.' Then, louder, 'I'm talking about my clients.'

'I know that.' After all these years, Colette was used to the brusqueness. 'And you can untangle them.'

This was a statement, but a question mark seemed to hang in the air afterwards, as though her mother needed reassurance that it was indeed that simple.

'Some of them.'

The hair was so fine and brittle that tiny fragments broke off as Colette brushed, rising up and mingling with the dust motes in the stale, sunlit air. 'There's this young woman I look after. She's being stalked.'

Her mother didn't respond and she was about to repeat herself when her phone buzzed in her pocket: Zoe Mulligan. Colette hadn't heard from her client since the day she'd opened that square chat, and read her bitchy little PS.

> #awks, but tech lady seems to think she's invited.
> We're already at capacity. Does anyone feel strongly
> that she should be there?

She hadn't received an invitation yet either.

'Hang on – just going to take this.'

As always Zoe sounded out of breath, overburdened, as though she were permanently struggling beneath a load of heavy shopping. Through the puffing Colette gleaned that there was some kind of problem, a device that had been broken, although what and how wasn't clear. Could she come and take a look today? 'It's a bit of an ...'

'... emergency,' Colette provided. She glanced over at the back of her mother's head. 'I can get to you in an hour and a half, if that works?'

It was a hike. It was a pain. But after what she'd promised Leila, it was also an opportunity.

'Do you mind?' Zoe glanced down at Colette's sandals on the personalised WELCOME TO THE MULLIGANS' doormat. She was barely through the door, her sandals were scrupulously clean, and Colette always offered to take off her shoes when visiting clients – given half a chance. But if there was one thing Colette appreciated it was order. 'Of course.'

Every time she saw Zoe Mulligan, she was struck by how tiny she was. A tiny, twig-limbed figure in a pink linen A-line shift dress and a long-sleeved red cardigan too warm for the stifling temperatures. In the past, she might have found this pocket-sized woman's fluffy white slipper boots endearing. Now that she knew the way Zoe spoke about her in private that was no longer the case.

Through the ceiling, the beat of a bass buzzed, and Zoe glanced up.

''Fraid you're going to be treated to Leila's playlist while you're here. It's been driving Guy up the wall,' she said through a rictus grin. 'You've met our new neighbour?'

When Colette nodded Zoe looked as though she were going to say something else, and then decided against it. 'Come through.'

The Mulligans' sitting room was patently too small for a family of four and crammed full of the kind of neat, white polypropylene units the organised parent used to stash away unsightly clutter.

Within a glass dome in the centre of the mantelpiece the family had been shrunk down to tiny smiling Mulligans, Felix's ginger head standing out in sharp contrast from the rest of the family. He was from a previous marriage, although how she knew this Colette couldn't remember. Certainly her client had never mentioned her first husband.

Thanks to Emilia's emails, Colette had been able to form a fuller picture of Zoe than anything she'd put together over the years the 'Boden mum on speed' had been her client. Zoe was apparently 'resentful' of being confined to one of these flats, rather than the gorgeous Georgian homes across the square. Could that be why she had taken it upon herself to be the square's head prefect? To raise herself up in some way? And Guy's antagonism towards their upstairs neighbour? That was useful information.

'How's that smart TV working out for you?' she asked, taking a seat on the sofa and inclining her head towards the sixty-five-inch screen she'd set up for the Mulligans at the end of last year.

'Good.' Sinking down on the armchair opposite, Zoe gave a series of little nods. 'I mean, it freezes sometimes. Quite a lot actually.'

Colette frowned. 'That what you'd like me to take a look at?'

'Oh, no,' Zoe shook her head distractedly. 'I'm guessing all tellies do that.'

'They shouldn't.' One of Colette's pet peeves was this idea that technology was flawed, fallible. When it was humans who malfunctioned and messed up. 'While I'm here I might as well?'

'Don't worry. We can deal with that another day. There's a few things I could do with your help with at some point: I want to check the safety settings on Felix's computer, for one thing. I'm not convinced we've done that properly, although my husband thinks I'm fussing . . . ' She glanced over at the laptop on the desk. 'And Guy's got some issue with these two-step verification alerts he keeps getting too, so—'

'It's honestly no problem to do all that now. I've got time . . . '

Again, Zoe shook her head. 'Better wait until he's home. I

did tell him you were coming today but he's so touchy about his laptop.'

Colette's ears pricked up. Touchy?

Why would her husband, who lived in such close proximity to Leila – who had a problem with her – be touchy about his precious device? She thought about the geek emojis Guy had seen fit to post on the square chat. *Maybe your husband's not the stand-up guy everyone thinks he is.* But Zoe was pointing to the iPad on the coffee table between them now.

'No, today I was actually hoping you could take a look at that and tell me if it's just superficial or if there's, you know, internal damage.'

'Wow.'

The screen wasn't just smashed in the usual way, the way it was designed to when dropped, but dented, the centre obliterated by a white oblong.

Pulling on her gloves, Colette checked to see if the touch interface had been impacted.

'How did it happen?'

'Just me being clumsy.' Zoe made a face. 'Knocked it off the kitchen table. 'Course, the bloody thing landed screen down.'

Colette looked up at her client. Had the spasm at the corner of Zoe's mouth not betrayed her, that last sentence would have. As with all lies, it's the unnecessary detail that's the giveaway. Smashed devices were Colette's bread and butter. She'd seen thousands of them over the years, heard a thousand explanations. Which was how she knew that when a screen lands face down on a hard floor or pavement, it'll smash the way Emilia's phone had, effectively exploding at the point of impact.

Zoe's iPad hadn't landed face down anywhere, she was sure of that. Whatever it had come into contact with had been softer, blunter: something like an elbow, from her experience, or some kind of human extremity, powered either by momentum or force.

'Well, the good news is that the controls don't seem to be damaged.'

'Thank God for that.'

'And I can have the screen replaced for you. But it might take a couple of days.' A couple of days in which Colette could scour the device for clues, peer inside this woman's life, just as she'd peered inside Emilia's and Adrian's.

Zoe winced. 'Can they really not do it on the spot? I could nip down to that FixxInn place on the high street . . . '

'I really wouldn't recommend any of those places.' *You get me over here for an 'emergency', and you're seriously now talking about taking your iPad to a FixxInn?*

It was the equivalent of a diner telling a Michelin-starred chef he was too hungry to wait; he'd pop down to McDonald's instead.

'I know, but I haven't got a couple of days. All my party planning is stuff on there, as you know.'

Zoe reached over to reclaim her device, decision made. As she did so, her cardigan sleeve rode up to reveal a plum-coloured strip of bruising across the wristbone, and in a single speedy movement her client pulled the fabric down again.

'You've been amazing with all that, by the way,' she babbled on, standing up. 'And I'm so grateful to you for coming over today. I'll be in touch about the other stuff, yeah?'

As she made her way down the stairs of Addison Mansions

a few minutes later, a fast-moving montage began to play out in Colette's head.

Leila telling her about the arguments she'd overheard, blowing through pouted lips for emphasis: 'I mean, couples argue ... but: wow.' Zoe lying about how she'd smashed the iPad. Guy's closed face and the regularity with which his eyes flicked over to his tiny birdlike wife during any dealings Colette had had with them both – checking on her, controlling her? Zoe's long sleeves, despite the sweltering weather. That fresh bruise on her client's wrist.

By the time she reached her car, parked directly outside Addison Mansions, Colette knew what she had to do. Because there wasn't just one breed of creeper and crawler in the world, country or any given London square, but a whole thriving variety. There were those whose vileness was flagrant, out in the open, like Adrian Carter, and then there were the Guys of the world: the starched collars you saw manspreading on the Piccadilly Line beneath their *FT*s. And what? We just assumed they were good men because of the clean shave and waft of Penhaligon's?

Reaching for the pull-along briefcase on the passenger seat beside her, Colette unzipped the front compartment and pulled out her laptop. Had her clients realised that – armed with the necessary security details – anyone could sit outside their properties and access their browsing histories, they would have been horrified. It was a horrifying thought. But as with Leila, this might be about a woman's safety – and wasn't that too much of a coincidence? 'Call Me Ade' didn't fit the stalker profile, but if Colette was right, Guy sure as hell would.

She needed to move fast. There were too many people she

knew in Addison Square, any one of whom might wonder what she was doing sitting there, her laptop on her knees.

Having connected to the Mulligans' WiFi using the password she had herself set up for them, Colette scrolled down through that day's search history, and the one before. Sky News, Ocado, Aviva, Mumsnet, the *FT* Broker's Forecast, Pure Collection, Amazon, an article from *The Times* on FIGHTING CLEAVAGE WRINKLES, cashmere cardigans, cashmere round-necks – Zoe liked her cashmere – PREMATURE MALE HAIR LOSS: the list went on. But just as it had that first time, with Emilia's phone, this felt necessary, important.

Like so many of the families Colette looked after, the Mulligans never thought to erase their search histories. But finding nothing out of the ordinary there and spotting the neon yellow of a traffic warden's vest at the bottom of the lane, Colette was about to snap the laptop shut when her index finger stopped halfway down the screen.

There, in between WILD RADISH GOURMET MEALS DELIVERED TO YOU and COBRA KING 12-PIECE GOLF SET were the words she hadn't dared formulate even in her own mind. SPOUSAL ABUSE: HOW TO GET HELP.

CHAPTER 19

HAMMERSMITH POLICE STATION
EXTRACT OF RECORDED INTERVIEW
WITH MRS ZOE MULLIGAN

Date: 17 July
Duration: 53 minutes
No. of pages: 26
Conducted by Officers of the
Metropolitan Police

DC BAXTER: Did you know Leila Mercheri had a stalker?

ZM: No. I mean, not until your colleague mentioned it earlier. But it doesn't surprise me.

DC BAXTER: Could you clarify?

ZM: Well, she's the type, isn't she? All these women in magazines talking about their stalkers. Terrifying thing to go through, obviously, but you do sort of wonder . . .

DC HARRIS: Wonder what?

ZM: You know, if they've exaggerated a few things. Made a mountain out of a—

DC HARRIS: This was hardly a molehill. It started off with a fake Instagram account, digital spying and the dissemination of intimate images - incidentally classed as online hate - and quickly went far beyond those to a series of more serious criminal offences.

DC BAXTER: But perhaps Mrs Mulligan already knows this?

CHAPTER 20

ZOE

'What's all this?'

Looking up from the recipe book open on the kitchen counter, Guy smiled.

'Kids are at the cinema, remember? They're not being dropped back until eight, so I thought I'd make you that beef thing you love.'

Beef stroganoff. Glancing at the pan spitting fawn-coloured specks of cream all over the stove top – the heat was up way too high, flames curling up around the edge of the pan – Zoe gave an inward sigh. She didn't love it.

They'd once had it at the little Italian on the high street a couple of years ago, and because it had been such a good night, free of the usual tensions, she must have said something that had left him convinced it was an all-time favourite.

She'd never had the heart to tell him otherwise, and certainly couldn't now – not with Guy having gone to so much effort. Not with him wearing her BAKING QUEEN apron.

'I could smell it from the stairs. Why do you never turn the extractor on?'

Crossing the kitchen, she reached over him and pressed the knob above the oven. As she did so she noted the spattered pages of the recipe book beside him, the jumble of empty containers – the tension in her husband's jaw.

'Just thought it might be nice for you to have the night off, with all that party prep you've been doing.'

Their eyes met. Zoe was inches away from him. She only had to lift her hand to rub his arm. Make some kind of appreciative, wifely gesture. Yet she couldn't do it. The events of the other night were still too fresh in her mind; the bruises still there, beneath the clothing that concealed them: kept their shameful secret. Only the iPad bore no traces, now as good as new.

'It's a nice thought.' Just saying that felt like such a strain. 'Bit hot for stroganoff, though, isn't it?' Her husband crossed his arms across his chest. 'I mean, it's a winter dish.'

'Zo ... Can we please just have a nice dinner together?'

'Of cour—'

A beat from above cut her off, and they both froze. Then another thudded through the ceiling, and Sho V was on his way, the pounding only alleviated, once a bar, by the briefest semitone rise.

'Fucking hell!'

Guy threw down the spatula into the pan.

'I have spoken to her.'

'Well, I don't think you've been clear enough, have you? But I tell you what: I'm going to make it extremely clear.'

'Guy, no.' Instinctively Zoe moved a little closer to the stove, to her husband, angling her body so that it was between him and the kitchen door. 'Don't do it when you're like this. Wait until you've calmed down. She's our neighbour. I ... we don't want things to be awkward every time we cross each other on the stairs.'

'It's pretty fucking awkward not to be able to enjoy a quiet supper with my wife!' He was waving his arms above the stove now, above the still spitting pan. 'What, you think we should just sit here and be terrorised by the rave going on upstairs, night after night?' His left arm was too close to the stove top and bare beneath his short-sleeved T-shirt. He'd burn himself if he wasn't careful.

Reaching out she grabbed it and pulled it back, away from harm. But the gesture was misinterpreted. She knew that immediately from the look in his eye. And suddenly it was her arm above the pan, inches from the broiling cream, from the licking blue flames.

The struggle was brief. Maybe a couple of seconds. Time ceased to mean anything to Zoe in these moments, at once speeded up and slowed right down, so that she was able to contemplate the sizzle as the flesh was pushed down into the pan, and held there. Such a celebratory noise, reminiscent of summer barbecues and happy family gatherings. Then the smell: stronger and sweeter than steak, with a tang of something old, leathery. But the yelps of pain? No one would hear them. They were drowned out by the music.

CHAPTER 21

COLETTE

Four missed calls. In the time it had taken Colette to install a smart doorbell for a client off the Earl's Court Road, Colette's phone had managed to amass half a dozen WhatsApp messages and four missed calls.

In moments like these her first thought was always the same: *Mum's died.* Then, as she sat in her parked car sifting through them, the aircon on full blast, she saw that they were almost all from Leila.

She was still on the second panicked voicemail when a new message appeared at the top of her screen:

Been trying to call you. New post gone up. Think maybe it's time to call the police. Can you call asap?

Clicking on Instagram, Colette found RealLeila... and the new post. It was a reel, a bright white square in amongst the patchwork of darker tiles, showing a woman's face – Leila's – against a pastel-striped cushion. Her eyes were closed, her lips slightly parted. Colette pressed 'play' and watched as the camera zoomed in close enough to see the corkscrew of hair resting across her cheekbone flutter with every exhalation.

At first Colette thought it might be a promotional video: an advert Leila had agreed to do for a garden furniture company, perhaps, because she could see now that the young woman was lying on a sun lounger, although she didn't recognise the location. Then the realisation of what she was looking at turned her stomach: wherever she was, Leila really was asleep – and unaware she was being filmed. The caption? SLEEPING BEAUTY.

As she called up Leila's number, Colette felt angry on her client's behalf, but beneath that was a beat of personal alarm. If Leila went to the police, would her investigations be dragged into it? Her job compromised?

A string of French swearwords sounded when Leila picked up. It was quite the greeting, then again who could blame her?

'I know.' Through the windscreen a shaft of sunlight targeted her between the eyes, and Colette flipped down the visor. 'Do not call the police. Sit tight. I'll be with you in twenty.'

She could see the fear on Leila's face as soon as she opened the door. Her features were drawn, her eyes darting. Before she closed it her client peered out, checking the landing and stairwell.

'That post ...' Ushering her into the flat, Leila paused to shove aside a row of stiff Net-a-Porter bags blocking the hallway. 'Freebies,' she muttered. Then: 'Who the fuck is doing this? Why? What have I ever done to anyone?'

Despite her sympathy, the question seemed naïve.

Leila's disregard for the noise complaints made by her downstairs neighbours wasn't just casual, but deliberate. In fact, the last time this had come up in conversation Colette had been taken aback by Leila's gleeful assertion that 'Every time they say something, I turn up the volume a notch.' Then there were the exchanges she'd read in Adrian's inbox a few hours ago: the arrangements being made for a meeting in Soho that very evening. Leila's flirtatious tone and provocative sign-off:

can't wait. Lx.

Her disregard for Emilia was shocking, and Colette had started to wonder how far her client would go to get what she wanted.

'I'm still catching up here. Where was that video shot?'

Wordlessly, Leila opened the front door again and led her up two flights of stairs to what Colette could now see was the roof.

'There's a roof terrace? I had no idea.'

It was no more that fifteen square foot and shielded from neighbouring properties by neat rows of tall, waxy plants in rectangular ceramic planters. The central area was decked and just large enough for two teak sun loungers with pink and white canvas mattresses and matching cushions.

'I think I'm the only one who ever comes up here. I was

here yesterday for a couple of hours, took a nap. That's when this fucker must have . . . '

Pointing to the lounger on the left, furthest from the door, Colette said: 'You were on this one.'

'Yes. How did you . . . '

Crossing to the other side of the deck, where what must be either an old chimney or some large, unsightly vent had been hidden behind a wooden panelled structure, she took out her phone and pointed it at the bed.

Leila let out a strangled laugh.

'Don't tell me they were behind that.'

'They were behind that, watching you sleep.'

Dropping down onto the lounger, Leila covered her face with her hands.

'This is . . . ' Her voice came out muffled. 'How could I not have heard them? Seen them?'

'I can't answer that.'

'There's something else,' she went on weakly. 'A couple of things have gone missing over the past few weeks. Little things. One of my perfumes. A T-shirt I sometimes sleep in.' Pulling her hands from her face she shouted: 'Who's doing this?'

Colette chose her words carefully: 'I'm not sure.'

But I suspect it's someone who doesn't like women. Someone who's abusive towards his own wife. Someone like your downstairs neighbour.

CHAPTER 22

LEILA

The leather trousers were a definite, but was the camisole too much? Turning, Leila took in the side view in the mirror: beneath the scalloped lace the outer curve of a breast could be made out, and unless she tucked it in, a chink of flesh was revealed by the split above her waistband. Too much, she decided. Better to go with the first option, the safer option.

Dressing for men like Adrian was a science. You needed them to be awestruck enough to give you what you wanted, but not actively salivating, not so distracted that they forgot why they were there in the first place – failed to deliver. But as she slid her feet into her new Isabel Marant boots, there was no doubt in Leila's mind: tonight, the deal was going to be sealed.

Adrian had practically said as much when he'd rung, later than was appropriate and very definitely drunk, the night before. He had news, and was she around for a drink tonight?

Without a second thought, Leila had cancelled her plans. He'd had her showreel for six days now, she'd been counting, and the lack of any feedback, alongside the events of the past week – not least the nightmarish realisation that someone had filmed her as she slept – had left her on edge. She'd even started to worry that Emilia might be behind Adrian's failure to get back to her. That Mrs Carter had noticed her husband's interest in her and warned him off. Which was why she'd put that Karve flyer through the door of number 46 earlier this week, offering Emilia a free three-pack of post-natal classes at Karve. Scribbled a warm note about how effective they'd proved for women wanting to shift the baby weight. Jealous wives could be problematic, in her experience. Important to keep them on side.

With one last look in the mirror, Leila walked out the door, a smile on her face.

'Wow.' As she wove her way through the tables towards his, Adrian was so quick to stand that he nearly knocked his chair over. 'You look ... '

Leila gave the necessary laugh, as though the effect she was having on him, on every man in that dimly lit Mayfair hotel bar, was unintentional. A happy accident. Then she spied the bottle of Dom Pérignon in an ice-bucket beside the table and was forced to bite her lip to stop her smile from spreading.

'Well, this is nice.'

Baring his teeth, Adrian reached for the bottle. 'Let's pour you a drop, shall we?'

They clinked glasses, her neighbour holding her eye a little too long, and as she asked Adrian about his week, his work, she tried to still the foot wagging impatiently beneath the table. *Go on then, don't make me wait.*

Finally, when she'd drained her second glass and couldn't listen to Adrian crowing about the 'mega-buck deal' he'd just negotiated for some talk-show host a second longer, Leila went for it.

'So you have news?'

She didn't like the fleeting look of bewilderment. But he was a busy man, with any number of deals being negotiated in the course of any given week. 'Ah yes! The Chloe thing.'

The Chloe thing?

'You'll have another glass, won't you? We're going to need another bottle at this rate.'

'I'm OK for now.'

'Nonsense.' He raised his hand. Was he actually going to click his fingers at the waiter? Oh yes. She cringed. He was.

'You said you had news?' she pushed.

'I did? I did! Yeah. They really liked your showreel.'

The anxiousness evaporated.

'Seriously?'

'Absolutely.'

'That's amazing. So what happens now?' He blinked at her. 'I mean, do we have a meeting? Work out the details?'

'The det—' Spearing an olive with a toothpick, he chewed for a moment, wagged his head from left to right. 'Yeah. We're not quite there yet. They're obviously looking at a few people, so . . .'

Beneath the table, Leila pushed her toe against the table leg in an attempt to sublimate her annoyance.

There was nothing 'obvious' about that. Not when Adrian had told her she was the only one they were interested in. He'd forgotten that. Easily done, she conceded sourly, when something isn't true.

'Just that I thought I ...'

Before she could finish her sentence a front-of-house guy appeared, placed a heavy, tasselled key beside Adrian's glass and said in a casual tone: 'In case you need somewhere quieter for your meeting, Mr Carter.'

The pause was so brief – just long enough for Adrian to meet her eye; take in her confused expression – before he too donned a look of confusion.

'Oh. You know, we're fine here.'

They started on the second bottle, but the conversation was stilted, the cooling of Adrian's body language palpable. Within ten minutes he was asking for the bill, throwing out a limp 'You were right. I don't think we did need that second one' – and before she knew it, Leila was sitting in the back of the cab she'd been bundled into, thinking: *what the hell was that?*

CHAPTER 23

SYLVIA

'You can take that look off your face.'

'What look?'

Sylvia followed Leila's gaze to her own white-knuckled hand, gripping the armrest of the massage chair, and laughed.

'That "I'm about to get tortured" look,' the young woman replied with a sigh. 'Mani-pedis are supposed to be fun.'

Ever since Leila had spotted her gnarled feet last week, she'd been obsessing over them. Finally, Sylvia had given in. With Leila forced to vacate her flat for another sales viewing, she had allowed herself to be dragged into the nail salon across the road.

In tones so staccato they sounded accusatory, the Vietnamese lady seated on a tiny stool at her feet barked out a series of baffling questions, culminating in: 'OPI, Shellac or Gelish?'

Not having a clue what any of these things entailed, Sylvia turned back to Leila.

'Yes to the Gelish,' the young woman retorted, without looking up from the phone she had been tapping upon incessantly since they'd sat down together. 'And my friend wants Emflowered on her hands and feet.'

'I do?' Sylvia stared at the tiny bottle being held up for her approval, shrugged and said, 'OK.'

It was the gaudiest shade of pink she could imagine. But now that she'd abandoned herself to the ludicrous world of 'self-care', she might as well go all the way: lacquer herself up like a working girl in the gaudiest shade of pink she could find. Peptobismol pink.

'Think of how good you felt after that first class you did at Karve.'

Sylvia nodded in agreement.

'I have to admit that I wasn't expecting that. And that other one I did, the yoga ...'

'... yogilates.'

'That was wonderful. I'd like to do more of that.'

'This is all part of the same idea: self-care.'

At this her elderly neighbour actually shuddered, and they both chuckled.

'Maybe just *try* to enjoy it? You might surprise yourself.'

The wind chimes were designed to relax her, as were the patronising admonishments of the squat gilt cat raising and lowering his paw – 'calm down, dear' – in the alcove opposite. And she was getting close, but then Leila started talking.

'So you know how there's been a bit of, um, friction, with my downstairs neighbours.'

'You mentioned it.'

'She complained about my music again the other day, which I always keep down. But it turns out it's him who has a problem with it.'

'Guy?'

'Yeah. Zoe gave that away. What's the deal with Mr Mulligan?'

Sylvia twisted to face her.

'Guy's a sweetheart.'

'Really? 'Cause she seems so tense.' Under the bright lights Leila's eyes weren't brown, as she'd always thought, but an ancient moss green, flecked with gold. 'I wondered if maybe there was something wrong ... with their marriage.'

'In what way?'

'These arguments they have. Always at night. And out of nowhere. Like ...' She'd brought her hands together in a simulated explosion.

Sylvia frowned, finding this hard to believe. 'You're sure it's not just the telly?' She shrugged. 'But maybe they bicker, in private. Archie and I certainly did. Guy's in finance, you know? Gentle. Quiet. And Zoe's wonderful. A devoted wife, mum – very kind-hearted.'

'But one of those community obsessed types, right? Always trying to get you involved?'

'Well, she's the head of the square committee, and this anniversary party next Saturday: it's a big deal.'

'I got that.'

Leila fell silent, and Sylvia closed her eyes. She loved their time together. There was something so invigorating about the girl's zest for ... everything. But she clearly watched too much reality TV, because what she'd said the other day in the square about Hugo and Emilia, what she'd just intimated about Guy and Zoe's marriage: it was as if she wanted to see drama everywhere.

'What about Adrian Carter?'

Sylvia opened her eyes again.

'I told you he's been helping me out with work?'

'That he's taken you on as a client? Yes. That's great. He's got some pretty well-known people on his books, so I'd say you're in good hands there.'

'That's what I think, but ... '

'And of course he'll love you.' Sylvia gave a good-natured laugh.

'Ye-es. I'm getting a bit of a vibe ... '

'Oh, I don't mean that he ... Just that Adrian appreciates women. He's what we used to call a bon viveur. Before it became a crime.'

Leila raised an eyebrow and it occurred to Sylvia that she might be one of those #MeToo women.

'Depends what his wife thinks about it. You think they have an arrangement?'

Sylvia was shocked. 'God, no. We're not like you lot. No offence.'

'None taken. Maybe she's more the "grin and bear it" type.'

The 'grin and bear it' comment stung – not just on Emilia's behalf but hers. Sylvia had grinned and borne it, hadn't she? For decades. But now she was free, she reminded herself. With no one there to question those many square laps, the close monitoring of a certain neighbour's movements. *Being able to live in the same square as you, to see and talk to you almost every day? Even if you don't know who I am; even if I'll always be the old lady across the way to you, that makes up for a lifetime's unhappiness.*

Holding up a hand she saw that the colour was even brighter than it had looked in that tiny bottle. Archie would be appalled. But she was having fun, enjoying being this new, brash person – enjoying wondering: what will you think of me, when you see me out and about with my neon talons? Will you notice?

Blowing on her own nails, Leila ordered her to 'lean in. Let's do a little story.'

After shooting a short video of the two of them across which she'd scrawled in lime green cursive: *Doing nails is our cardio,* Leila slipped her lacquered feet into flip-flops, and announced, 'I've got to get back. Check they've locked up properly after the viewing. Didn't bother me when I first agreed to it. Now . . .' She shuddered.

'I don't blame you. Not nice, that feeling of strangers in your personal space.'

A shadow crossed Leila's face. 'Yeah. See you tomorrow.'

The salon door tinkled shut, and Sylvia reached for the little remote control attached to her chair, pressed the button marked 'pummel' again, and smiled. Then a buzz from her handbag broke the silence. And there it was. A 'blowing heart' emoji she registered with an internal scream. *How can this be happening to me? A thank you for the money.* Because her blackmailer was nothing if not polite.

CHAPTER 24

COLETTE

'It would've been so simple if it were just papers, wouldn't it?' grumbled Sylvia. 'Documents that could be filed away safely in a drawer. But no, Archie had to be the only pensioner I know who did everything *online*.'

The way her client said the word – in an undertone suggesting a rarefied world inhabited only by the foolhardy – made Colette smile. But it had given her a heart pinch the week before, when Sylvia had finally called to say, 'I'm ready to transfer everything. Let's do it.'

The four-bedroom family home had always seemed too big for this childless old couple. Now it felt like a mausoleum.

Archie's Barbour was still hanging on its peg in the hall, above the ocean-liner white Nikes that had looked comically large on her late client's feet. The kitchen and sitting room were still filled with condolence cards, and the study she'd spent so much time in over the years was now desk-less. Towards the end everything had been moved into the master bedroom to make it easier for Archie to prepare for 'the handover'. Few people had the foresight to think of such things and as Colette took in the neatly labelled row of blue folders on his desktop – HOUSE EXPENSES, BILLS, HEALTHCARE – she said a silent thank you to her late client.

Swivelling around from the desk at the window, looking out over the square, Colette focussed on his widow. With her athletic build and that clunky jewellery she always wore, Sylvia was a picture of stoicism: a survivor. But there was something unnaturally straight about the way she was holding herself, perched on the side of the bed her husband had died in, their beloved terrier at her feet. And her nails . . . What on earth had she done to her nails?

'How are you doing?'

'Oh, I'm alright. The clear-out's helping. I just wish there wasn't so much still to sort out. And that I'd paid more attention to all this while Archie . . . but he always took care of that side of things.'

Going through dusty concertina files wouldn't have made things any easier, Colette assured her. She had everything she needed right here, including a list of logins and pass-words Archie had left on a stickie for their online accounts. 'But it'll take us a while to work through it all.'

After Adrian and Emilia Carter, the Ryans were Colette's longest-standing square clients. It was largely thanks to them that she'd built up a network spanning the four corners of this little community, and she'd found herself worrying about Sylvia lately. She was holding up admirably in public, even keeping up the querulous tone when talking about Archie that she'd used with him when he was alive, but Colette suspected that this was her way of dealing with her grief, of keeping her late husband alive in some way. Beneath the grumblings, that grief would be raw, messy.

'So if we're going to "drag you into the twenty-first century", as Archie warned me we might have to do,' said Colette, with a lame attempt to inject some levity into proceedings, 'then I think it makes more sense to set up everything you need on your iPhone.'

'The iPhone I do in fact have.' Pulling it from the folds of her skirt, Sylvia held it up to be admired. 'Oh, and you'll be impressed: Zoe's even got me on What's Up. And I have to admit that the square chat thingy's been pretty useful. Especially with the party coming up.'

Zoe. Colette had been racking her brains for a way to get back into the Mulligans' flat, to confirm what she increasingly believed to be true.

'You're coming, I hope?'

'Me?' *I'd have to be invited to come.* 'I'm not sure ...' *That anyone besides you wants me there.* 'Honestly, I haven't got an invite. Which is absolutely fine. I realise it's mainly residents and locals.'

Sylvia seemed genuinely irritated by this, and a little embarrassed.

'Let me talk to Zoe. See what's happened. I know you were on the list,' she added, flushing.

Bless you for lying about that. And bless you for fighting my corner on that square chat, while everyone else sneered.

Feeling her expression tighten, Colette turned back to the screen. 'Listen, it's great that you're on WhatsApp, but

164

there are a few more staples I'll stick on your phone for you today: Amazon, Waitrose, and maybe the Shop app too. That'll make sure you don't miss any deliveries. Honestly, I think you'll find it so much easier than doing all that on the desktop. But the accounts are most pressing, so let's get those sorted first. I just need you to put in that call to the bank now, and then I can get started on transferring everything to your name. You filled out the Third-Party Mandate, so it should just be a brief conversation confirming access – then we're good to go.'

As Sylvia ran through the security questions from the landline on the bedside table – tonelessly delivering maiden name and addresses lived in many lifetimes ago to the man at Barclays – Colette tried to avert her eyes from the Archie memorabilia scattered around the room: the wedding photograph on the desk and Churchill biography sitting there, poignantly, on Archie's bedside table. She was relieved when Sylvia finally handed the phone to her so that she could conclude the conversation.

'Great. So if you give me your phone and remind me of the passcode,' she handed Sylvia the legal pad, 'I'll get those Apps downloaded. Do feel free to get on with . . . ' What did a recently widowed septuagenarian have to get on with on a sunny Wednesday afternoon? ' . . . things.'

Sylvia nodded, equally relieved, it seemed, to be released.

'I'll take Reggie out for a stroll.' Then, pausing at the door: 'You know, it was a great comfort to Archie to know that you'd be there, after. That someone he trusted would be able to take care of all this.'

Colette smiled. 'What I'm here for. Now off you go.'

*

Thanks to Archie's fifty-year-career as the head of a plastics company specialising in flexible packaging, Sylvia had been left well catered for. In fact, the balances on their accounts were startling.

Nevertheless, as she checked the transferral to Sylvia's name had been made on all three accounts – skimming quickly through the statements as she did – Colette couldn't help but marvel at how frugal the Ryans were. Much of these were the last few months of Archie's life, so they were hardly going to be living it up, but that generation seemed to be against the accumulation of 'stuff' on principle, and aside the Cromwell hospital bills that had ballooned over November and December as they'd tried to mitigate the ravages of Archie's bowel cancer and that one outsized, emotionless figure to Dignity Funerals in March, the outgoings had been steady and predictable. BT, Amazon and Waitrose seemed to recur on a loop, with the expenditures rarely exceeding £100.

Aware that this 'overstepping' was in danger of becoming a habit – old Sylvia was hardly going to figure on her list of stalker suspects – Colette was about to log out of the account when something caught her eye. A trio of zeros, strikingly perfect in their little row. Unfeasibly perfect. Because how often did round numbers occur on bank statements? In Colette's experience this only happened with credit repayments, and whilst these were certainly regular – once a week over the past three weeks – these £5,000 payments were also to an unnamed payee.

OK so the Ryans didn't have kids, Colette reasoned, but perhaps they had other dependents. Nieces, nephews or even close friends that Sylvia might want to help out now that Archie-the-purse-string-holder was gone.

Colette tried to quash a sense of unease that rose, like nausea, from the pit of her stomach. She'd read about the people who preyed on widows at the most vulnerable moment in their lives. The lawyers, insurers and executors exploiting women like Sylvia, either by pushing them to sign up to services they didn't need or overcharging them.

Remembering how quick her client was to tell everyone that she was 'financially illiterate', how it was Archie who had 'dealt with the money stuff', Colette winced. To an opportunist, she'd make the perfect victim. With a quick glance out the window, she reached for her client's phone.

There were things you couldn't help but see in her job, and this wasn't one of them. She was honest with herself about that, at least: it was another boundary crossed. But she'd promised Archie to help keep his wife's affairs in order, and something was very definitely out of whack here. She could feel it. If Colette could just find an explanation for those figures, it would put her mind at rest.

Like most people her age Sylvia clearly preferred talking to messaging. Her WhatsApps contained nothing but the square chat, and aside the photo of a lost Burmese posted by a resident an hour ago, there had been no new messages since Colette had caught up on them, on Emilia's mirror phone, that morning.

Her iMessages weren't any more revealing. O2, NHS reminders, some excruciatingly bureaucratic 'FYIs' from Zoe and a few jokey one-liners from Leila. Then, right at the bottom, a thread with someone named 'Me'.

Sylvia must have deleted any older messages, because the first was thanking her client for something. Ignoring her question 'who are you?' the second simply said:

More of the same or I tell.

Yesterday, at 5.04 p.m., another 'thank you': a blowing hearts emoji. Then at 10.16 a.m. that morning the most recent message had come in, and Colette frowned down at the GIF of a mother rocking her baby and the sentence, complete with typos, beneath:

> You'll both be there at the square party. Juste
> thinking it would be a shame for it to come out then?
> I'll be in touch.

Checking the dates of the thank yous against Sylvia's statements, Colette saw that on both occasions those £5,000 sums had left her client's bank account hours earlier.

The sound of a dog barking outside broke her train of thought, and with a series of quick swipe-ups Colette erased her digital footprints.

Downstairs the door slammed.

'How are you getting on up there?' Sylvia called up from the hallway.

'Perfect timing! Just finishing up.'

When her client appeared in the bedroom doorway, however, bright-eyed and grumbling at the dog entangled in her legs, Colette was momentarily lost for words.

Scouring Sylvia's face for some sign of what she'd just uncovered – fear, confusion, even a desire to be busted – she found nothing.

'Nice walk?'

'Lovely. Just wish there were even a bit of a breeze, you know?'

Colette nodded. 'I think we're all done with this heatwave. Anyway, everything's now under your name and your Apps are on here.'

Should she just come out with it? *I couldn't help noticing these payments, Sylvia. Who is doing this and why? Is it to do with Archie's death? Did he get himself into some kind of a bind that you're paying for? And that GIF? What's that about? Who is 'Me'?*

It wasn't that much of a breach. She'd been given permission to check the accounts had been transferred. But when someone in her position admitted to even the smallest overstep, it was like a doctor being caught with wandering hands or a dentist failing to sterilise their equipment: game over.

'Is there anything else I can help with today?' She tried to communicate a silent message to Sylvia. *I can help – if you let me?*

But the old lady was brisk. She had a yoga class to get to. Thanking Colette for going 'above and beyond', she ushered her out of the front door.

For a minute, Colette just stood there by the gate listening to the gossipy cries of two parakeets perched atop a silver birch, the faint laughter drifting over from the pub on the corner – until the word she'd been suppressing pushed its way to the surface.

Blackmail. Sylvia was being blackmailed. Why, Colette couldn't begin to fathom. But it was by someone close enough to know a secret the old lady was willing to pay to keep quiet. Someone who, from the sound of that message, would be at the anniversary party. Someone living in this serene West London square.

CHAPTER 25

❦

HAMMERSMITH POLICE STATION
EXTRACT OF RECORDED INTERVIEW
WITH MRS EMILIA CARTER

Date: 17 July
Duration: 48 minutes
No. of pages: 24
Conducted by Officers of the
Metropolitan Police

DC HARRIS: Did you know that your husband was mentoring Ms Mercheri?

DC BAXTER: For the tape, Mrs Carter is pulling a face. Could you tell us what that expression meant?

EC: 'Mentoring' is one word for it.

DC HARRIS: What's another?

EC: [Does not answer]

DC HARRIS: When did you discover that mentoring wasn't all your husband had in mind?

EC: I think I would like a lawyer now.

DC BAXTER: Have you ever heard of a Gemma Reeves, Mrs Carter?

CHAPTER 26

HUGO

'Hey, Ollie, isn't that your friend Theo?'

Hugo lowered his menu and followed his wife's gaze across the crowded pub. It was indeed Theo, being ushered towards a corner table by Adrian. Behind him was Emilia, carrying Hattie in her arms.

He sipped his pint, watching out of the corner of his eye as the Carters were led to the only free table in the corner – a little round one that was going to be a squeeze. Emilia was dressed down in a faded grey T-shirt and jeans. As lovely as she'd looked at their picnic last week, he preferred her this way. But he really wished their neighbours had picked another pub.

'Do you think we should . . . ?' For a second Hugo thought Yasmeen was going to suggest they swap tables. Then he understood. 'God, no.'

'Might perk Ollie up. And there's plenty of room.'

They'd got to the Addison before the evening rush and been given the biggest table there, Ollie promptly scattering his felt tips across half of it. He'd been colouring in, wordlessly and intently, ever since and had scarcely looked up when Yasmeen pointed out his friend. Hugo felt a heart tug of the kind that came almost daily now, when he expected a smile or a laugh from his boy, and got only that distracted, absent face. 'But do we really want to have supper with Adrian Cart—'

Hugo was too late. His wife was already signalling at the Carters, and he took in what happened next with alarm: Theo bounded over to them, followed by a grinning Adrian. Emilia, meanwhile, stayed where she was, head bent down towards Hattie. She was obviously as keen as he was to avoid an uncomfortable merger.

'Since when did this place get so rammed, eh?'

Everything about Adrian smacked of self-importance. The way he held himself, legs planted wide apart, pelvis tilted forward. The five-day stubble he was currently sporting, most likely a pit-stop towards something yet more cretinous. Even the ringtone blaring out from his shirt pocket now: dark strings, a touch of percussion – Christ, it was the *Mad Men* theme tune.

Frowning down at his phone, Adrian rejected the call, looked up and said, 'I reckon it was that write-up this place got in *The Times* a while back. Great for them ...'

'... not so great for us locals,' Yasmeen concluded with a laugh. 'Seriously: you're not all going to fit over there, are you?'

Theo had already slid onto the empty chair beside Ollie's, craning his neck to look at his friend's drawing, and Hugo knew what was coming. He was about to give his wife a gentle kick beneath the table when he heard her say, 'Come on. Silly us having all this space. Join us.'

Next thing Hugo knew, Adrian was braying, 'Not a bad idea. Boys would love it,' chairs were being moved, a highchair brought over, and with a look of reluctance that matched Hugo's thoughts Emilia was carrying Hattie over to their table.

'I feel awful, hijacking your dinner like this.'

It wasn't until they'd all ordered that she looked directly at him. But Adrian and Yasmeen had immersed themselves in a conversation about local property prices, the boys were playing hangman, and something about Emilia waiting for that moment to speak, the dip of her voice, felt so intimate that he felt a stab of desire.

'Don't be silly,' he murmured back.

Their conversation felt stupidly stilted. As though the words were just an excuse to look at one another. But there was something else adding to his awkwardness: he'd never mentioned their picnic to Yas. What if Emilia referred to it in passing tonight? His wife wasn't a jealous woman, and what could be more innocent than a picnic with the kids – *only he hadn't mentioned it.*

Yasmeen asked him a question: something about their involvement with the party.

'God, it's next Saturday, isn't it? I can't even remember what we were signed up to do. We did try to get out of it, but Zoe's been like a dog with a bone with that party.'

'Oh, we've all been tapped up,' Adrian groaned. 'Can you believe she actually tried to get me to enlist one of my clients as a host? For a summer party?'

'Bicentenary,' Hugo corrected him.

'Sorry?'

'It's the bicentenary.'

'Right. Anyway, where do these people get off?'

Emilia winced at the 'these people', but Adrian, oblivious, went back to monopolising the conversation.

Yas was making a valiant effort, nodding and asking the appropriate questions, but when the first two bars of *Mad Men* rang out a second time and Adrian wandered off with an 'I'm going to have to take this', Hugo stood.

'Don't know what's happened to our waitress. Gonna get another pint. Anyone else need a top-up?'

They were two deep at the bar and, giving up, Hugo headed off to the Gents, locked himself inside a cubicle, leaned back against the door and closed his eyes.

What had seemed like a harmless flirtation suddenly felt like a lot more. How had that happened? Then again what if this was all in Hugo's head? Something he'd conjured up to get himself through the day? If that was the case, it was even more likely Emilia might casually mention their picnic in conversation. Because it meant nothing.

Pulling his phone from his back pocket he tapped out a message:

FYI didn't mention our drink to Y.

To a friendly neighbour this would simply sound like an over-cautious husband.

Hugo had his hand on the lock when he heard the toilet door swing open, a burst of pub chatter, and a familiar voice dripping with sarcasm: 'You're not quite getting this, are you?'

Adrian. Whoever had been calling had finally got through.

Hugo froze, waited. 'You really think people are going to believe you, some talentless wannabe who never got a single call-back? Because it'll be my word against yours, Gemma.'

A pause. 'Yeah, you do that. Let me know how you get on when no one wants to hire you, love. Because I'll make damn sure that happens.'

Silence. Then the sound of the door opening and closing again.

CHAPTER 27

❧

EMILIA

FYI, didn't mention our drink to Y.

Her phone had been face up on the pub table when Hugo's message appeared, and quickly Emilia flipped it over.

With Adrian off on a call and Hugo still at the bar – an excuse to send that message? – the two women had been left alone, and Emilia watched Yasmeen launch into a defence of Zoe without hearing a word.

All the noise and laughter in the room had cut out when she read Hugo's message, and slowly the possible permutations of that single sentence sank in. If their picnic had made Hugo feel guilty, that meant she hadn't imagined it: that charge between them, stronger than passing attraction, thrilling enough to be wrong. Or was this just a husband in a small panic over a jealous wife? Looking at Yasmeen now, it was hard to believe that could be the case.

In a green jumpsuit that tied at the shoulders, one slender brown arm – bare but for three hammered gold bangles – resting on the table, she looked as serene as ever. How could this woman who jetted off across the world several times a month feel threatened by her? In paranoid moments Emilia had even pictured the couple discussing her, Hugo's accomplished, glossy-haired wife laughing – 'Dear oh dear. Someone's got a crush' – and cringed.

'I mean, it's not like I'm ever going to be involved with the committee,' Yasmeen was saying now. 'Not with my job. So if Zoe Mulligan wants to do the hard graft and let us enjoy the benefits . . .'

'I was thinking exactly that the other day,' Emilia managed. 'And just think of all the little improvements she's made since she's been in charge: the film nights, the croquet thingy, that Little Free Library . . .'

As Hugo re-joined the table Emilia watched Yasmeen run her hand across the base of her husband's back, just above the waistband of his jeans, where beneath his T-shirt the skin would be lean and taut, perhaps with the blurred remnants of a tan-line from summers past. It was the gesture of a woman who still enjoyed touching her husband, for whom marital sex was probably still a pleasure, rather than a chore, and Emilia had an unwelcome vision of them together, Yasmeen on top. Because she would have to be, wouldn't she?

'A bit spiky, isn't she?' Adrian murmured as they climbed into bed.

'Yasmeen?' Sitting up beside her horizontal husband,

Emilia reached for the lotion on her bedside table and began to rub it into the backs of her hands, over her knuckles and along her fingers. 'She's alright.' She had no desire to defend Hugo's wife, but Adrian's suspicion towards any career woman always got her shackles up. 'Very lawyer-like.'

'And my God, Doormat Dad's pussy-whipped.'

'Because he looks after his own child?' she countered. 'Anyway, I hate that expression.'

Rolling towards Emilia, her husband slipped his hand beneath her T-shirt and began to move his fingers back and forth across her stomach in a way designed not so much to arouse as warn, like a bleeping lorry backing at high speed, of an imminent sexual move on his part – the first since she'd read those emails with Leila.

'Who were those calls from earlier?' The pressure of her husband's hand increased.

'Calls?'

'In the pub.'

'Pain in the arse actress. All sorted, though.'

He was lying. Emilia knew it. And for a second she was tempted to say something, only Adrian was just doing what he did. What he'd always done. The focal point for her anger wasn't her husband but the piece of work on the other side of the square. A woman who had actually gone to the trouble of putting a note through the door offering her free workout classes. Free *post-natal* workout classes. Ha! *My daughter's ten-months old, you little bitch. So, what? It's not enough for you to humiliate me by flirting with my husband in front of all the neighbours, to use him to further your own ends? I only hope one day you feel as belittled as I do now.*

'You done with all that lard?'

Beneath her T-shirt, Adrian's hand had moved up, claimed a breast.

'Yup.' She put the lotion back on the bedside table.

'Although, maybe I like you greasy.'

Adrian went from man to boy when he wanted sex, complete with juvenile leers. At some point she had found this endearing. 'And you're "in your window", aren't you?'

'My what?'

'You know what I mean.'

Emilia glanced at the man beside her, taking in the single raised eyebrow and flecks of russet in his beard, which was being groomed into what his ludicrously overpriced Mayfair barber called 'a French fork': a style that was 'both elegant and masculine', he'd assured her. Only her husband was neither of those things, she thought coldly. And Emilia was no more ready to sleep with Adrian than have another baby with him.

'Actually, I promised I'd FaceTime Caro tonight.'

As she said it, Emilia knew what she was going to do.

'It's almost midnight.'

'California time.' She shrugged.

'Right.'

The hardening of his mouth irked her. What right did he have to be hurt after what he'd been up to, was up to? He'd been jumpy for weeks, taking his phone with him everywhere, muting it when it rang in front of her. Was it all about Leila? Or was there something else he was hiding? Reaching for her own phone, Emilia slipped it in the pocket of her dressing gown and turned off the light.

'Back in a bit.'

Alone in the kitchen, she tapped out a message, pressing 'send' before she had a chance to read it through.

Can't believe we gatecrashed your Saturday night.

It was as if that single line Hugo had sent her earlier had freed Emilia up in some way. Because then she began tapping out another. She had to know; surely she was allowed to ask:

Why that message earlier?

Why didn't you want Yasmeen to know? I need you to say it.
Both messages remained unread, and for what felt like forever she sat there in that silent kitchen, staring at her phone and listening to the hum of the fridge – until she was forced to admit defeat. Hugo had gone to bed. She should do the same. She was creeping back up the darkened stairs, taking the image of her neighbour with her, when her phone lit up.

You still awake?

That banal question meant everything. Emilia sank down on a step and, cradling the phone above bare knees, spelt out:

Yes.

Without a second thought she repeated the question she'd asked minutes earlier:

That message – why?

Three little dots appeared. Then disappeared. Then reappeared.

Not sure Y would understand.

We weren't doing anything wrong.

The little dots were back. Emilia held her breath, closed her eyes. When she opened them again it was to a dangerous new world of possibility.

So why do I feel like we are?

The messages took on an unstoppable quality then, both of them typing simultaneously.

'I feel that too.' Boom. They were off. And the thrill passed through her like an electric current. 'I've been thinking about you. About what it would be like. What you would be like.'

She could almost hear Hugo's sharp intake of breath.

'What would it be like?'

From her neighbour's gentle demeanour, she would never have guessed he would get here so fast.

'You would take your time. At first.'

'Then?'

'Slow down. I said you'd take your time.'

'Take my time where?'

'There.'

A burst of light almost made her drop the phone. Then her husband's voice from upstairs called out: 'You coming to bed?' With a quick swipe and a tap, she deleted the thread.

CHAPTER 28

COLETTE

'That article you sent me really got me spooked.' Zoe's eyes were wide.

'Sorry. That wasn't my intention,' Colette lied. 'It was only that you mentioned you were worried about Felix's online safety . . .' *And I needed an excuse to come back.*

Her client was standing in her hallway, wearing an A-line green dress, smocked around her concave chest, and as she scoured the few inches of bared flesh above the neckline, noting the long sleeves, Colette tried to find any trace of the abuse she alone knew this poor woman was enduring in private.

Was she wearing more make-up than usual? A thick layer of it covered her angular jaw and cheekbones, and her smile seemed tense, but wasn't it always? Unless you knew what Colette now did, you would never have guessed that this picture of togetherness lived in a world of chaos behind closed doors.

'Those video games in particular . . . ' From the expression on Zoe's face – as though she'd bitten into something sour – her client felt the same way as she did about these.

'I meant, I always check first, on Mumsnet and so on, which ones are age appropriate, but all that stuff about groomers, how exposed kids are. Anyway, I thought it best for you to come while Felix was at school. I don't want him to think we don't trust him . . . '

'I'll take a look. And I can check out those alerts on Guy's laptop too, while I'm here?'

'Oh.' Zoe smoothed her hair. 'I'm not sure he'd like that. Not when he's out.'

Really, why might that be?

'OK.' This was disappointing, but Colette couldn't immediately think of any way around it and allowed herself to be led into Felix's bedroom.

Zoe had warned her about the mess, which turned out to be negligible, but as she was taken through to a small powder-blue-painted room that was a jarring mix of child and teenager – a vast Emirates Stadium poster hanging beside a model aeroplane – the smell of puberty hit Colette at the back of the throat.

'So when it comes to phones and computers we have a full transparency policy with Felix and Freya,' Zoe explained.

Colette got the feeling she was supposed to show her admiration – give her client a red tick: *Good effort!* Which wasn't unusual. Like the patients regaling their GPs with details of their impressive daily step counts and 'moderate' alcohol intakes, her clients were often keen to impress upon her how carefully monitored their kids were. In reality this was rarely the case – particularly where teenage boys were concerned. That generation were far more tech-savvy than their parents, and whatever security measures Colette put in place today would likely be reversed by Felix the moment he came home. But it wasn't her place to say that.

'Always a good tack.' She nodded.

Having keyed in Felix's password, Zoe smiled.

'I'll pop the kettle on. Leave you to it.'

As Colette waited for the boy's Xbox to load, stretching out her legs beneath the low desk, her foot made contact with something hard, and peering down she saw a Microsoft Xbox Elite Wireless Controller, still in its box, tucked between bin and wall. Those things weren't cheap. And if the aim was to get young Felix to spend less time gaming, buying him expensive kit wasn't ideal. Unless his parents hadn't bought it for him. But where else would Felix get that kind of money?

A virtual combat game, *Mind Control Delete*, was clearly his poison of choice, and she was blowing on the tea that had been set down on a coaster beside her when a two-note whistle announced the arrival of a message. Clicking on it Colette saw that there wasn't just one, but a whole string of new messages, and instinctively, she scanned them. She was here to ensure this boy's safety, after all.

THE MAD MAN:
Node 5 starting 2 get tough!

WORTBOY:
That was the most I've felt like an actual Ninja in my life.

ASATRIGHT:
That don't sound right, dude. Here if you wanna talk.

DOOMSDAY:
Anyone else realised this is the exact same story
as Tetris?

At first, the messages appeared to be from friends, but a quick look at the Communication & Multiplayer settings confirmed that both the 'Privacy' and 'Child Defaults' buttons were off, and a closer examination revealed that it wasn't just the Xbox settings that were not secure, but the basic configuration of Felix's desktop. The web browser hadn't been set to show only pre-approved websites or necessitate parental approval for online purchases, and no content restrictions had been implemented. Just as well they had called her in, because from what Colette was seeing it wasn't just video games that Felix was getting stuck into on a daily basis. In fact, as far as thirteen-year-olds went, this one seemed more clued-up than most. But something Colette had just read snagged in her mind, and she scrolled back up.

The thread with ASATRIGHT went back almost a month, and with no references either to common friends or school to anchor this person, Colette began to feel uneasy. She was about to call out to Zoe, when she saw it: a one-liner from Felix to his anonymous friend:

I got shit going on at home. Real shit. Dark shit.

So he knew what his mother was going through. Of course he did. But please God, let Guy not be abusing the kids too?

She'd read a piece in *IT Weekly* about it not being uncommon for children to reach out to strangers online for advice when things got serious, for them to feel reassured by the anonymity it offered. Her finger hovered over the Communication & Multiplayer privacy button. She was here, if only nominally, to safeguard Felix online, but was turning off what had clearly become an outlet for him really safeguarding? Not when Colette knew what was 'going on at home'. Leaving the privacy button off, Colette moved on to Felix's search history.

From across the hall in the kitchen she could hear the sound of running water and clink of china. Quickly, she scanned down. Then she sat back, took her glasses off and stared at the screen.

> Leila Mercheri YouTube
> Leila Mercheri workouts
> Instagram: RealLeila Leila Mercheri nude pics
> Instagram: RealLeila login
> BDSM Buddy
> Leila Mercheri boyfriend
> Fetishchat.co.uk edit profile

And back to Instagram:

> RealLeila

CHAPTER 29

LEILA

'You've gone a bit quiet.'

Frowning down at the message she'd just typed out, Leila proceeded to delete it letter by letter.

Then she drained the dregs of her Lean Green cold press, rearranged her legs on the sofa, and tried again.

'Everything OK?'

No. That was just as needy – with a side of stupid. Clearly everything was not OK. She'd known that from the moment the front-of-house guy at that Mayfair hotel bar had picked up the tasselled room key and left; from Adrian's flinty eyes as they'd waited for a taxi a quarter of an hour later and the toneless way he'd trotted out her address to the driver – without even explaining why he wasn't coming.

But Leila had only grasped how pissed off her neighbour

was now, after four days of being pretty much ghosted. And she wasn't sure if she was angrier at herself for having played the whole thing so badly or Adrian, for trying such a crude move – *before he'd delivered the goods.*

She'd been in enough transactional relationships to know that there were rules, codes of behaviour on both sides. It was understood that you didn't give a man more than the pleasure of your company until he'd proved himself to be in good faith. If you were as artful as she was at this, they never got any more than that. And they weren't left angry or bitter either. But with his blank face at her mention of the showreel that night, his bungled explanations as to why there had been zero progress – and then the pounce, Adrian hadn't just been clumsy: he'd broken the rules.

Sometimes awkward scenes like that one could be beneficial – speed things up. The men went home, did the maths and realised that empty promises weren't enough, that they were going to need to pull their finger out. But given Adrian had only replied (briefly) to one of her emails since that night and none of her texts, that was not going to happen here, and Leila had been finding it increasingly difficult to silence the voice inside her head whispering: *What if he's not the right kind of player?*

She'd met plenty of the wrong kind: the bullshitters who never intended to come up with the goods, wasted your time and were nasty and unpredictable when you let them know how disappointed you were. Did Adrian fall into that category? Leila had no way of knowing, no frame of reference here in London or girlfriends on the circuit to ask: 'What are we talking: harmless perv or classic A-grade predator?'

Then a memory floated back to her: a fellow dancer back in Paris telling her about a website set up a year or so after #MeToo. 'Call Him Out' had been an ingenious idea – a sort of Yelp for sketchy men – where women in the entertainment industry could input a man's name and get anonymous feedback from anyone who might have had bad experiences.

Money was running out. Time was running out. In three and a half months she'd be kicked out of this flat, and she badly wanted to find a way to stay in Addison Square. She needed this TV job to come off – or at least to know if it was a possibility. She needed the answer to one question. Reaching for her laptop Leila found the site and posted:

> Anyone had any run-ins with a telly agent named Adrian Carter?

On the coffee table her phone vibrated once, loud enough to make her start. She had the absurd thought that it might be Adrian looking over her shoulder, but no: the name on the screen was her landlord's.

'I thought I'd better make this call myself, Ms Mercheri, you know, rather than get the agency to do it.'

As he prattled on about how important 'maintaining good relationships with my Addison Mansions neighbours has always been to me' Leila moved through to the bedroom, stuck him on speaker, chucked him on the bed and began to pick out her workout outfit for that afternoon's Karve class. She was holding a pair of Merlot Everlux leggings in one hand when she turned and stared at the phone, open-mouthed at what she was hearing. 'I'm afraid there's been a complaint made against you. Specifically, the noise levels.'

In a mellifluous voice imbued with just the right amount of pained surprise, Leila said: 'I'm so sorry to hear that.' And she was. But not half as sorry as the Mulligans were going to be.

CHAPTER 30

COLETTE

Pulling up outside Addison Mansions, Colette asked herself again whether she was making the right decision.

Since leaving Zoe's the day before, she'd been over and over it in her mind. Yes, Felix was a child, a mixed-up teenager, high on hormones and unable to process his anger at the 'shit going on at home'. God knows how traumatised he must be by his abusive stepfather. But he'd been terrorising Leila.

Besides, Colette had been given a job to do, made a promise. Now that she'd found out who was responsible, was she really going to cover up for Felix? No, when she'd messaged her client early that morning telling her she had 'an update' and could she come over – she'd known she had no choice.

Glancing up at Felix's window, a new worry formed: what would Leila do with the information? Would she tell his parents or, worse, the police? The young woman hadn't wanted to involve them at the start of this, but so much had happened since then. With everything Colette now knew about her, she wouldn't want to be in Felix's shoes.

She was pulling the key from the ignition when her phone pinged. Leila.

> You on your way? Juste checked my IG. There's a load of total weirdos claiming to be 'Daddy Doms' on there. Apparently my profile's juste gone up on a new BDSM site. Help! Can't take much more of this.

It wasn't the contents of the message that had her doing a double take at the words on her screen. Leila's spoken English was practically flawless, but there were occasional grammatical errors and misspellings in her messages. Usually what were called 'false friends': words that sounded like their French counterparts but were spelled differently. And Colette knew exactly where she'd seen that 'juste' before.

She registered the grim significance of the extra 'e' with the understatement only true shock can prompt: a little internal 'ahh' – almost a sigh.

That baffling GIF: *You'll both be there at the square party. Juste thinking it would be a shame for it to come out then? I'll be in touch.* It all made sense.

Leila trying on shoes in Sylvia's bedroom as she helped her with her clear-out – assessing the old lady's worth, identifying her prey, uncovering some secret – what? – the old lady was desperate to keep. That expensive video equipment, all those Net-a-Porter bags. They hadn't all been 'freebies', had they? They'd been Leila, enjoying her weekly windfalls ... alongside coffees, strolls and manicures with her oblivious victim.

Her face still stiff with shock, Colette typed out a reply:

> Re the update: may have spoken too soon. Get back
> to you when I know more.

Then she got out of the car, walked straight past Addison Mansions and rang Sylvia's doorbell.

Movement within; the familiar pause as, behind the door, the old lady peered through the spy hole – then the drag and drop of the chain.

'Colette?' Sylvia blinked at her. 'Come in.'

It was absurd to have this conversation on the doorstep, yet she didn't move. Once she stepped across the threshold there would be small talk, offers of tea to be turned down. This couldn't wait another second.

'I came across something during the course of my work today.' She'd known she would start with that, but now what? 'Something that ...' She stalled, trying and failing to find words that might lessen the shock, blunt the betrayal.

A frown. 'Colette, are you sure you won't come in?'

'I know about the money,' she blurted out. 'The weekly payouts.'

She watched Sylvia's breath catch at that, her hand rise to her throat.

'I have no idea how long it's been going on or what's being held over you.' Whatever it was had brought fear to her client's face. How bad could it be? *What* could it be? 'But I do know who's doing it and I . . . I couldn't not tell you. Not when I see how close you two are, how much time you spend together. How convinced you are that Leila's a friend.'

In a low voice Sylvia repeated, 'Leila?'

CHAPTER 31

HAMMERSMITH POLICE STATION
EXTRACT OF RECORDED INTERVIEW
WITH MRS SYLVIA RYAN

Date: 17 July
Duration: 83 minutes
No. of pages: 42
Conducted by Officers of the
Metropolitan Police

DC BAXTER: So when you discovered that
this woman you had befriended and trusted
had been blackmailing you out of tens
of thousands of pounds, you still didn't
report Ms Mercheri. Why?

SR: [No response.]

DC Baxter: Mrs Ryan?

SR: Because I didn't want anyone to know.

DC Harris: About the real reason you moved to Addison Square?

DC Baxter: For the benefit of the tape, Mrs Ryan is nodding.

SR: Do you have a child, Detective Constable?

DC Baxter: A boy, yes.

SR: Can you imagine what it would be like to be forced to give him up at birth? Even if you wanted and loved him?

DC: I can't say that I can.

SR: Well, let me tell you something. When you give up a child, you give up your right to be in their life – forever. And I decided I would rather pay the money, any amount of money, than blow up my child's life.

DC Harris: But after your IT consultant, Ms Burton, told you who had been sending

you those messages and blackmailing you,
you confronted Ms Mercheri, didn't you?

SR: [Faint] Yes.

DC Baxter: Why?

SR: I hoped to appeal to her better
nature. *Ha.*

DC Harris: And that's amusing because?

SR: Turns out Leila didn't have one.

CHAPTER 32

LEILA

'Shall we sit?' Sylvia nodded at the bench in the shade by the playground. 'Drink our coffees?'

When the old lady had suggested a stroll, Leila had agreed immediately. She had an hour to kill before her first Karve class and the flat felt airless, stifling. As she'd left a disembodied voice from her telly was announcing that 'the Heatwave Alert Level has risen to 4, with illness and death occurring not just in high-risk groups but among the fit and healthy.'

Above them, the July sky was a brutal blue, but at least she could breathe out here. Besides, she needed a distraction.

Leila wasn't used to being fobbed off, and right now the two people she urgently needed to hear from were full of excuses, unreachable. Her heart had leapt when the tech geek had told her she had an update – and sunk when she'd admitted she'd 'spoken too soon' just a few hours later. What was that about?

Then there was Adrian, who was at least now replying to her messages, but without really engaging. Certainly his tone wasn't as flirtatious as it had been before that night in the hotel bar. As for the question she'd posted on Call Him Out, nobody had replied.

'You remembered the way I like it,' she murmured, stretching out her legs and taking a sip of her iced almond milk latte. 'You are sweet.'

For a moment they both drank in silence, Leila admiring the delicacy of her new Tiffany bracelet, the glint of diamonds on her wrist. Then, because she'd started to enjoy the 'name the flower' game they played on their square walks, she pointed at the magenta flowers springing up on both sides of the arbour before them: 'What about those? The pinky-purple ones.'

'Anemones,' Sylvia replied without a moment's hesitation. 'In fact I think that particular variety's called "Summer Breeze".'

'And those sapphire ones over there?'

'Delphiniums.'

'OMG, you're amazing. I bet you can name every plant here. Let me see ...' She scanned the nearby flower bed, giggled. 'What about—'

'Actually I have a question for you.'

Leila closed her eyes, breathing in the hot scents of summer: 'Go on.'

'Did something happen to you? Were you damaged in some way growing up? Or are you just a psychopath?'

Leila's eyes flew open, the laugh frozen on her face. Swivelling her neck, she stared at Sylvia.

'I feel like such a fool.' Nothing in the old lady's expression matched the words coming from her lips – smoothly, seamlessly. Her grey eyes were as serene as always, her brow unfurrowed. 'I mean I did wonder, at first: what does this vibrant, gorgeous young person see in me? What possible motive can she have for befriending me? But I was flattered, I suppose. And lonely.'

'Sylv . . .'

Her neighbour held up a hand. 'It never occurred to me that the messages started after you moved here: that you were the one sending them.'

Quickly, Leila weighed the situation up, decided straight denial was worth a shot.

'I literally have no idea what you're talking about.'

'Don't bother.'

'Seriously. I . . .'

'I may be an old fool, but you can't get anything past Colette.'

Swallowing a surge of fury, Leila nodded. She'd been so careful, and all the time tech lady was supposed to have been helping her that bitch had been sticking her nose where it didn't belong? Big mistake. But right now all that mattered was what Sylvia planned to do with this. Leila had to think fast.

'I was going to ask you the same question,' Sylvia went on. 'How did you find out? I've been racking my brains, trying to think. Eight years I've been living here, with nobody suspecting a thing. Then, what, within a few weeks of moving to the square you . . .' Stopping abruptly, she raised a hand to her forehead. 'God, I'm so stupid. You found the box. That day, in my bedroom, when we were going through my things, when I gave you those shoes: you found the box, didn't you?'

Leila sighed. There didn't seem much point in explaining that she had genuinely enjoyed their budding friendship – in the beginning. That with younger women always so wary of her and men of every age only ever after one thing, it had been a relief to find someone so welcoming, someone without an agenda, in her new community. Because who else was there in Addison Square: Emilia? Zoe? Yasmeen? So there had been no 'motive', and a 'psychopath' – really? But Leila had always been able to spot an opportunity when it landed in her lap. In her mind that was something to be proud of.

Sylvia had been downstairs with the IT woman on the day she'd found the box and unearthed a secret the old lady had kept for God knows how long.

She'd been so generous with her things as they'd gone through her wardrobe, apparently oblivious to how much some of them were worth. Then again, this woman was loaded. The size of that house! And it wasn't like she had anyone to pass these things down to. Quickly, Leila had understood that it only took her enthusing over a vintage suede jacket (that would go for a couple of hundred on Depop) or a pair of '70s YSL pumps, for Sylvia to say: 'Go on, have them. Please. It's not like I'm ever going to wear them again.'

Leila had been going through the little stash of treasures she'd amassed on the bed when she'd spotted a vintage Céline handbag at the bottom of Sylvia's open wardrobe. Pulling it out to check that the gold hardware was unscratched and run her hand over the butter-soft leather, she'd spied the box beneath it.

It was a large shoe box, tantalisingly bashed up at the corners, and as the chatter had continued in the hallway downstairs, Leila had pulled it out and opened it.

At first, she'd been disappointed. All the box contained was a collection of documents, photos and cuttings, a tiny woollen hat and a hospital wristband, the name printed upon it blurred and faded by time – but still decipherable. Sylvia Ryan had a child and that child had no idea that their birth mother lived across the square.

She'd read as much as she could before hurriedly putting the box and handbag back when she'd heard the front door slam. That night, still balking at her discovery and working out the finer details, Leila had decided how to make use of it.

Taking a swig of her coffee, Leila shrugged. 'I found your box, yes.'

CHAPTER 33

SYLVIA

The shrug threw Sylvia so completely that for a moment she was speechless.

Then her thoughts came out shambolically, illogically. 'And you didn't think to ask me about it? Your first impulse was to make money from me, to *blackmail* me? Is this what you do? Or am I the first?'

Another sigh. 'Do you have any idea how much dancers make, Sylvia?'

'No.' Sitting back, the old lady crossed her arms. 'Tell me.'

'Not enough to live on. Not really. Which is why I do the classes, and the influencing. To get by.'

'But all those companies who pay you, those ambassador-ships: you told me that . . .'

Leila dismissed this with a wave of the hand.

'It helps, but it's still not enough.'

'And that's your excuse?'

'No.' The young woman thought about this. 'More of an explanation. But what about you?' She cocked her head to one side. 'What's your explanation for giving up your child? For lying about it to everyone. Did you even tell your husband?' She leaned forward on the bench, so close that Sylvia could see her own reflection in Leila's pupils. 'If you tell anyone what I've been doing, everyone will know. And remember this, Sylvia: I've kept your secret.'

In amidst this baring of souls Sylvia suddenly saw a glimmer of light. Because the humiliation, the money – those things she could recover from. When all was said and done, the only thing that mattered was Leila keeping quiet. Maybe if she understood, if Sylvia told her everything, she would let it go. She was so tired of the lies. She'd been telling them for half a lifetime.

'We tried for so many years to have a baby, Archie and I. And I tried everything, every old fertile wives' tale. I drank cough syrup like it was water, I ate yams, I spent as much time around other couples' kids as I could, hoping motherhood would rub off on me. None of it worked.'

Sylvia half expected an 'I'm sorry', before remembering that Leila didn't do that. Oddly, it made it easier.

'Archie was disappointed, of course, but for me it was more than that. I suppose because I didn't love him.'

There was no judgement on Leila's face. She just nodded and waited.

'Oh, I thought I did, at the start, but very quickly I realised it had been a mistake – that he was a mistake – and a child would have made up for that. Made the life I'd chosen bearable. Anyway, this was back in the seventies, when people didn't do the thing of finding out who was to blame, who was defective. Back then people accepted this was their lot.' Sylvia took a breath. 'So when I sought solace elsewhere, just for one night – with someone who meant nothing, who just happened to be there – it didn't occur to me that I might get pregnant.'

'How old were you?'

'Thirty-three. Old then. And that's when I made my second mistake, my biggest mistake, and came clean. I had thought that once Archie calmed down, he would see it as the blessing it was, but . . . ' She shook her head. 'Anyway, getting rid of it was abhorrent to him and to me. So when I got too big to hide it, too pregnant for Archie to bear the sight of me, I went off to stay with my mother, had the baby there – and gave my baby away to a couple who had been trying for years. A good, solid couple, who were great adoptive parents until they died, within months of each other, a few years ago.'

Leila nodded. 'That was why you moved here. To be near . . . '

A few feet away a lawnmower started up, drowning out the end of her sentence. They hadn't seen the gardener arrive. They hadn't noticed Zoe either, encircled by a small troop of men and holding a clipboard to her chest, over by the gazebo.

Leila glanced at her watch, and the coldness of the gesture filled Sylvia with dread. She'd told her everything, even betraying a confidence by blurting out Colette's name when she'd promised to keep her out of it, and it hadn't made a dent. The young woman was standing up now, she was going to leave, go about her day as normal, with everything she needed to explode Sylvia's life – if she chose to.

'Wait. Are you going to ...' She'd brought Leila here to confront her, hoping that by doing so she would end this. That they'd be quits. Now, she only felt doubly vulnerable. 'Are you going to tell anyone?'

'No.' Leila slung her handbag over one arm, and Sylvia noticed that it was new, expensive looking, presumably paid for by her. 'But I'll need more money. You of all people get it, don't you?'

'Get what?' It came out hoarse.

'That we do what we have to. To get by.'

CHAPTER 34

ZOE

'I can't talk now, Guy. I'm in the middle of something.'

Mouthing 'sorry' to the Dynamic Marquees men assembled around her on the square garden lawn, Zoe stepped away and tried to hurry her husband along.

'It's under the shelf in the hall.' *Use your eyes!* 'Listen, if you can get Freya to have her shower, I shouldn't be more than twenty minutes.'

Ending the call, Zoe lifted her sunglasses, swiped away the damp crescents beneath, and sighed. A few feet away the three men were bent over the marquee design layouts she'd spent months finessing – the ones they'd had on a shared Google document since May. Yet from their puckered brows you'd think it was all news to them and Zoe felt an itch of irritation at the 'no can dos' she sensed coming.

Today's trials had started early, with Freya adamant she hated tennis camp – 'It's the first week of the holidays, Mum! Why do I have to go?' – and that dirge-like beat grinding overhead as they ate breakfast. Leila had never kicked off before 9 a.m. before and Zoe no longer thought Guy was being ridiculous when he said she was doing it on purpose. In fact she was pretty sure this was Leila's defiant response to the complaint she'd lodged with her landlord.

'So we all good?' she asked the marquee men brightly. If her Goldmans years had taught her anything, it was that questions expecting the answer 'yes' were more likely to get a positive result.

'Well,' the main man began tentatively, 'we might have a little problem. One or two little problems, if I'm being honest.'

Zoe had been right about the 'no can do's but she listened patiently before telling the men that yes, they were going to need the two separate exits at the back of the main marquee, *as previously agreed*, and was in the middle of explaining why having one of those exits directly behind the stage wouldn't work, *on account of how guests would need to access it*, when she noticed two figures seated on the bench by the playground.

In the spandex uniform that accentuated every sleek curve, tightly packaging chest and thighs, Leila was instantly recognisable. But it took her a moment to make out Sylvia.

What was it with these two? What on earth could they possibly have to talk about? Leila was smiling, so maybe it was some kind of pep talk. She could imagine her playing the guru, doling out empty positivisms to this little local 'project', when the greatest pain the young woman would ever have experienced was probably a failed audition or 'poorly performing' Instagram post.

As she led the disgruntled men out of the gardens, Zoe threw Sylvia and Leila one last bemused glance.

Back at the flat, she was greeted by a familiar scene. In his bedroom Felix was busy slaying men with deft clicks of his mouse, while in the sitting room Guy could be heard talking on the phone. If Freya was on the iPad – if she too was on a screen . . .

Zoe slipped off her new white plimsolls – dismayed to find them feathered with green from the lawn – leaned against the wall and forced herself to breathe in through the nose for a count of four. She could hear the lady on the relaxation podcast telling her to 'exhale forcefully through the mouth, really empty your mind as you make that whoosh sound for a full eight seconds!' But all Zoe could think about was that poisonous Xbox and her ruined shoes. She would have to put them through the machine. Even then the stains might not come out.

Rounding the corner Zoe found her daughter, as predicted, on the iPad and still in her tennis gear, bare legs curled up beneath her.

'Off that please, Freya.'

'There's only seven minutes of this episode left!'

'I don't care. Off.'

On the other side of the room, hunched over his desk, his shirtsleeves rolled up and his hair in disarray, sat her husband.

'So much for getting her showered.' Guy looked up and met her eyes. She knew that look, and everything it meant for later.

'I'll put the supper on, shall I?'

*

What a person – two people – could get used to, was astonishing. Couples got used to being apart for years, they got used to cheating and lying and living separate lives. But for Zoe, meals were sacred: the foundations that kept their family upright, no matter what else might be going on. When one of the school mums had admitted to eating supper with the kids at a different time to her husband, Zoe had been horrified. How could anybody normalise something so … uncivilised? Then the voice inside her head had jeered, *As opposed to what you've normalised?*

The first time had shaken them both to the core, taken weeks to get over. And if anyone had told her then that she and Guy would come to accept such a thing into their lives, continue to function as a family even as it happened again and again, she would never have believed it.

Now, after all these years, what took place between them when the kids were out or in bed had become a part of their relationship. Only like sex, those physical acts took place in a private parallel world. One never referred to in broad daylight, the bruises carefully hidden from view as they went from bluish-purple to green and then yellow, before disappearing entirely. A clean slate.

Sometimes months would pass peaceably, and Zoe would convince herself that whatever that dark period in their marriage was about, it was over. Then the pressure would start to build again, like the heaviness before a thunderstorm gaining in intensity until she would almost yearn for it to break.

Sitting there with Freya, listening to herself answer her daughter's questions about intransitive verbs – 'So "Mummy threw the ball", see?' – Zoe knew it was about to. Yet over the next two hours a shaky equilibrium was re-established.

She watched her family enjoy the supper she'd made, agreeing with Guy that the lamb cutlets were 'perfect': moist, succulent and pink on the inside, without being bloody. Then, after the kids had gone to bed and she and Guy were sitting there watching telly, her husband made a comment, something casually demeaning about the home makeover shows she loved but he only tolerated.

By then the wine they'd had with dinner had peeled back a layer, left them exposed. But Zoe had the foresight to get up and lock the sitting room door before going back to her position on the sofa.

Sure enough, before Zoe knew what she was doing, she was back on her feet, hissing at Guy, clawing at his face and pummelling his chest. The rage, as always, had turned her into someone else, and there was only one clear thought in her head: *I want to hurt you.*

His cowering and flinches, instinctual after all these years, only made her angrier, showing her up for what she was: the person she'd thought she would only be with Felix's father. A person who had remained dormant throughout the first four years of her marriage to Guy, before emerging again, more vicious than before.

So when, trying to shackle both of her wrists with his hands, Guy spat out, 'You need help! You're fucking unstable and one day you're going to kill me!' Zoe saw her hand reach for that heavy glass snow globe on the mantelpiece and watched herself swing it at her husband's head.

CHAPTER 35

HUGO

Something about manual labourers always made Hugo feel unworthy, he decided, as he jogged past the man bolting together a corner of the marquee frame on the square garden lawn.

The circuit he'd chosen was almost entirely shady and he was only on his third lap, but this was his first jog in months and already he was sweating more than any of the men who had been heaving in steel beams and rolls of canvas since he'd started. So by unworthy, what Hugo actually meant was unmanly. Possibly even ridiculous, with his pale middle-class calves and hamster-wheel-like attempts to keep fit. These guys didn't go home and *jog*, did they?

Feeling the hollow pang of a stitch start up in his right side, Hugo slowed to a panting halt, watching in fascination as one of the men – bald, with a warped Everton crest inked around his forearm – fitted the curved end of an eave into a bracket.

'How's it coming on?' he called out, cringing a little at the instinctive softening of his 't'.

Everton man straightened up.

'It's coming.'

'Looks vast.'

Vast.

'Fifty by forty.' The man scratched at a stubbled jaw, looked up at the sky. 'Not that you'll need it. Looks like Saturday's going to be like this.'

Out of the corner of his eye Hugo saw Zoe heading towards them across the lawn, looking even more uptight than usual. Of course: Guy's accident. Sylvia had told him all about it yesterday. This was why he didn't play squash. Because at some point everyone who did seemed to end up taking a racquet to the face and a trip to A&E.

Hugo knew he should do the neighbourly thing and ask how Guy was doing, but Sylvia had said he was on the mend and pretending not to see Zoe was generally the best course of action. He threw out a cheerful 'What a summer, eh?' and jogged off.

As Hugo started on another lap around the outer edges of the garden, ducking to avoid the occasional low-hanging branch, he imagined himself recounting the exchange to Emilia. Would the pitch of her laugh drop, the way it did when she found something so funny she lost all self-consciousness? And how on earth was he going to stand beside his wife in forty-eight hours' time making small talk with a neighbour he'd . . .

He still shrank from calling it 'phone sex' – even in his

head, five days later. They'd broken off halfway through, for one thing, and he had no idea whether that had been Emilia's choice or whether she had been interrupted. In any case phone sex was for teenagers, not frazzled parents. And it made him sound like a cheater. Only Hugo had never felt less frazzled in his life. He'd had to go for this jog to try and dull the wired feeling he'd woken up with every day since they'd done ... whatever it was they'd done together. But he was a cheater, wasn't he? The moment he'd sent the WhatsApp message that had started it all, he'd cheated on Yas.

Are you still awake?

Hugo's mind skittered over the messages he and Emilia had exchanged. The words they'd each tapped-out in vow-breaking sentences. *'Slow down,' she'd written. 'I said you'd take your time.'*

That had been Emilia? His neighbour, wife of Adrian-the-Twat and mother of two? It still didn't feel real.

As he ran on, thoughts of her naked sprang up. The heavy breasts, the extravagant outward curve from waist to hip. The thought made Hugo slow to another wheezing standstill. Pressing both palms against the trunk of a nearby tree he stretched his right calf muscle and his left. Then he pulled his phone from his pocket and tapped out a new message:

Where are you? I'm in the garden.

Since their pub night and those messages there had been no further contact between them; no chance sightings of Emilia. Now, he needed to see her. Touch the real her.

He carried on running, panting, until suddenly there she was, letting herself in through the side gate, pink-cheeked – as though she too had run to meet him.

He stopped, took her in; remembered the men hammering away just across the lawn. Then there was Zoe.

'Follow me.' What he was doing was insane, but as he led Emilia towards the shed behind the greenhouse all Hugo cared about was being alone with her. Prising open the stiff wooden door, he felt his T-shirt sticking to the back of his neck, the pulse in his temple.

He barely registered the sacks of compost piled high against one wall, the stacked tennis racquets. Pulling the door shut, he pressed Emilia up against it and kissed her.

That feeling you get when you're so thirsty you can't think beyond that first glug? When you can't imagine ever being sated? That's what their first kiss felt like.

Hugo had been clumsy, gone in too hard, sending Emilia's handbag sliding down into the crook of one arm as he opened his mouth to her, tasting the creamy vanilla of her lipstick. Because after the other night he knew what she was, what she liked, even if this was the first time he'd ever touched her.

Pulling back, he followed her eyeline up to a single balled-up spider hanging from a gossamer thread at eye level, and forehead to forehead, they laughed.

Then everything happened so fast he wasn't sure who was hitching up clothing or yanking it down.

After that there was only the rhythmic rattle of the door hinges, Emilia's ragged breath in his ear – and a single shrill cry when she finished.

They listened out for any footsteps outside. Nothing but a distant hammering.

'Sorry.'

'Why are you apologising?' She laughed.

They spoke over each other as they righted their clothing, sober and self-conscious after that moment of madness. But Hugo wanted her to understand. 'I haven't been able to stop thin—'

Outside a woman's voice rang out. Zoe was shockingly close, inches away from the shed door, calling out to the marquee men, 'Back in a bit with some squash!' And they both held their breath.

Had Zoe needed something from that shed, had she tried to open the door . . .

'I've got to get back,' Emilia whispered.

'OK. Just wait . . .'

She smoothed her hair, scouring the floor around her feet for her bag.

'Here—' He reached for it, threading her arm through the strap.

'How do I look?'

Hugo took in the pink-tipped nose, smudged mouth and the missed button at the top of her dress.

'Do you really want me to answer that?'

'Maybe not.'

'It's OK.' With one hand over her head, he pushed open the door. 'We're clear.'

She was leaning in for one last kiss when he looked over her shoulder and saw the shadow on the paving stones; the woman standing in the pathway watching them, a yoga mat beneath one arm. Then everything imploded.

There was at once an acute understanding of what they'd done and a foreshadowing of all the pain his actions were going to cause. He thought about the way Yasmeen would always try to make the bed with him still in it, about the time capsule school project he and Ollie were working on and his son's anxious face that morning, when out of nowhere he'd started asking him whether children could go to prison too – and he knew that a life without them was unimaginable.

'Sorry,' Leila murmured, eyes still fixed on them both. Only she didn't look sorry. She looked . . . gleeful.

CHAPTER 36

COLETTE

The invitation had stated 'black tie and gowns'. But Colette hadn't owned a 'gown' since school, so a summer suit it was. The M&S suit. Which looked even better in her hall mirror than it had in the fitting room, and alone in her flat, to the sounds of Michael Bolton's *Songs of Cinema*, Colette allowed herself a rare moment of vanity, admiring the tailoring around the shoulders, the neatness of her waist and sleekness of her freshly trimmed hair.

As the first few bars of Michael's duet with Dolly Parton started up, she pictured herself sauntering across the square garden lawn in just a few hours' time towards the huge cream marquee she'd glimpsed through the railings that morning. She imagined the faint surprise in her clients' smiles. A surprise she would pretend not to notice.

That's right! Colette wasn't a cyborg without a life or style, but a slick and accomplished woman who had agreed to spend that July Saturday in their company. Who was giving them her time.

In the mirror, her image frowned back at her, and Colette's eyes ran down the length of her reflection to ... her bare feet. Formal footwear had always been a problem. The linen trousers were a good three inches too long for flats, but along with dresses and skirts she didn't do heels. Never had. The closest thing she had in her wardrobe were a pair of chunky-soled winter boots. Adrian's smirking face popped into her mind. *'No, no, it's a good look; a strong look, um ...'* *'Colette – my name's COLETTE.'* But she had bigger things to worry about, like what to do about Felix Mulligan.

It had been five days since – still stunned by the significance of that 'juste' – she had fobbed Leila off with a WhatsApp, and in that time her client had called and messaged incessantly. What was the update Colette had for her? When would she know more? There had been another post. She was freaking out here! In the last few voicenotes there had been a hard edge to Leila's 'call me back please' and for a moment she'd panicked that Sylvia had told the young woman who had busted her. But no, she'd sworn her to secrecy.

One thing Colette was sure of: she couldn't denounce Felix. Not now that she knew what Leila had been up to with Sylvia, what the young woman *was*. Setting aside what the boy was going through at home, how damaged he clearly was, she had no way of gauging what Leila's reaction would be. If she was amoral enough to befriend a recently widowed woman in order to blackmail her, to string Adrian along for the sake of a TV slot and humiliate his wife, what else might she be capable of?

Leila would be there at the party – unavoidable. They would *all* be there. And Colette couldn't shake the feeling that tonight, the whole tinder box might go up.

CHAPTER 37

HAMMERSMITH POLICE STATION
EXTRACT OF RECORDED INTERVIEW
WITH MRS YASMEEN COOPER

Date: 17 July
Duration: 69 minutes
No. of pages: 34
Conducted by Officers of the
Metropolitan Police

DC BAXTER: How much do you know about Colette Burton?

YC: The techie? She's worked for us for years. Ever since we bought the house.

I forget who recommended her, but she basically does the whole square.

DC BAXTER: We're aware, but what do you actually know about her? What kind of person is she?

YC: [Long pause] Sorry. I'm drawing a blank.

DC HARRIS: Funny. We've asked your neighbours that same question, and nobody seems able to tell us a single thing about the woman you all trust with your most private information.

YC: I've never thought of it that way. But you've met her. She's sort of a non-person.

DC BAXTER: Do you know who's most statistically likely to be the perpetrator in any murder investigation?

DC HARRIS: For the tape, Mrs Cooper is shaking her head.

DC BAXTER: The person who found the body.

YC: OK.

DC BAXTER: Do you know who found Ms Mercheri's body?

CHAPTER 38

LEILA

The Square Party

L eila's finger hovered over the 'post' button. Then, as she so often did, she went back to the picture to triple check it couldn't, in some small way, be improved upon.

There she was, holding her phone up to the mirror in a bedroom that looked gratifyingly luxurious, very *ELLE Decoration*, the single piece of contemporary sculpture on the side table (by some feminist firebrand activist whose name and message she'd forgotten) proving her cultural credentials. Not that anyone would be focussing on soft furnishings or sculptures. Not with her in that dress.

The floor-length silk amber gown was cut deep enough

to make the wearing of any kind of bra impossible, and the unforgiving fabric would have reduced anyone else's body to an assortment of physical failings, an embarrassment of bulges. It had been duly tagged, alongside the studded nude leather sandals just visible at the bottom of the frame, the single drop chain earring, and the most expensive part of the outfit: that *insane* gold and emerald Jade Trau necklace. *Thank you, Sylvia.*

With a sigh of satisfaction Leila pressed 'post'.

As she left the flat and made her way cautiously down the stairs, the hem of her dress in one hand, Leila heard the band start up in the square. Beneath the simmering rage, she felt a shiver of excitement at the thought of the evening ahead.

She couldn't give a damn about the party. No. It was the confrontations she was actively looking forward to. There were people who feared conflict, who would do anything to avoid a face-off, but Leila? *Bring it on.*

The Mulligans were going to regret that call they'd put into her landlord, for starters. Because although he'd refused to tell her who had made the noise complaint, Leila had immediately known it was her downstairs neighbours. That she hadn't laid eyes on either Guy or Zoe since then only confirmed it. That was the British for you: nothing terrified them more than the prospect of a moment's social awkwardness. Well, Leila would redefine awkward for them.

Then there was Colette, who thought she'd been so clever, spying on her even as she pretended to help – but apparently forgetting one crucial fact: if anyone knew what the IT lady had been up to, she would never work again.

That little head-to-head would be brief, however, compared to the one she intended to have with Adrian. Because the night before, almost a week after she'd posted her question on Call Him Out, a woman had replied.

> What I could tell you about Adrian Carter, **wrote one 'Gemma R'**. He was my agent. Told me I was in the last three for a key role in *Casualty*. Strung me along for weeks, took me out for drinks and dinner. Then, when I wouldn't sleep with him, chucked me off his client list. Said I 'didn't have what it took'. But here's the best bit: I found out later that he never even put me up for the role. Yup, this guy should come with a hazard warning.

One sentence had alarmed Leila far more than the rest – *I found out later that he never even put me up for the role* – and she'd gone back to Adrian's client list online and scrolled down until she found the same publicity shot she'd found weeks ago, when Adrian had first mentioned Chloe Hartnell.

There she was, captured mid-laugh, one shoulder raised to her cheek, the glint of a tongue-piercing just visible in the recesses of her mouth. But something still hadn't felt right, so Leila had done what she should have done to begin with and the first Google search result for 'Chloe Hartnell' 'Agent' wasn't Adrian Carter, but a brassy blonde in her mid-to-late fifties ... at a completely different agency. One phone call had confirmed that Chloe had changed agencies over a year ago. That Adrian Carter was your classic predator and full of shit from the start.

Leila had felt stupid, naïve – something she was very definitely not – but more than anything else she'd felt furious. She'd called in the dress she was wearing tonight for Adrian. She'd been counting on clinching the deal they should have been celebrating that night in Mayfair. And she'd been played. So that particular confrontation? Although she hadn't yet decided what she would say or do, she would definitely bide her time, take him by surprise. Because this was the one Leila was going to relish the most.

As she reached the first floor landing she realised that her clutch was oddly light, felt the absence of something. Damn it. She'd left her phone on the bed. Retracing her steps Leila became aware of a key rattling in a lock above: her lock.

'What the ... ?'

Craning her neck she peered up the stairwell, caught sight of a small figure in a blue striped T-shirt at her door.

'Hey!' Cursing her long dress she took the last flight two by two, just in time to see a boy, Hugo and Yasmeen's boy – Oscar? Oliver? Yes! – turn in alarm and dash past her down the stairs. 'What the fuck do you think you're ...' He was fast. So fast she didn't even try to chase after him. 'Hey!'

A succession of thuds as the boy missed a step below, sliding down the last flight – then the slam of the front door.

The door of the utility cupboard opposite was ajar – the boy must have been hiding there, waiting for her to leave – as was her own front door. Pushing it open she stood on the doorstep, waiting for the pounding of her heart to subside. How the hell had Ollie got hold of a spare key? What was he doing there? Even as she asked herself the answer was obvious: someone must have sent him. The same someone who had been stalking her for weeks.

With trembling fingers, Leila grabbed her phone and headed back down the stairs. Outside in the lane she could hear the smoky voice of a woman crooning out 'The Look of Love', see a messy line of people tailing back into the road outside an entrance decked out with gold and silver balloons.

Still shaken, Leila joined the queue, surveying the guests with a distracted eye. In amongst the black-tie suited men, the women were columns of colour – deep plums, punch pinks and royal blues – leaning in to complement one another's hideous gowns and hair as they approached the suited security with clipboards on either side of the gate. And there, halfway down, was Colette, wearing an ill-fitting suit and some ... there were no words for whatever she was wearing on her feet.

Ignoring the murmurs of annoyance as she skipped past the people in front, Leila tapped her on the shoulder.

The expression of alarm on the IT lady's face was comical. Why not kick off the confrontations now? After all this wasn't just about Colette's betrayal; she was holding back on something, Leila was sure of it. And after what had just happened she was more determined than ever to find out what.

'Great outfit. Really ...' she bared her teeth, 'original.' The woman stammered out a thank you. 'You're not easy to get hold of. I've been trying. But you know that.'

'Sorry.' Pushing the bridge of her rimless glasses into her nose, Colette looked around helplessly for an escape. 'I'm afraid I've been ...'

'... busy elsewhere?' The two women edged forward, and Leila lowered her voice. 'Looking into Sylvia's little problem, maybe?'

Colette blinked once, twice. She had her.

'Look,' she started. 'I don't know what's been said, but ...'

Pulling a tube of gloss from her clutch, Leila ran it lightly across her lips, cut in: 'Let's shelve that – for now. Because guess who I just caught trying to get into my flat with his own key? Well, a copy of mine. Hugo and Yasmeen's kid.'

Whatever Colette had found out, it wasn't that. The look of astonishment on her face was too genuine.

'Clever, when you think about it. Who's going to notice a little kid? So I'm going to ask you straight: do you know who sent him? Who's been stalking me? I want you to think *really* carefully before you answer.'

The IT lady looked as though she might hyperventilate. Then, in a whisper, 'I have made some headway. I just needed to ...'

'Thought so.' Leila cut in. 'And?'

'And ...'

From the gates one of the security guards called out, 'If everyone can have their invitations ready, that'll speed things up!'

Leila knew exactly how to speed this situation up. 'Remember that promise you made to me? You know, when you made that little speech about new laws? About stalking and cyberstalking? I made you a promise too, didn't I? To keep it between us. But if you're not going to keep up your side of the—'

'It's Felix,' Colette said softly, looking not at Leila but down at the invitation she was clutching to her chest with both hands.

'It's ... sorry, what?' That little freak in the flat below. *He'd* been doing all this? He and his little sidekick?

'The fake account, the photos, the missing stuff. He had access to the roof balcony, of course, although how he and Ollie got hold of the keys to your flat, I don't know ... But it's all Felix.'

Leila stared at her. Of course it was. She should have guessed. The whole thing had had 'fucked-up Incel' written all over it from the start.

'But that's good, right? Better some teenager with a harmless, um, crush than, than ...'

'Hardly harmless.' That it was a kid – kids – was humiliating. But that kid had been terrorising her. 'He's broken the law. Quite a few laws.'

'I know. But we don't want to involve the police. We don't *need* to involve the police. This is a mixed-up child. He just needs to be told that the game is up, to stop his nonsense ...'

'Nonsense? Do you have any idea what this has been like for me?'

'Stop all of it, I mean. And take everything down too: RealLeila and whatever else. But please,' the woman was begging now, 'let me deal with Felix? I'd rather his parents didn't know. It's ... complicated. So first thing in the morning, I promise I'll ...'

'You'll talk to him tonight.' They'd reached the front of the queue. 'If not, I'll corner the little shit and the parents myself.'

Colette looked so relieved that Leila couldn't help herself. 'Actually, you know what? I think I'll do that anyway.'

'But you just said you ...'

Turning the full beam of her smile onto the security guard, Leila held out her invitation. 'I know, but I'm like you: not great at keeping promises. Only no one wants a

dishonest IT lady, do they? So you might want to start looking for another square to work in, another city,' she flung
back, striding down path without looking back. 'Maybe
even another job.'

CHAPTER 39

✦

COLETTE

At the end of the curved entrance path illuminated by parallel lines of garden torches a cluster of waitresses in black shift dresses and feathered headbands were holding out trays of drinks. 'Champagne or cocktail?'

Only yesterday the garden had looked its usual pretty, placid self – aside that huge marquee at the end of the lawn. But in twenty-four hours the place had been transformed. Tiny teardrop-shaped gold and silver paper lanterns had been threaded through the branches of the chestnut and plane trees. Strings of foil flowers now hung down in curtains across the open sides of the tent, so that lit as it was from within the structure gave off a metallic glow against the night sky.

In between the shallow stage occupied by the jazz band

and the dining area, an art deco dance floor had been laid down. On it a single couple were swaying in the deliberately exaggerated way of every dance floor trailblazer, conscious that comedy cancelled out embarrassment. The man was heavy-set, his suit jacket straining with every movement, and even from a distance Colette could see that the left side of his neck and jaw was taped up with surgical gauze: Guy.

She'd heard about the 'accident', and experienced a brief moment of elation at the thought of Zoe fighting back – immediately quashed by another thought: at what cost? She couldn't see her now, and as her husband dipped a woman in a burgundy, sheer-sleeved dress, she noted the cinched in waist and side slit up to the thigh ... Was that Emilia?

But as she wandered distractedly across the lawn, Colette couldn't focus on the beauty of the scene, the dresses or the music. She didn't hear the rhapsodic descriptions of the 'Mint Juleps' and 'Pink Shimmies' being offered to her – only Leila's words echoing in her head.

She couldn't find it in her heart to be angry at Sylvia for telling her. But she was worried about what the old lady had said on her doorstep that day: how deluded she was to think that she 'could deal with Leila herself'. She thought of Emilia being made a fool of by one of her own neighbours, Guy's wrath at the public scene the young woman had all-but promised to make tonight, and what that might mean for Felix and Zoe.

Then she thought of Leila's face as she'd flung out that final threat just minutes ago – 'Maybe even another job' – the thing that defined Colette's existence an airy afterthought.

A single word came to her: enough.

CHAPTER 40

ZOE

She could do this.

They were only an hour into the night, and every time Zoe had been asked, her reply had come out smoothly. When the guy carrying the amps earlier had exclaimed, 'Bloody hell. What happened to him?' at the sight of Guy, her tone had been imbued with wifely sympathy. But after the fourth, fifth and sixth time, Zoe had heard a new edge to her voice, a light stuttering that wouldn't have been noticeable to anyone else but sounded flagrant to her.

Still, Zoe hadn't spent months meticulously planning this event, ensuring everything from the shape and placement of the Japanese lanterns to the quality of the oysters was perfect, for it all to be overshadowed by a few questions. Tonight was going to be a triumph. Her triumph.

At that moment a shoal of guests parted on the lawn before her to reveal Leila, and Zoe broadened her smile in readiness for their polite verbal combat.

'Wow,' she forced the word out as her neighbour approached. 'You look gorgeous.'

'What about you!' Pursing her lips Leila gave a silent whistle. '*Magnifique!*'

It was excessive and they both knew it.

'An old dress but, well, it never lets me down.' Zoe jutted out her chin.

'I have to say that this,' Leila went on with an expansive gesture, 'is all pretty incredible. Bravo. And look at all these people. Two hundred, you said? Who are they all?'

'Oh, current and previous residents, friends and family, local figures and business owners ... A lot of hard graft, but I think it's paid off. Anyway, I'm just going to check in on the catering team ... '

'Before you do ... ' Leila placed a hand on her arm. 'I got a call from my landlord the other day.'

'Oh?'

'Yes.' The young woman tilted her head to one side. 'He said he'd had a complaint about the noise.'

'OK.'

'Which is pretty pathetic.'

'Now listen, I—'

'No, no. Let me finish. Obviously this was you. And I guess I just feel sad, you know, that you didn't feel you could come to me first, if there was a problem?'

'Oof.' It was a stupid noise, a stupid reaction, but Zoe couldn't hold it in. 'I came to you more than once. I told you how loud the music was. Oh, and I know you love it, particularly that one song.' And suddenly she heard herself growling out: '*I'm coming in quick, quick, quick. Coming in slick, aye, aye.*' Catchy, but not exactly Beethoven, is it?'

Leila removed her hand from Zoe's arm and, still smiling, crossed her arms. 'What happened to Guy's face?'

Zoe's face felt tight. Her mouth dry. The words wouldn't come. All she could do was stare at this woman in her ridiculously skimpy ... that wasn't a dress: that was a piece of lingerie, with clearly nothing beneath it.

Yes, the Fitbit Leila always wore seemed at odds with something so diaphanous, but the rest of her accessories were delicate and tasteful, and most gallingly, Leila barely seemed to be wearing any make-up: just a slick of gloss and something shimmery across her cheekbones. But she was imagining the faint smirk, wasn't she? The challenge in Leila's posture?

'He was playing—'

'—squash, I heard.'

So why ask?

'Took a backhand to the face – poor thing. Honestly, it looks worse than it is. But he won't be playing again in a hurry!'

'And the hand?'

'Sorry?'

'His hand's bandaged up too.'

'Oh, that's from a while back. DIY accident. Men. Can't leave them alone for a second, can we?'

During her first marriage Zoe had become a cover-up pro – both in terms of content and delivery. Mostly the physical evidence could be hidden from public view. When it couldn't, when the provocation had been too extreme (because Zoe would never raise a hand unprovoked), she knew that it was all about keeping the lies simple. Using or embellishing everyday accidents, domestic or otherwise.

Sometimes she would add a little wifely eyeroll at the pathologically 'clumsy' men in her life as a way of lightening the facts. Often, she would tell people that 'it looks worse than it is.' Which was largely true. And in the odd moments of paranoia, it had always been easy to reassure herself: at five foot two, with her build, she was hardly 'the type'.

So why wasn't Leila saying anything?

She gripped her radio tighter, willing it to crackle into life. 'I really should go and . . . '

'But you see,' Leila narrowed her eyes, 'we crossed on the stairs, me and Guy, the day it happened. Late in the day. Did he tell you that? We didn't stop to chat, just said a quick hello, but here's the funny thing: there was nothing wrong with his face. Then that night, since we're talking about noise, there was a hell of a lot coming from your flat.'

In a robotic voice Zoe repeated, 'It was an accident on the squash court.'

The amplified voice of the singer rang out across the garden: 'I'm told you're about to be seated, so that's all from us, guys. Have a great night!'

Watching as constellations of guests from every corner of the garden began to make their way towards the marquee, Leila murmured: 'Imagine if they knew?'

CHAPTER 41

> ❦

HUGO

Supper was lasting forever. They were still on their main courses, and Hugo made a vague noise of assent to whatever Colette was saying.

That Emilia had been seated on another table was one saving grace. She'd tried to catch his eye earlier, when they'd been settling the boys at one of the kids' tables in the corner, but Hugo had refused to allow himself even a glance. The idea of there being any complicity between them was repugnant to him now. Which was laughable, given what they'd done.

He only wished Yas were closer by, but his wife was a little further down the table, beside Sylvia, immersed in conversation with some local councillor. Meanwhile Adrian, opposite, had come up trumps, with Leila on his left, and a middle-aged woman on his right he'd barely addressed a word to since they'd sat down.

Before the starters had even been served, the ghastly Mr Carter had undone his bow tie and left it hanging around his neck. Now, he leaned in so close to Leila that his shoulder was touching hers, and as the young woman gave a coy laugh, her eyes met Hugo's across the table and she raised an eyebrow.

Sucking in a breath, he turned back to Colette, who had paused mid-sentence and seemed to be observing him: 'Sorry – you were saying?'

That eyebrow. His marriage, his family, *his life* depended on what it meant. He and Emilia had spent the past two days having hushed phone conversations behind closed doors, trying to work out the best course of action, and every time Hugo thought back to the young woman's face as they opened the door of that shed, he felt his stomach fall away.

They'd taken such risks! Christ, they hadn't even used protection. And the dread of the past two days had stripped away all the magic, killed his feelings for Emilia dead.

Could she hear it in Hugo's voice? In their snatched conversations he'd been aware that his tone had become cold, detached, even impatient when Emilia had suggested knocking on Leila's door and explaining what they both had to lose: 'It's not Adrian. Our marriage is a joke. He's made sure of that. But this is my home, Hugo – and everyone would know. The kids would know. So maybe if I could just explain that to her?'

Had she lost her mind?

'And what? Tell her "it wasn't what it looked like"?' he'd snapped. 'No. For God's sake, don't do that.'

To her insistence that 'we can't just leave it', Hugo had replied flatly, 'What other option do we have?'

That morning, when Emilia had again called in a panic, he'd felt a flash of confidence.

'I don't think she's going to say anything. What's to be gained?' And Emilia had been forced to agree that there was nothing. Leila was only interested in Adrian, or rather what he could do for her, and she already had him in the palm of her hand. What did it matter if his wife was playing away? Maybe it would help her cause.

'She'd have to do it out of pure malice,' Hugo had gone on. 'And I can't imagine that's who she is.' But was Leila's eyebrow telling him otherwise?

Up on the stage, Zoe was tapping the microphone, her 'Hello, everyone!' drowned out by a screech of feedback.

'Gosh, sorry! Let's try that again – and don't worry. I'm going to keep it short, let our little film do the talking while you enjoy your desserts. Then we can head out into the garden for the fireworks.'

The lights in the marquee dimmed and an aerial image of London filled the screen. Noting that a few guests – Leila included – had taken advantage of the darkness to slip away for a cigarette or to the toilets, Hugo swivelled on his chair to check on Ollie.

He could see Theo reaching across the table to pop one of the small balloons in the centrepiece, the other children following suit – but where was his son?

With a nod at Yasmeen, who had clocked his absence at the exact same time, he murmured to Colette, 'Just going to see where Ollie's got to' – and snuck out of the marquee.

There was no sign of him in amongst the cliques on the

lawn and Hugo was about to turn down the path leading to the Portaloos when he spied a strip of blue and white T-shirt behind the gazebo. Through the trellised arch at the back he could see that Ollie was not alone. Bent over him in her gold dress, gripping his son's arm, was Leila.

Rounding the side just in time to catch her snarling 'I want it back,' Hugo heard himself say with impressive restraint, 'Can you please take your hand off my son?'

CHAPTER 42

COLETTE

Along with the rest of the crowd assembled with upturned faces on the lawn, wine glasses in hand, Colette let out an 'oooh' as the rocket lingered there for a moment, deciding whether or not to indulge them, before disappearing with a hiss into nothing.

Then came a fountain of gold and silver, showering the trees with sparks, hot silver snakes, fleets of red and green jumping jacks spinning wildly, shells that exploded into a million scintillating stars, leaving sulphurous streaks against the night sky.

The display was heartstopping, awe-inspiring, and it left Colette completely cold. She needed to find Felix, tell him that Leila knew, take care of that first – then, the rest.

Scouring the lawn for a red-headed teenager, Colette saw

Zoe, on edge, talking into her headset over by the marquee. And there was Sylvia, moving from one gaggle of guests to another. Spotting her, the old lady hurried over: 'Have you seen Leila?'

'No – not for a while. Sylv—'

But already, a determined look on her face, she'd moved on.

A few feet away, over by the gazebo, another vignette caught her eye: Hugo, kneeling on the grass in front of Ollie. Straining her ears, she heard him ask, 'Why would she think you have her keys?' and felt sick. If Leila had told Hugo about his son's involvement, had she already outed Felix too? Was that why he was nowhere to be seen?

She felt a sudden urge to warn everyone that their balancing acts were too precarious – that everything was about to come crashing down.

The fireworks were still going strong. Crossing the lawn towards the sinewy side path that snaked around the edges of the square, Colette continued her search.

She was about to round the northwest corner when the sound of a woman's heavily accented voice, low and sardonic, stopped her short. The only thing between her and Leila was a squat horse chestnut, its crown low slung and threadbare, like the centre-parting of a cheap wig, so that even in the darkness Colette could make out two pale faces through the branches.

'*Adrian.*' Leila was doing her best to keep her tone casually disparaging, but she could hear the alarm creeping in. Then there was a rustle of bushes, as though someone – Adrian – had been shoved back.

'What the fuck?'

Standing on her toes Colette could see the back of Adrian's

head bent over Leila's, his voice muffled by her hair, 'You're commando under there, aren't you? You naughty girl.'

'Seriously, get the fuck off.'

'I don't think you realise how much time I've been putting in to helping you out.' His head had jolted back, his voice turned cold. 'You think I've been doing that for fun?'

Another rustle, louder this time, accompanied by a crunch of branches. The tree shook with the impact. Then a yelp. But Leila wasn't calling for help, she was laughing: great high-pitched shrieks.

'You don't even represent Chloe. Not anymore. And if you really think I'd give a man like you *signals*?' A fresh burst of laughter. 'Jesus. You're even more of a cretin than Gemma said you were.'

For a moment all she could hear was Leila's light panting. Then: 'I wish you could see your face, Ade. Yeah, you remember Gemma Reeves, don't you? That actress you worked with earlier in the year who 'didn't have what it takes'? We've been talking, me and Gemma. But don't worry: she's not about to go public about what you did. Says there's no point – that people are never going to believe one woman. But if there's two all that changes, doesn't it? If there's two *everything changes*.'

The sound of light steps left Colette no time to retrace her steps. Then Leila appeared, pulling the strap of her dress back up over her shoulder.

Without even acknowledging her presence the young woman muttered 'fucking dinosaur' and headed off towards the main gate.

Above, the fireworks reached their crescendo in a final bombardment, and a deep sonic thud reverberated through the square. Then the first few bars of 'Dancing Queen' rang out, that joyous piano glissando prompting a cheer, and from all over the garden shadowy figures started to make their way back into the marquee and onto the dance floor.

CHAPTER 43

EMILIA

Locking the Portaloo door behind her, Emilia leaned against the sink and stared at her flushed face in the mirror. All these years spent in fear of reflective surfaces, to the point that she would open the bathroom cabinet as she brushed her teeth, preferring the racks of Paracetamol and Antacid to the sight of her own face.

Now, she didn't recognise the woman staring back at her. The one in the figure-hugging burgundy dress with expensive hair and emerging cheekbones. The one who had had sex with her neighbour in a shed. And who knows? Maybe Emilia would have thrown herself into an affair, guilt-free – after putting up with Adrian for all these years, why the hell shouldn't she? – if it hadn't been for Leila.

It had to be *her* standing there as they'd opened that door, didn't it? It wasn't enough that this unscrupulous young woman had made her an object of pity in her own community. That tonight, she'd been forced to endure the familiar smarting as Adrian had flirted his way through supper and ignore the compassionate glances of her own neighbours as they asked themselves 'Is she seeing this?', 'Does she know?' On top of all that, Leila had had to ruin the one moment of abandon Emilia had ever allowed herself.

It scared her how much time she'd spent thinking about the young Frenchwoman over the past two days – weeks, if she was being honest. How many hours she'd spent stoking her anger with every image and mention of her she could find online. Because somehow her lithe figure and goofy smile had come to represent all the petty humiliations and casual debasements of her marriage. There Leila was, blithely using people to get what she wanted, *getting what she wanted*, oblivious to the collateral damage. Yet Emilia had made one misstep – and she'd been there, waiting, holding it over her now. Once again, Leila had the power.

Thanks to the emails Emilia was still checking whenever she got the chance, she knew that something had happened, or rather not happened, between them. Adrian was a sulker, always had been, and she could tell from the way her husband was taking so long to reply to Leila and the change in tone – suddenly, after a date in Soho he'd lied to Emilia about – that he'd tried something and Leila had rebuffed him.

Far from endearing Leila to her, this had only made Emilia despise her more, sharpened her mortification. She'd played along with her husband, teased him for weeks, but now it was *oh, Adrian, whatever gave you that idea?*

She didn't care what Hugo said. Rummaging in her clutch

for her phone Emilia saw that it was nearly 10 p.m. She tapped out a message:

> I'm going to get her alone. I'm at least going to try.

With an unsteady hand she reapplied her lipstick, and as she unlocked the loo door and tottered along the tenebrous path, she was aware of the sense of dislocation the cocktails and the wine had given her, as if she was floating above herself watching the evening happen.

In the distance she saw a familiar form in black tie – Hugo – making his way up the path towards her. Then, a column of gold appeared in between them, heading towards the square garden entrance. Was Leila leaving?

'Leila! Wait.'

Lurching towards her, she begged: 'Just give me one second. Please.'

Without slowing her pace the young woman glanced back at her, throwing out a caustic and senseless, 'Leave me alone. What the fuck is wrong with you all?'

But as Emilia hurried after her through the gates, she knew only that she needed to do this, that she would make Leila listen.

CHAPTER 44

SYLVIA

The dance floor was packed, the music hurting her ears. And it seemed to be getting louder, each track more frenetic than the last, as though the man in bulbous earphones behind his turntable was deliberately trying to whip the guests up into a collective act of madness. How could he know that in her world, at least, peak insanity had already been reached? That the pounding in that once peaceful square was echoing in her head and heart?

How long ago was it that she'd gone to find Leila: an hour? More? When her last demand had come in yesterday, Sylvia had immediately known she couldn't pay it, and there had been a kind of relief when she'd seen that exorbitant figure – three times the previous sums. Because it had brought everything to a head. Looking at her tonight, flirting with

Adrian at the dinner table just a few feet away from his wife, she couldn't believe anyone had been fooled by this woman even for a minute. She was making a mockery of all of them, flagrantly, joyfully. And that had cemented Sylvia's decision to end this.

Since she'd returned to the marquee, the scene seemed to have descended into something ghoulish and carnivalesque: into chaos. Over by the bar two waitresses were sweeping up the debris of broken glass, and at the edge of the dance floor an intoxicated young man who had been lying prone and cackling on his back a second ago was being pulled to his feet. Around him the whooping throng danced on, bodies jostling, hands reaching clumsily for necks, waists and hips, mouths shouting lyrics into one another's faces.

Sylvia badly wanted to go home. She wanted to shower. But she couldn't; not yet. Checking her phone, she saw that it was earlier than she'd thought, yet the night had thickened around them all.

If she could just get some air. Find somewhere quiet to sit and think. Dazed and disorientated she headed out across the lawn. Like her the older crowd had gravitated to the south side of the garden and, nodding at a group of locals enjoying their cigars, she walked on in search of a quiet bench.

A burst of American accents as she passed another gaggle of guests, ignoring the attempt of a New Yorker who spent just a few months a year in her square home to wave her over. She'd been aiming for the most discreet bench in the gardens, situated in a carved-out enclave of the central shrub bed, but as she approached Sylvia made out a huddled figure at one end of it.

'Emilia? You clever girl. You've nabbed the best seat in . . .'

Emilia raised her face and Sylvia saw the tear tracks down her make-up, the wild eyes. She had looked so beautiful earlier. Now she looked broken. 'Hey!' She sat down beside her, pulled her in. 'What's going on? What's happened?'

Emilia opened her mouth to speak and closed it again as a fresh bout of tears came.

'What can I do?' Leaning in closer, Sylvia took Emilia's hand.

'Nothing.' Her voice was toneless. 'What I've done can't . . .'

Above the music, Sylvia heard her name called out. Followed by her friends, the New Yorker was making her way over.

'Too loud over there, isn't it?' The lady smiled, oblivious to the emotional scene she'd interrupted. 'I wanted you to meet my friends.'

Somehow the two women managed to nod their way through the introductions. Then one of the men logged Emilia's state.

'Anyway, let's leave Mum and daughter to it, eh?'

Passing the back of her thumb across her damp cheek, Emilia managed a sodden smile.

'Oh, we're not . . . Sylvia's my neighbour.'

As the group headed off across the lawn one of the men threw back: 'I could've sworn! Something about the eyes.'

Emilia's hand grew limp in hers and Sylvia pressed it. Just once. Slowly her daughter turned to look at her, lashes still webbed with tears, the expression in her eyes moving from bewilderment to understanding.

CHAPTER 45

COLETTE

Back in the marquee Colette ordered a glass of wine and stood at the bar, trying to locate a familiar face in the mass of swaying, hopping and gesticulating figures on the dance floor. She hadn't been able to find Felix, and now they'd all disappeared, including Leila, who she'd last seen heading home after her altercation with Adrian. That she hadn't dusted herself down and reappeared by now was somehow surprising.

'We've run out of white!' the barman shouted over the din. 'But there's more on the way. Mrs Mulligan's chasing it up.'

At that moment Guy appeared on the other side of the marquee, hugging a box of Chablis.

'Here you go.'

As the two men manoeuvred the box over the bar top

beside her Colette got a blast of warm ammonia. That Guy hadn't taken off his suit jacket despite the warmth of the night and the sweat soaking the top of his collar seemed absurd.

Still breathing heavily, he leaned back against the bar, pulled his forearm over his brow, and closed his eyes.

Like everyone else, he'd clearly had too much to drink and had Colette not known what he was she might have felt sorry for him. The tape holding the gauze in place up his neck and jaw had come unstuck, revealing marbled purplish bruising beneath. When he opened them again she saw that his eyes were bloodshot, glazed – haunted. She wasn't even sure he'd registered her presence.

Colette opened her mouth to say something, but muttering something incomprehensible her client lumbered back out into the darkness of the garden.

The barman slid a warm glass of wine across the bar, but as she checked her watch and saw that it was already 11.16 p.m. the simmering sense of unease Colette had been unable to shake since Leila had left reasserted itself with force.

She would be in her flat, reapplying make-up or fixing her hair. Shooting one of her reels. Or maybe she was already on her way back, but Colette had to be sure. Abandoning the wine she headed off across the lawn towards Addison Mansions.

There was so much she couldn't remember, afterwards, beneath the buzzing strip lights of the police interview room. Had there been anyone else in the lane? Had the front door to Addison Mansions been ajar? Had she noticed the brush of russet along the white paintwork of the stairwell?

Maybe she did see it. Maybe that was why Colette chose to

check the empty ground floor flat where the food and drink was being stashed first, rather than go straight up to Leila's flat on the third.

She did remember her first sluggish thought when she pushed open the door: that someone had spilled something over by the marble island in the centre of the kitchen. Something dark and syrupy – red wine, perhaps. That it had made the most God-awful mess across the plastic sheeting partially covering the floor, pooled in the swirls and twists of the floorboards.

She remembered too that there had been a disturbed quality to the air as she walked through the hallway into that open-plan kitchen. As though the molecules had only recently been disturbed, the oxygen from another person's lungs only recently expelled into the atmosphere. That was when she saw the foot, encased in a studded nude sandal, sticking out from behind the island.

Everything about that foot was wrong in a way that instantly turned her stomach to slop. Its stillness was wrong; the angle of it unnatural. She took another step.

How Colette wished her memory had chosen to blur what she saw next, softened the image of Leila lying there, silk dress ruckled to just above the knee, where it was still gold and pristine. Above the waist it was matted and discoloured a dirty crimson, sticking to the young woman's body in puckered lines of blood-soaked fabric – blood that had pooled in the plastic sheeting beneath her head and neck.

One arm was outstretched, the wrist encircled with its smartwatch, and Colette's eyes went from Leila's faintly cupped fingers to the spattered skirting board and wall beyond.

That a human being could cause this much mess when cracked open seemed indecent.

She took a breath, inhaled the metallic tang that was oddly familiar. Then she pulled her phone from her pocket and pressed the same digit once, twice, three times.

CHAPTER 46

HAMMERSMITH POLICE STATION
EXTRACT OF SECOND RECORDED INTERVIEW
WITH MS COLETTE BURTON

Date: 17 July
Duration: 93 minutes
No. of pages: 47
Conducted by Officers of the
Metropolitan Police

DC BAXTER: According to one square resident, Ms Mercheri had mentioned overhearing arguments in the flat below. Did she ever say anything about the Mulligans to you?

CB: She did. And I—

DC BAXTER: Ms Burton?

CB: I think it was more than arguments.

DC BAXTER: Based on?

CB: A few things. On one occasion Zoe had this bruise on her wrist that she seemed anxious to hide. She was always covered up, in long sleeves, even when it was nudging thirty degrees.

DC HARRIS: So—

CB: So I'm pretty sure that Guy Mulligan was violent with his wife; that Zoe was a victim of domestic abuse.

DC HARRIS: But you never reported this?

CB: I only began to suspect a few weeks ago and I— It was a delicate situation. I wasn't sure how to handle it.

DC BAXTER: OK. Listen, we appreciate you coming in again. You've been very helpful.

CB: One thing: I'm sure you're aware, but Leila had a smartwatch. She was wearing

it on Saturday night. Have you retrieved
the data yet?

DC BAXTER: Not yet. It's with forensics.
These things always take a few days. But
as soon as we have that—

CB: What I'm saying is that I set it up for
her, so I know Leila's pin. If it can help
speed things up?

DC BAXTER: You have Ms Mercheri's pin?

CB: Unless she's changed it, yes.

DC BAXTER: I can let forensics know.

CB: If you have her phone here, the data
can be accessed on that.

DC BAXTER: Would you be able to show me?

INTERVIEW PAUSED.

INTERVIEW RESUMED.

DC BAXTER: For the benefit of the tape,
I have used the password Ms Burton has
provided to access the victim's smartwatch
data. She is now pointing out the heart
monitor function on Ms Mercheri's watch.

CB: Photoplethysmography.

DC BAXTER: You what?

CB: The name of the technology. Every time your heart beats, the amount of blood that reaches the capillaries in your fingers and face swells and recedes. Because blood absorbs light, the watch is essentially testing how much red or green light it can see through the skin on your wrist. Not a new technology, actually. First used in the 1930s.

DC BAXTER: So we go to last night here?

CB: Yes. That's Leila's heart rate. You can see that it's steady. Regular. At 7 p.m., 8 p.m. she's in the square garden, at the party.

DC BAXTER: Then she goes back to Addison Mansions. We think around 9.30 or 10 p.m . . .

CB: Right. And we've got a brief spike here that could mean anything but that slump there, that flatline—

DC BAXTER: That's our time of death: 11.19 p.m. What about all these jagged spikes here, just before?

CB: That's an elevated heartbeat. The kind you might get with physical exertion of some kind. That was Leila—

DC BAXTER: Ms Burton?

CB: That was Leila fighting for her life.

DC BAXTER: Which tells us exactly what we needed to know. I have to go. We're going to make an arrest.

CHAPTER 47

GUY

The Day Of The Party

'I told you half an hour ago to get more Chablis. Now we've run out.'

Leaning against the bar top, Guy looked away from his wife and nodded. The grim line of Zoe's lips when he'd 'disappointed' her – something he did four, five, six times a day – the strip of corrugated skin up by her hairline when she raised her eyebrows and glared. If he caught her eye now, there would be only one thought in his head and she would see it. *I hate you. I hate what you've done to me and I hate what you've done to us.* So he kept looking resolutely away.

Did his wife have any idea how many people he'd had to

lie to tonight? And that was just since the party had started. That wasn't counting the others earlier today, yesterday: the postman, the pub landlord who'd stopped him in the street – 'Hey, man, what happened to your face?' – his secretary at work; everyone at work. Sometimes he wondered what would happen if he told them the truth: *She likes to knock me about, my wife.*

On the marital abuse sites he'd looked at and the message boards, it was almost all women, which only made the shame darker, deeper, into something he had trouble even acknowledging to himself. Because, as one of the comments on a *Daily Mail* SURGE OF DOMESTIC VIOLENCE AGAINST MEN article had said, *What kind of man would let that happen?*

'I'll go now.'

'Great. You know where it is. Ground floor flat kitchen, far right. Door's on the latch.'

Detaching himself from the bar, Guy raised his hand to his jaw. Why was the pain always at its worst two or three days later? The painkillers were barely touching the sides today. It felt as though his whole cheek was thrumming, although it was most tender along the bone, where that glass globe had shattered, slicing through the flesh.

That hadn't been easy to explain to the A&E doctor at Charing Cross, which was why Guy had changed his story halfway through. He'd started reciting the squash 'accident' Zoe had come up with, but something about the way the young doctor had paused and looked at him after peeling off the dressing told Guy it wouldn't wash.

'You've got some pretty deep cuts here?'

It wasn't a statement but a question, so Guy had admitted the lie, and bungled his way through another one.

To be honest, he'd had a run-in down the pub – been glassed by some thug. But he couldn't have his wife finding out. She would only blame him. And although he wasn't a good liar and resented having to tell so many, Guy was pretty sure he'd got away with it. The doctor had bandaged him up, made a few notes on his system, sent him off for an X-ray and discharged him.

'A whole case, yeah?' he heard his wife call after him now as he headed out onto the lawn towards the gate.

Addison Mansions was brightly lit and quiet as he pushed open the front door, surprised to find it not on the latch but ajar. But the thought was overtaken by the relief of finding himself alone, the lack of people and questions. Glancing at his watch he saw that it was coming up to 11 p.m. A couple more hours and tonight would be over.

Up above, a door slammed. Soft flat steps on the stairs, then Leila appeared on the landing.

'Evening,' he nodded, pausing to let her pass.

The young woman had a vaguely antagonistic expression on her face. As she moved gracefully down the stairs, he saw that it was more than that. Leila was riled up, her mouth set in a hard line, her eyes glinting. Another angry woman. Where did all this anger come from? Then he remembered the noise complaint they'd lodged – been forced to lodge.

'I've been sent back to get wine,' he said limply.

She stopped on the ground floor hallway, flicked her eyes up and down Guy's body and said, 'How long are you going to put up with this?'

For a second he thought this might be about the wine – some attempt at humour.

'Listen.' He grinned. 'I just do what she tells me.'

But Leila's face was solemn, and before she opened her mouth again he knew.

'I can hear your arguments. I know what she's doing to you.'

'I think maybe you—'

'No. You need to do something. Look at you. Look at the state of you.'

From a deep-buried place inside, Guy felt a rumble of gathering rage. He opened his mouth to trot out the squash story but instead heard himself say, 'Not here.' Gesturing at the open flat door beside them, he motioned at Leila to follow him inside.

She didn't stop talking. Not when he asked, 'Now, which one of these boxes do you reckon is the Chablis?' More playing for time than anything else. Not when he tried to explain that whatever she'd got into her head was wrong, and that either way it was none of her business. And all the while there was a nonchalance to her attitude, as she stood there by the marble island in the middle of that half-built kitchen, that was really starting to grate.

'OK,' Leila was saying now, in a tone so languid she almost sounded bored. 'So if you won't do it for yourself, do it for your kids. Do you have any idea how fucked up they are – well, Felix anyway?'

He stared at her.

'What are you on about?'

An hour ago, he would never have envisaged talking to a woman, a relative stranger, like this. But he was aware of a shift taking place, from the old Guy to a man he didn't recognise.

'Your son, stepson, whatever: he's been stalking me, terrorising me, taking pictures of me sunbathing in the square, sending his little mate to steal stuff from my flat, videoing me as I sleep.'

It struck him that this woman might actually be deranged. Then he pictured the back of Felix's head as he sat at his computer, slashing and punching and blasting away those little red figures. He thought about all those unexplained 'walks' around the square that had only started a couple of months ago; the night he'd caught him eavesdropping on a conversation he and Zoe had been having about Leila, and that peculiar friendship with Ollie – one the younger boy never looked as though he was enjoying much. *Because he was being bullied into doing Felix's bidding, into breaking into their neighbour's flat?*

'He's a freak, just like his mum.' Leila was still talking, and suddenly she was Zoe, the yapping drilling into the tenderest parts of his brain. 'I'll report him, get the police to look into it – into your whole fucked-up family.'

Another rumble inside. A warning that came too late.

Leila needed to stop talking. Maybe he even said it out loud, 'Stop talking.'

But she wouldn't.

'Does some part of you actually enjoy it?'

That's when the rumble rose up, uncontainable now, and Guy's right hand balled into a fist.

CHAPTER 48

EMILIA

Two Days After The Party, Late Afternoon

'I should have rung.' DC Harris had looked surprised to see her standing there in reception. Now she just looked flustered. 'We won't actually need to talk to you again. Sorry to have made you come back in. Anyway, you're free to go.'

Did that mean they knew who did this? Emilia would find out soon enough. Presumably they all would. At least she'd been spared another interrogation.

The first time her relationship with Hugo had been mentioned, in that initial interview, it had felt like a punch in the gut, the implications hitting her in a series of aftershocks. He had told them. Because who else could it be? Which meant he had told Yasmeen. Which meant it was over. And perhaps she'd already known that. But the second time she'd been interviewed, when they'd brought up Sylvia? That had been a far bigger shock.

'You were aware that Ms Mercheri had been using information she had discovered about Mrs Ryan to extort tens of thousands of pounds from her?' the male DC – Baxter – had asked. 'Information concerning you and your parentage?'

'What?'

'Because Mrs Ryan is, in fact, your birth mother, isn't she?'

Those words – 'birth mother' – had no immediate meaning to her. They cancelled each other out. You couldn't call yourself a mother just because you'd given birth to someone. As she'd lain awake in the early hours of Sunday morning, unable to make sense of what had just happened and suddenly grotesquely sober, Emilia had thought about the mother she still missed every day: the woman who had raised her.

Ever since her sixth birthday she'd known that there were two people out there who had passed on their DNA to her and then called it a day – given her the broad shoulders and wide hips that had always made a mockery of size tens and twelves, even when she was at her slimmest; the thick hair she was constantly being told was 'her best feature' – but those people didn't deserve to be called a 'mother' and 'father'.

Sitting beside her on that bench on the night of the party, Sylvia hadn't presumed to call herself that either. Which was something. Watching as the American who had unwittingly broken open Emilia's life story disappeared across the lawn repeating, 'I could've sworn!' she had waited for Sylvia to say something. But eventually, there had only been 'I don't expect you to understand – or forgive. But watching you for the past eight years, seeing your darling children grow? That has been the greatest privilege of my life.'

After that there had been sirens, flashing lights, and the night had faded to black.

Released now, dizzied and blinking, into the harsh afternoon sunlight, Emilia took a deep breath, steeled herself. Because now, she had to go home and tell her husband about Hugo.

She could hear Hattie bawling from outside the front door and paused, her key in the lock. Then she turned it.

'Sorry. Took a while,' Emilia mumbled as she crossed the sitting room floor, wincing at her daughter's cries but grateful to have a reason to avoid Adrian's eyes.

He wasn't in his usual slumped position in the far corner of the sofa but perched on the edge, Hattie in her bouncer at his feet, looking up at her.

'What did they say?'

Unstrapping her daughter she held her close, breathing in her clean, redemptive scent.

'They sent me home. Didn't need to speak to me again after all. So maybe they've got whoever did it. Maybe it'll turn out to have been a burglary gone wrong? Random.'

'What's "random" mean, Mum?'

She turned to her son, lying on his stomach on the floor by the telly, reading his comic.

'Without meaning,' she replied automatically. 'Unplanned.' And were these the last few minutes of normal family life? Should she be cherishing them? It was almost six already.

In a minute she would have to make the children's supper – then put them to bed. How could she do those things after having told Adrian?

'How about I put on *The Minions*?' she said to Theo. 'Then maybe you could look after your sister for a moment while your dad and I have a chat.'

Out of the corner of her eye she saw Adrian's face change – subtly. A tightening of the muscles around his mouth. He had no idea what she was about to tell him.

Knowing her husband he would be thinking in the short term – and about himself. It wouldn't have occurred to the man who never bothered to lower his voice when he swore that they should be discussing Leila's death in private. But he knew this wasn't good.

Gently, she replaced her daughter in the bouncer and said a silent prayer. *Please don't start crying again. I can't bear any of this, but if you cry I think I might scream.*

Intuiting this, Hattie allowed herself to be strapped in, and Emilia found the film and pressed 'play'.

'Shall we ...?' Emilia motioned towards Adrian's study down the hall.

'Sure.'

From his desk chair her husband blinked up at her, and it occurred to her that she'd never seen him looking like this: vulnerable.

Then, after she had listened out for any noise from the children, after she had shut the door but remained standing in front of it, unsure of what to do with her arms, Emilia began, 'I had a fling.'

It was the wrong word. Too carefree. But there was no right word.

'I could tell you that it didn't matter,' she said quickly. 'But I wanted it. I enjoyed it.'

When she finally lowered her eyes, Emilia was surprised to find that a part of her was curious to see how Adrian would react. After everything he had done – dalliances she had no interest in hearing about now – would he even care?

Beyond incomprehension, his face told her nothing, so she pushed on.

'You must have known I wasn't happy? You can't have been happy. Not with everything you ...'

'Who knows about this?' he interrupted, and Emilia thought it strange, significant when it came to their marriage, that any talk of happiness was being ignored, and that this was his first question, rather than 'Who was it? Who did you cheat on me with?'

'The police.' A beat. 'And Leila. Leila knew.'

Adrian leaned forward, all focus now.

'How?'

'She saw us. A few days ago in the square. Me and ... Hugo.'

Adrian pulled a face. Not the face you'd expect a husband to make when he finds out his wife has been sleeping with the neighbour; the kind he might make if his wife said something inappropriate at a work dinner.

'Doormat Dad? You've been ... with him? Jesus Christ, Emilia. This is so fucking embarrassing.'

Whatever she'd expected, it wasn't this.

'That's all you care about?'

'You realise everyone is going to know. If the police do, then it's only a matter of time before we're a laughing stock.' He slammed his palm down hard on the table. 'Fuck.'

As staggered as she was, Emilia suddenly saw this as the

gift that it was. She was terrified of what the next few hours and days might bring. She had no idea where she would be in a month or a year, or even who she was, after the past few weeks. But there was someone just minutes away who loved her unconditionally; had loved her for all these years, without her knowing. And that 'we' – the idea of any kind of future with Adrian – was repellent to her.

'You don't understand,' she said quietly. 'I'm leaving you.'

CHAPTER 49

COLETTE

Three Days After The Party

As she recounted the moment she'd heard, Sylvia's voice grew faint at the end of the line.

'That's when they said who'd been arrested – when they said it was Guy. And this was, what, three hours ago? But I haven't moved, Colette. I've just been sitting here trying to make sense of it.'

'You're still in shock. We all are.'

Colette had known what Guy Mulligan was doing to his wife, yet even she felt winded by the news.

As though reading her mind, Sylvia asked: 'Do you know anything? Have you got any idea why he would have ...? I can't even say it.'

Colette stared at the sediment at the bottom of her coffee cup, sighed and moved the phone to the other ear.

'I know that Guy Mulligan wasn't the person people thought he was.'

A pause as Sylvia considered this, then: 'Do you think you could come over?'

The heatwave had finally broken, the temperature dropping to 20 degrees overnight, the sky a pewter-grey slab overhead. In the half-empty streets, pedestrians were sluggish and distracted – staring down at their phones at zebra crossings as the little green man counted down to zero – and Colette pulled into Addison Square less than an hour later.

There is nothing sadder than the scene of a party after it has ended. But the three-day-old scene of a party that has ended in tragedy isn't just forlorn but chilling, and Colette was asking herself why the square garden hadn't been cleared sooner when it hit her: only now that Leila's killer had been found would it have been allowed.

Outside the main gate a pyramid of recycling bags had been amassed beside a stack of folded trestle tables and through the railings Colette glimpsed the partially imploded marquee, the skeleton of which was being carried out by workers, limb by limb.

That the square was so still, windless, and that the workers were loading up their lorry in silence – with no casual jokes or curses and no radio blaring – only added to the sense of wrongness.

'You came.'

The relief on Sylvia's face was so acute that for a second Colette thought the old lady might break down right there on her doorstep, but collecting herself just in time, she ushered her in.

Neither of them said a word as they sat down at either end of the bay window seat in the kitchen – Reggie curled up between them – and waited for the kettle to boil. Then, when it clicked itself off and Sylvia still didn't get up, Colette started talking. She told her what Zoe had been enduring in private for God knows how long, though not precisely how she'd found this out. She told her how guilty she now felt that she hadn't reported Guy, what Felix had been up to and how scared she'd been for the boy on the night of the party, after telling Leila what she knew. Then, abruptly, she stopped.

As ashamed as Colette was to have kept Guy's secret – would Leila still be alive if she hadn't? – there was something she felt almost as bad about.

'Between us, when I went in to talk to the police on the night, I told them about Felix . . . I seriously thought, at first, that it might be him.'

Sylvia nodded.

'After what you've just told me, I can see why.'

'Anyway, apparently they went to the flat, ransacked his bedroom, and it was all for nothing because as it turns out Felix spent the last two hours of Saturday night sitting behind the greenhouse necking a bottle of Baileys with two other boys.'

'Ah.'

'But imagine what that must have felt like for him, when the police turned up? And after what he'd been living with, is it any wonder he was messed up, found some weird outlet?'

'Did the police charge him with anything?'

'No.' For that Colette had been grateful. 'They let him

off with a slap on the wrist, told him he was lucky to be a minor. Then, well, things were overtaken by events. But I think it helped his cause that the Mulligans had had Leila's key legitimately the whole time. Apparently it had belonged to the previous tenant.'

'Mr Bevan.'

'Right. So all Felix had to do was help himself.'

For what felt like longer than it was, they both sat there looking out of the window in silence – Colette trying and failing to silence the small voice inside, asking: *is any part of you glad that this woman who caused you such pain is gone?*

Because she couldn't ask that, Colette eventually said: 'But you told the police about Leila – what she'd been doing?'

'I had to. I had to tell them all of it.'

Another long pause, this one painful. Whatever Sylvia had paid all that money to keep secret, surely it didn't matter *now*?

'Wouldn't it help to talk about it?'

The old lady's eyes flicked down to Reggie and she gave the dog an absent-minded stroke before saying in a flat voice: 'I have a child. A daughter.'

Even in her dazed state, Colette could see the joy saying these words out loud gave Sylvia, a blaze of it breaking through the brume.

'I gave her away. I was made to.' A desolate shrug. 'But I still gave her away.' Colette nodded but didn't speak. 'I gave Emilia away.'

This time Colette was unable to stay silent.

'Emilia?' Looking into Sylvia's face, it was so obvious. The answer was there, had been there all along. It was in the old lady's build, the shape of her eyes and arch of her brows. It was in the rich texture of her hair.

'She's mine. She's the reason I moved here.' A single tear welled and fell. 'I'd missed so much of her life, and I thought that if I could see her every day, every other day, or even catch a glimpse of her and my grandchildren once a week, I'd at least have that.'

'But you never told Archie?'

'I didn't tell anyone. Only Leila found out.' She tossed back her head, angry now. 'There's this box. I kept everything the hospital let me take away that day in there. It was all I had of her. And Leila was spending so much time at the house, helping me with the clear out.' She groaned. 'I'd been so stupid. I genuinely thought she was fond of me. So when you told me what you did . . .'

'Why not tell Emilia, after Archie passed?' Colette murmured. 'Wasn't that the perfect time to try and have some kind of relationship with her?'

Sylvia shook her head. 'You're not a mother, are you? I don't say that with any judgement. Just that when you are, you would do anything to spare your child pain, disruption, and although she'd always known she was adopted, Emilia already had a mother and father she loved. Even when they later died, it felt so wrong to bulldoze her life after all these years. It would have been so selfish – and why shouldn't she hate me? She'd have every right to.'

'So you kept paying out. You were going to keep paying out.'

Sylvia shook her head.

'No. The night of the party, I'd decided I'd had enough. That's why I was trying to find Leila. I was going to tell her that I was done, that I was going to go to the police. Only she'd disappeared. She . . .'

. . . *was back at Addison Mansions, with Guy.*

There was one last thing Colette wanted to know.

'Will you tell her?' she asked gently. 'Emilia?'

Sylvia gave a watery smile.

'Emilia already knows.'

CHAPTER 50

HUGO

Four Days After The Party

'So Adrian Carter's moving out.'

'Yeah.' Head bent over her legal documents, his wife continued to move her middle finger slowly down the printed lines on the page.

'Guess I'll get over it. In time.'

The finger stopped.

'Will you get over her, though? Because *she's* still here.'

'Yas. Look at me.'

Hugo reached out across the kitchen table, but before he'd even touched her she snapped, 'Don't.' A small sigh. 'It's bad enough thinking about us living across the square from a murderer and a wifebeater for all these years. I have flashbacks of us clinking glasses with Guy Mulligan, *laughing with him*. Of him kicking a football about with Ollie in the garden. And I want to peel my own skin off.' She shuddered. 'I feel like we should have known, don't you? Like if we'd only seen him for what he was all of this could have been avoided. Then when I think about seeing *her* every day, being forced to live alongside that woman on top of everything, well, that just makes me want to pack up my stuff and go.'

There had been no choice. After all that, he'd had to tell Yas anyway.

He'd known that the moment he'd heard those keening police cars turn into the square and, along with the other guests who had gathered in the lane, watched the first responders hop from the ambulance and troop through the doorway of Addison Mansions. They'd been surprisingly agile for bulky middle-aged men, up the stairs in a second. But there had been no need to rush. Leila was already dead.

You'd think that one fact would blow everything else out of the water, render what he and Emilia had done insignificant. But that hadn't been the case – at least, not for them.

Sitting there at their kitchen table in the early hours, Yasmeen asking a series of stream-of-consciousness-like questions he couldn't answer – 'Did they say there'd been signs of a break-in?' 'Had anything been taken?' 'Why wasn't the front door locked?' – he'd known everything would come out.

'I need to tell you something.' They'd been keeping their voices down, conscious of the child in the next room who had miraculously slept through the sirens. 'It'll ... I'm going to have to tell the police, so ... '

Yas had taken off her dress as soon as they'd walked through the door, her make-up too, as though everything had been tainted by the horror of the night, and it seemed doubly cruel, somehow, to be telling his wife this when she was in her pyjamas.

'So what? You're scaring me.'

'Emilia and I, we had … we were … '

He hadn't needed to say any more. The initial blankness on his wife's face had given way first to confusion, then disbelief before settling into a sneer of disgust.

'No.'

'I don't know how it happened.'

'No.'

'You'd been away so much and—'

'Don't you dare!'

'I'm not saying … that. It's my fault, of course it's my fault. I'm trying to explain how, why. We were spending all this time together.'

'With the kids! How did you manage that? What, did you stick them in front of the telly while you went off for a quick … ? Oh God, oh God.' She'd covered her face with her hands: 'Did you actually fuck her?'

'Shhh.'

'Don't shush me! If you didn't want our son dragged into this pathetic – I don't even know what to call it – you should have thought of that before.' A pause. 'So did you? Or was this just a snog behind the swings?'

Whatever involuntary admission had played out across his face had made her eyes widen: 'All this *blossomed* in the square, did it? Ha!'

For a moment they had sat there at this same kitchen table

in silence, Yasmeen still visibly in freefall; Hugo allowing the reality to percolate, repeating to himself over and over again, like a mantra: *this is the worst bit.*

Four days on he knew that wasn't true. The pain was duller now but it had a festering quality, and every day seemed to bring a starker understanding of the damage done.

Even if his wife did manage to forgive him, their marriage would forever be sullied by his actions. It would never be the same, and what would a new version look like?

'I'll never stop trying to make it up to you.' He needed her to know that. 'I'll always be grateful you stayed.'

Yasmeen looked up: 'Don't be. I might still leave.'

CHAPTER 51

COLETTE

One Week After The Party

'There I was assuming the police were rubbish. Plods,' said Adrian. 'Turns out they actually know what they're doing. I mean, how long did it take them – forty-eight hours?'

'About that.'

She waited for the arrogant addendum.

'Always thought there was something off about Guy Mulligan.'

When Adrian had called her, Colette had toyed with the idea of saying no. No, I won't come over. No, I won't spend another minute in your study, surrounded by pictures of you and those gurning TV personalities who probably can't stand you either. Then he'd muttered something about 'a move', about 'disconnecting' his tech, and the chance to pack up Adrian Carter and send him off had been too good to miss.

'You taking the printer too?'

Colette crouched down by the two cardboard boxes in the middle of his study: one containing his bubble-wrapped desktop, keyboard and mouse, the other mostly cables.

'Only we might need another box.'

With a groan Adrian rose from his chair and peered down at the kit at his feet.

Those oxblood velvet slippers took her back a month. How could it only have been a month? In that short time everything had changed. She'd judged and misjudged, been proved right and wrong so many times she no longer knew which way was north.

Yes, Adrian was a low-life, human plankton of the basest kind, but he hadn't been capable of what she had briefly imagined.

'Yeah, let's pack up the printer,' said Adrian, dropping back down into his chair and taking a sip of the coffee he'd made himself alone.

Colette wasn't sure why it had taken her this long to realise what was different about him: he'd shaved off his beard. In all the time she'd known him, Adrian had always had some form – every form – of facial hair. Without it he looked exposed.

'Emilia won't need it?'

It was clear that she wasn't home, and at no point either on the phone or since Colette had arrived had his wife's name been mentioned. Anyone but Adrian would have felt obliged to provide an explanation, however brief. Not that Colette needed one. Emilia's messages and emails had confirmed it all. Their marriage was over. Adrian was going to stay in a mate's empty flat in Bloomsbury, 'until we get things sorted properly. And he's going to be vicious and petty and mean. But anything's better than staying married to him.'

'You know what, um . . .' *Colette, but we're past that now, aren't we?* 'I think my wife might have to find another way to print out her return labels. Although if she thinks I'm going to carry on funding her online shopping habit, she's got another think coming.'

'OK.' *Deep breath.* 'And you had said you might need a few things boxed up separately to take to the office?'

'Ah. On that: slight change of plan. I'm actually going to be taking an, um, leave of absence. So it's all now going to the flat.'

'Really?' Colette held his eye, drinking in every last drop of discomfort. 'That sounds like a good idea.'

Because she also happened to know that 'Call Me Ade's leave of absence was, in fact, a 'suspension pending investigation'. For a reason she would never have explained to her, Gemma Reeves had finally made good on her threat.

'So it's just the one box we need for the printer?'

'Yup. Should be a few spare ones out by the bins.'

Picking her way down the narrow stone steps outside to the basement, Colette reminded herself that this would probably be the last time she'd ever see Adrian Carter. Beside the wheeled plastic green and black bins there were indeed two boxes. Only one was big enough. The other, an empty wine box marked CHABLIS: DOMAINE LOUIS MOREAU in curly writing she left behind. But as Colette climbed back up, she stopped. Deep within her consciousness something chimed.

Esprit de l'escalier, the French call it. To think of something, after the fact. Guy, with his box of Chablis. The face of her watch as she stood at the bar telling her it was 11.16 p.m. Leila's heart monitor showing that final slump at 11.19 p.m. and DC Baxter's voice: 'That's our time of death.'

If Guy had left her to bleed out – taking care to remember the box of wine – the line would have sunk down gradually to nothing in the final minutes of Leila's life. Yet it had reached its desperate crescendo at almost exactly the time Guy was standing beside her at the bar. They'd been so focussed on the time of death that both she and DC Baxter had ignored the brief spike of Leila's heartbeat sixteen minutes earlier, when Guy would indeed have been in the flat – with Leila. But whatever had taken place between them, he'd left her alive.

She flashed back to the words Felix had messaged a stranger online: 'I got shit going on at home. Real shit. Dark shit.' To the wound on Guy's face as he stood beside her at the bar and the look on his face: haunted – or hunted?

Then the barman's voice floated back to her. 'We've run out of white. But there's more on the way. Mrs Mulligan's chasing it up.'

She needed to call the police.

CHAPTER 52

HAMMERSMITH POLICE STATION
EXTRACT OF RECORDED INTERVIEW
WITH MRS ZOE MULLIGAN

Date: 22 July
Duration: 131 minutes
No. of pages: 65
Conducted by Officers of the
Metropolitan Police

ZM: He kept saying the same thing over and over: 'She fell.'

DC HARRIS: For the benefit of the tape, could you please explain that this is Ms Mercheri you are talking about?

ZM: Leila. Yes. Of course.

DC BAXTER: And once again you're aware that your husband has made a full confession? That he waived his right to legal representation and . . .

ZM: Yes.

DC BAXTER: OK. So take me back to the ground floor flat. Your husband had left to get more wine around 10.45 p.m?

ZM: Something like that. But he was taking so long. It was such a hot night. People didn't want red. So I went to find out what was going on. To deal with it myself.

DC BAXTER: And you found your husband where?

ZM: In the kitchen, where we'd stashed the wine and catering equipment.

DC HARRIS: You said he was standing there by the island.

ZM: Yes.

DC HARRIS: Mr Mulligan wasn't doing anything or saying anything?

ZM: No. I think I said something though,
or started to: 'One thing I ask you to
do . . .' Something like that.

DC HARRIS: But you didn't finish, because
at this point you saw the victim.

DC BAXTER: For the benefit of the tape Mrs
Mulligan is shaking her head.

ZM: I didn't see Leila. Not then. But Guy's
face . . . he was white. Shiny with sweat.
And sort of holding himself upright, with
one hand on the countertop.

DC BAXTER: And that's when he told you
that she fell.

ZM: 'She fell.' He kept saying it, over and
over, and I didn't understand what he was
talking about until I looked down. Then I
saw her. Leila. All that blood.

DC HARRIS: What happened next,
Mrs Mulligan?

ZM: They'd crossed on the stairs. That's
what Guy told me. And she'd 'made
a comment'.

DC HARRIS: About?

ZM: About his face. The bandage on his face. Leila told him she could hear arguments – from her flat upstairs. That she thought I was . . .

DC HARRIS: . . . physically abusing your husband. Which was the case, wasn't it?

ZM: What? No.

DC BAXTER: We had a call, Mrs Mulligan, from an A&E doctor at Charing Cross.

ZM: No.

DC BAXTER: Seems he treated your husband for his facial injury on July twelfth. But he wasn't convinced his story added up. Then, when he read about Ms Mercheri's murder, saw that it had taken place at Addison Mansions, he recognised the address.

ZM: [Indecipherable]

DC HARRIS: What was that?

DC BAXTER: For the benefit of the tape, Mrs Mulligan appears to be in some distress. And perhaps I can help. Because here's what your husband told us happened next. According to him, Ms Mercheri said that if he didn't speak up, she would.

ZM: [No response]

DC BAXTER: At which point – and again your husband has confirmed this – their conversation moved through to the empty ground floor flat.

ZM: [Indecipherable]

DC BAXTER: Could you please speak up?

ZM: I said she called me 'a monster'. [Suspect laughs] Guy told me. As though she knew anything at all about us, about our marriage.

DC BAXTER: And what did your husband reply to that?

ZM: He said Leila wouldn't let it go. That she kept pushing him. That when he told her it was none of her business, private, she'd said, 'Does some part of you actually enjoy it?' That's when he . . . hit her.

DC BAXTER: It was a punch, wasn't it, with a closed fist, not a slap?

ZM: I wasn't there. All I know is what Guy told me: that she fell.

DC HARRIS: Only she hit her head on the way down, didn't she? Forensics have established that she caught it on the corner of the island. You can see that quite clearly in these photographs. For the tape, I'm showing Mrs Mulligan images C, D and E.

DC BAXTER: The depressed skull fracture was 'so deep that it resulted in the bone of the skull vault being folded inward, into the cerebral cortex.' That's what the pathologist's report says.

DC HARRIS: Quite a wound. But not, as it turns out, enough to kill her.

ZM: What?

DC HARRIS: Were you aware that the victim wore a smartwatch?

ZM: [No response]

DC BAXTER: I'm going to show you another image. This one's data extracted from that smartwatch, specifically the data monitoring Ms Mercheri's heart rate. You

see that brief cluster of jagged lines,
right there?

ZM: [Faint] Yes.

DC BAXTER: That was her heart rate flaring
up at 11.03 p.m. on Saturday night, when
your husband punched her. When she fell
back and cracked her head on the corner of
that island. It's short, isn't it? Little
over a minute. Which is why we didn't
think anything of it at first. Because
look how it compares to that second and
final set of jagged lines, just before
11.19 p.m., when Ms Mercheri's heart stopped
beating? Look at how wildly it's pounding
there, how much longer the struggle
lasted, how hard she fought for her life.

ZM: [Does not answer]

DC BAXTER: When you found your husband in
that kitchen, Ms Mercheri was still alive,
wasn't she? In fact, all the time your
husband was telling you what had happened,
she was still alive.

ZM: No.

DC HARRIS: Really? Because here's the funny
thing: we have a witness placing him back

at the party, at the bar with his box of
Chablis at 11.16 p.m. That's while that
final struggle was going on.

DC BAXTER: So I'm going to ask you again,
when you realised that Ms Mercheri was
still alive, what happened then?

ZM: I wasn't . . . I didn't know. Not until
she moved. It was so slight. The smallest
twitch of the head. Then she made a sound.
A sort of gurgle. And Guy said, 'Thank
God.' Like . . . like he was relieved.

DC HARRIS: You sound surprised.

ZM: Because I don't think he'd understood.

DC HARRIS: Understood what?

ZM: That it was already too late. He was
telling her not to worry, that we were
going to get help. So I told him what was
going to happen. That he was going to take
one of the boxes of Chablis back to the
party and let me take care of this.

DC BAXTER: What did Mr Mulligan
say to that?

ZM: He started making a fuss. I knew he

would. But there wasn't time for that. I told him to go. I pushed him towards the door. [Pause] She'd managed to raise herself up at this point, Leila, on one elbow; she was trying to speak. And the way she looked at me . . .

DC HARRIS: Mrs Mulligan?

ZM: She'd never liked me. But in that moment there was so much hope. I think she genuinely thought I was going to save her. Then, when I just stood there watching, she knew. She started clawing at the plastic sheeting around her, sort of thrashing around. And I tried to push her back down, shut her up, but she was making these moaning sounds. So I kicked her. Just once. Hard enough to end it.

DC HARRIS: [Faint] 'It'?

DC BAXTER: You do know, Mrs Mulligan, that your husband tried to keep you out of it? That even after everything you'd put him through, he was willing to take the blame?

CHAPTER 53

COLETTE

Ten Days After The Party

'She had a good life.'

Brenda had always had the remarkable capacity to deliver a platitude as though it were the freshest, most original thought on earth. Adding death to the mix had only made things worse, and Colette wished the carer would get called away to tend to another Carmel House resident and leave her to finish packing up Gillian's things alone.

Most platitudes did of course have the benefit of being true, but not this one. Her mother hadn't had a good life; she'd had a bitter one. Aware that she was expected to confirm this, however, Colette channelled her inner Brenda: 'She's gone to a better place.'

'She has,' she clucked, folding the mohair blanket Colette had bought her mum in a fit of guilt the previous winter, and handing it to her. 'And ninety-one! That's a ripe old age. You know I always pray they'll die in their sleep, after a nice meal.'

There were certainly worse ways to go, and Colette wondered whether she would have felt as tranquil as she had when the call had come in two days ago, if Leila's murder hadn't thrown the news into such sharp relief.

It had been early afternoon. She'd just got back from the e-dump where, alongside a hastily gathered assortment of defunct tech, she'd finally ditched Emilia's phone, and was in the process of logging Adrian out of his TeamViewer. Her keyhole into Addison Square was no longer needed. In fact, Colette didn't want to go near it ever again.

She'd known before picking up – from the time on her screen. Her mother would normally still be napping at 2 p.m. Unless her heart had stopped at some point during that nap. Delivered alongside the news was the fact that her mother had 'enjoyed a quiche Lorraine for lunch', and that by a stroke of luck they'd served up stewed pears and cream for dessert: 'her favourite.'

Colette looked down at the suitcase lying open on the bed. She'd worried it might not be big enough, but they were almost done, and it was only half full. Pulling the quilted dressing gown from its hook behind the door, she remembered the desk drawer. Aside from a pack of playing cards, some medication and a pack of strawberry liquorice well past its expiration date there was only the Mason Pearson hairbrush, thick – as ever – with silver down. This time she didn't clean its bristles but tucked it carefully into a corner of the suitcase, as it was.

As Colette was zipping it up and saying a silent, unregretful goodbye to Carmel House, her phone buzzed in her pocket.

'Emilia. How are you?'

Brenda was still opening and closing cupboard doors and checking beneath the bed as she assured her client that now was a good time, and actually she had an opening this afternoon; she could be in Addison Square around 4 p.m.?

Pulling the suitcase off the bed Colette thanked her mother's carer from the heart. Brenda smiled, nodded and offered: 'Give yourself time. It doesn't always hit people for a while.'

It wasn't Emilia who opened the door but Sylvia, with Hattie on her hip.

A row of bags lined the hallway and a pile of skirts and blouses – still on their hangers – that she recognised as belonging to Sylvia were draped across the chair in the corner. Despite the day she'd had, Colette felt the corners of her mouth twitch into a smile.

'Seemed a bit silly,' whispered her old client, 'when we've been spending so much time together, to be on the other side of the square. And with Adrian now gone and Emilia needing the extra pair of hands around the house we thought it made sense for me to come and stay for a while, didn't we, Hattie?' Kissing her granddaughter's head, she motioned at Colette to follow them downstairs.

In the guest bedroom Emilia was busy making up the bed while Theo attempted to turn a pillowcase into a sleeping bag, and when she turned Colette was struck by her radiance. It had only been ten days since she'd last seen her at the party – almost that since she'd been back to Addison

Square – and yes, she'd looked beautiful that night, but over-painted and fraught.

Now, her skin was make-up free but luminous, and although she seemed to have regained the weight she'd lost and more, it suited her.

'Perfect timing.' Emilia pointed to the small TV bound up in its own wiring on the bedroom floor. 'I brought this over from Sylvia's earlier. I was hoping you could do your thing, connect it all up to the Sky box and so on. Then I think this'll be rather cosy, don't you?'

The job took less than half an hour, and when Colette was done Emilia asked whether she might join them for tea.

In all her years at number 46, she had never once been in the kitchen, let alone sat around the table being offered ginger biscuits.

'They were there again this morning,' Sylvia said with a groan. 'When I made that last trip to the house. You'd think they'd give it a rest now, wouldn't you? At least until the sentencing. What more can they possibly have to write?'

The journalists and cameramen who had descended on the square after Guy and Zoe's arrests hadn't yet tired of the 'Square Slaying' that had nonetheless been covered exhaustively in tabloids and broadsheets alike. They collected in coteries outside Addison Mansions and the pub, clutching their take-away coffees and puffing on vapes. They rang people's bells. One of them, Sylvia recounted, had even cornered Emilia on the high street, offering her money for 'an exclusive interview about her killer neighbours'.

As intrusive as this must be for a little community that was still reeling but slowly, cautiously, trying to return to normal life, Colette could see why.

The case had all the ingredients to whip the media into a frenzy. A beautiful Parisian dancer whose image had been reproduced in papers and gossip magazines across the country, even making the front page of the *Sun*. Somehow they'd managed to dig up some early 'glamour shots' of Leila. And Colette couldn't help thinking how ironic it was that this fame-hungry young woman wasn't around to enjoy either this or the Instagram follower count that had doubled since her death.

Then there was the 'murderous husband and wife team' who had been 'pillars of the community' until what one journalist had described as 'their bloody binge'. An exclusive middle-class enclave 'turned into a living hell' over the course of a single summer night.

In their own lofty ways, the broadsheets had cashed in on this local tragedy, publishing a series of op-eds on domestic violence against men. Colette still couldn't believe it. Zoe. *Zoe?*

'Those poor children,' she said now. 'What'll happen to them?'

'Felix has gone to his dad, apparently.' Emilia pushed the milk jug towards her. 'And I think Guy has a sister who took in Freya. But I can't bear it for them.'

'Do they know when the sentencing will be?' asked Colette.

'Not yet.' Absently, Emilia brushed a smattering of crumbs off the table into her palm and tipped them onto her plate. 'I wonder if they'll be more lenient with him. Because if it hadn't been for Zoe ... ?'

Sylvia shook her head: 'Goes to show. You never know what's going on behind closed doors.'

And Colette nodded. *Even when you do, you might not get the whole picture. You're still outside, looking in.*

*

On the way back to Mortlake an hour later, Colette sat in her car on a gridlocked A316 humming along to Michael Bolton's 'The One Thing' and wondering at the human ability to find light, even in deepest darkness. Maybe because people had to. Maybe it was those good old survival mechanisms kicking in.

As she turned onto the ramp that took her down to the underground car park and waited for the roller shutters to rise, she made a decision.

CHAPTER 54

EMILIA

Six Months Later

'Do you want me to get you a scarf from the house?'

It was the second time Sylvia had asked, and Emilia made no attempt to conceal her eyeroll.

They were at that stage now. After those tentative early weeks and months when she and Sylvia had kept up the cordial, considerate tone of neighbours – occasionally trying to force their relationship forward in ways that had felt unnatural – they were finally at the stage where they could openly find each other annoying. Just the other day Sylvia had made a tsk sound when Theo had come home from school with a bag of M&Ms, chastised her for not giving him 'an apple or a cereal bar.'

'I'm fine.' She smiled at Sylvia, huddled up in her fur-lined parka on the square bench beside her. 'Stop fussing.'

For a moment they sat in silence, hands wedged between their thighs, looking out across the silvery lawn at the crisp, frost sheathed shrubs and skeletal plane trees. January was supposed to be such a bleak month, but at the start of every year Emilia was struck by the beauty of that wintery square.

'The doctor did say you had low blood pressure,' Sylvia started up again, 'so you need to keep yourself warm.' She threw Emilia's stomach a tender look. 'You and the baby.'

Emilia still felt as disbelieving as a teenager about the pregnancy: *but it was just the one time!* For reasons she couldn't explain even to herself she wasn't yet ready to tell Sylvia that the baby hadn't been conceived in the dying days of her marriage to Adrian, but in the garden shed. Maybe one day she would. She'd opened up about so many other things since Sylvia had moved in permanently, renting out her house to an orthopaedic surgeon in the unenviable position of having two under two. But Hugo? He would never know.

Emilia had been so certain she hadn't wanted another child, but that had been with Adrian, she now realised, and her pregnancy had been a force for good in so many ways. It had given her and Sylvia something to focus on besides each other and the forty-plus years they would never get back.

One night early on, Emilia had turned to Sylvia on the sofa, taken a deep breath and said, 'I don't want to upset you, but I can't imagine ever calling you Mum. I had a mum and it feels, I don't know, wrong to call someone else that just because she's no longer here. I'm so grateful to have you now, but ... Do you think you could find a way to be OK with that?'

That she could be in Emilia's life at all, Sylvia had assured her, was more than she had ever wished for.

'Did you see that they finally sold Guy and Zoe's flat? It was in my InYourArea mailout this morning.' Sylvia's increasing fixation with her phone had been the source of much amusement over the past months. When she wasn't extolling the wonders of 'the Facebook' and perusing interior décor pages on Instagram, she was reading aloud from the My Pregnancy App she had downloaded. But any mention of the Mulligans was still sobering, joy-leeching, and Emilia held back on her usual wisecracks.

'Did they really?'

'Yup. Got the asking price, surprisingly.'

She thought of Guy, who had been found guilty of assault occasioning actual bodily harm but not murder, and would serve a minimum of twelve months, the papers had said. Emilia hoped that he might be able to use the money from the flat to start a new life somewhere else. As for Zoe, she would have no use for money anywhere but the Bronzefield commissary until her late seventies – if then.

'The ground floor flat, however, still hasn't sold ...'

Emilia finished the sentence for her: '... and isn't likely to any time soon.'

They both watched in silence as a dense flock of birds took off, squawking, from the top of a chestnut tree. Then Sylvia stood. 'Let's walk. Warm ourselves up a bit.' But with a sharp tug on her arm Emilia pulled her down again. Because three figures had appeared on the pathway by the playground. A man and a woman and a little boy.

'Eleven o'clock,' she muttered. 'Hugo and Yasmeen.'

There was no need for dramatics. Over the past six months she, Hugo and Yasmeen had come to an unspoken agreement. Neither of them was willing to forfeit the square, so the only way this could work, the only way they could all continue to exist in such close proximity, was to restrict interactions to nods and waves.

Duly, she raised a hand and had her greeting returned.

The boys' friendship had been a casualty, but children were fickle creatures and after whingeing for a fortnight about the lack of playdates Theo had moved on.

Shivering, Sylvia tapped a few buttons on her phone and exclaimed: 'OK – that's it. Says here it's minus one. If you're not going to wrap up, we'd better head back.'

She tapped on the phone again. Sighed.

'Still doing that freezing thing.'

Emilia pulled herself to her feet.

'Did you ever get hold of Colette?'

'No, and I tried a few times. But it just rings once and then goes through to an automated message saying the number is no longer in service. Weirdest thing. She seems to have disappeared into thin air.'

CHAPTER 55

✦

COLETTE

Where were the cups? She had sliced open a dozen of the movers' boxes that morning and discovered books she had no intention of reading, summer clothes she wouldn't be wearing for months and a whole selection of Tupperware she couldn't remember ever having owned, but there were still no cups – and Colette urgently needed a coffee.

Kneading her lower back, she picked her way through the chaos of her sitting room and stood at the window, taking in the view. It wasn't as glorious as the one from her Mortlake flat, and certainly nowhere near as good as the online brochure had promised, but if she craned her neck she could catch a distant cleave of the Oxford canal, and Colette had always found it calming to be near water.

She'd chosen Jericho because it was fairly central despite being a suburb, had a number of 'exclusive modern developments' of the kind she liked and was far enough away from Addison Square for her to be able to start afresh, without any reminders. Then, when she'd Googled the word and found that the Biblical meaning of Jericho was 'a remote place', she'd seen it as a sign.

She'd been grateful that she had enough savings to buy the one bedroom third floor flat in this 'highly regarded waterfront development' without having to wait for her Mortlake property to sell. But until that money came through – and after – she was going to need some expendable income.

Checking her phone, she saw that it was half past four. Prontaprint had promised the new business cards would be ready by five. She could pick them up along with a coffee and put them through a few local doors – see if that yielded any immediate work.

Outside a freezing wind had picked up, sending eddies of deadened leaves above and around her, leaves that got caught in the wheels of her Tumi briefcase as she pulled it along the pavement behind her. But the coffee had helped, the cards weren't bad for a rush job, and as she turned off into an affluent looking cul-de-sac and started posting them through letterboxes Colette felt a wave of optimism.

She was already halfway round it and reaching out to slot her card through another polished brass letterbox when the front door opened.

'Jeez,' the man started. 'You gave me a shock.'

She took in the expensive-looking tracksuit and the signet ring and decided the cul-de-sac had been an inspired choice.

'Sorry.' She wasn't good at this. But giving him her

warmest smile Colette held up the card between two pink-tipped fingers. 'I was just going to pop this through your door in case you ever need an IT consultant.'

The man put his hand to the Hugo Boss insignia on his chest, inhaled sharply, and for a second Colette thought he might be one of those 'no junk mail' obsessives – that he was about to tell her off. Instead, he broke out into an unnaturally white grin. 'Your timing couldn't be better,' he reached for the card, glanced at it, 'I mean actually, literally, you might have just saved my life.'

She held out a hand. 'Colette Burton. Pleased to meet you.'

'Listen, I'm running late.' He slammed the front door behind him and strode briskly towards the Uber that had just pulled up. 'But your deets are on here, right? I'll be in touch, Colleen!'

As the car looped around the cul-de-sac Colette stood perfectly still, watching it disappear around the corner. Then, through the smile still pasted on her face, she hissed, 'It's Colette.'

ACKNOWLEDGEMENTS

I'm endlessly grateful for the help, encouragement, opinions and wisdom of my brilliant editor Rosanna Forte. I live for your occasional vitriolic outbursts about fictional characters.

As ever, I'd like to thank my wonderful agent, Eugenie Furniss, as well as Stephanie Melrose, Laura Vile and the whole Sphere team, who have been so dedicated and tireless. I am particularly grateful to Jon Appleton, for his patience, his forensic attention to detail and his queries about semi-permanent nail varnish.

For their friendship, support and ability to answer the kind of random WhatsApp questions only crime writers ask, I want to thank Jessica Fellowes, Colette Lyons (also generous enough to lend me her name), Charlotte Hellman Cachin, Maria Flor, Darryl Samaraweera, Eleanor Proudlock, Caroline Graham, Kate Regan, Julia Koeppen, Sean Thomas and Nick Cavanagh.

The most important person in my life for the past year, however, has without a doubt been Joe Andraos. Joe, I promise you a cameo in the TV series.

Lastly, much gratitude and love to my family: Mum, Dad,

Olly and Frank. Aunt Delyse, you are the best first reader there is. Piers, I promise you a month-long break before I start the next book. Elise, no eleven-year-old should be this good at coming up with twists. I can't wait for our first official collaboration.

PAYDAY by Celia Walden

The Richard and Judy Book Club Pick

They all wanted to destroy him.

But which one killed him?

'Impossible to put down' HELEN FIELDING

Available now from

SPHERE